Something glittered at her in the middle of the bed. Something small and shiny.

Kim began to tremble. Slowly this time, she pulled the sheets and mattress pad back, the blood from her hand leaving bright red streaks on the flowered cotton.

Now she could see it.

The tip of a shiny metal blade, sticking up from her mattress. Pointed and sharp, the rest of the knife was hidden from view, buried deep inside the mattress.

But she didn't have to look. She knew what the knife would look like. She knew the blade would match the scars on her thigh.

She dropped to her knees, staring at the steel tip. Then she yanked the cell phone off her waistband, dialed Sean's number, hit send and grabbed the gun off the nightstand.

She would be a victim no longer.

THE SHARPEST EDGE

STEPHANIE ROWE

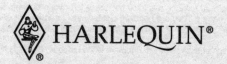

HARLEQUIN®

TORONTO • NEW YORK • LONDON
AMSTERDAM • PARIS • SYDNEY • HAMBURG
STOCKHOLM • ATHENS • TOKYO • MILAN • MADRID
PRAGUE • WARSAW • BUDAPEST • AUCKLAND

For Amanda, who makes our family better by joining it.

Acknowledgments:
Thanks, as always, to my wonderful agent, Michelle Grajkowski, for always encouraging me to spread my wings and believing in my ability to pull off the impossible. And to my talented editor, Wanda Ottewell, for refusing to give up on me. And to JR, for believing in me every step of the way. And a special thanks to my brother, Ben, for freaking out at Squam Lake that night, thinking there was a bear on the roof. You inspire me! Here's to many more such memories at the new abode. And to my parents: every success I have today is because of the foundation you gave me.

ISBN 0-373-22896-1

THE SHARPEST EDGE

ABOUT THE AUTHOR

A lifelong reader of romance, Golden Heart winner Stephanie Rowe wrote her first novel when she was ten, and sold her first book twenty-three years later. After experimenting with a legal career, she decided wearing suits wasn't her style and opted for a more fulfilling career entertaining herself and others with stories of romance, humor and, of course, true love. She currently shares her household with two dogs, two cats and her own hero. When not glued to the computer or avoiding housework, she can be found on the tennis court, reading, or inviting herself over to her mom's house for dinner. You can reach her at www.stephanierowe.com.

Books by Stephanie Rowe

HARLEQUIN INTRIGUE
896—THE SHARPEST EDGE

HARLEQUIN FLIPSIDE
13—STRESS & THE CITY

CAST OF CHARACTERS

Kim Collins—Ten years ago, to save herself, she left the man she loved. Will his reappearance in her life finally destroy her?

Sean Templeton—A cop who has returned home, determined to start a new life free from the pain of his past.

Jimmy Ramsey—A man with one thing on his mind: payback.

Max Collins—Will he awake from his coma, and what secrets will he reveal if he does?

Helen Collins—She will do anything to save the man she loves.

Allan Haywood—How far will he go to protect Kim?

Didi Smith—Will her access to inside information be enough to save others, or will it make her a victim in this deadly game?

Chief Vega—Will his loyalty to his staff make him blind to the real threat?

Tom Payton—Is the marina assistant's innocent persona legit?

Will Ambrose— A front-desk attendant who may not be what he seems.

Garth McKeen—A cop with either an agenda or not enough experience. Which is it?

Eddie—Does the old harbormaster know more than he should?

Chapter One

I will come for you.

Kim Collins bolted upright in bed, adrenaline spiking. What was that? A whisper in the wind? Or her imagination? A premonition of a future soon to be hers? The promise of a man whose only goal was to kill her?

I will come for you.

Her heart pounded in her chest, filled her ears, bruised her ribs.

He was here. She knew it.

She frantically searched the dark bedroom, her gaze darting back and forth, trying to cover every inch at once. She dipped into the moon's eerie shadows, double-checking the location of each item. Nothing amiss. Even her suitcase still lay open on the floor, half-unpacked after her arrival from California two days ago. All was quiet.

Except the six-inch scar on her thigh.

It throbbed with pain. Pulsed with fear. Ached with ugly reminders.

But the room was silent. The house was still.

Relax, Kim. It's another nightmare. Nothing in the room had moved since she'd gone to bed. See? She was imagining things.

It was nothing but a dream.

Or, rather, a nightmare.

Kim pushed her hair off her face, her fingers twisting in the wet strands, damp from the humidity and the fear. The sweat of terror. Too real. Too often. And now...she was having those dreams almost every night.

The knife.

The blood.

Her scream.

The overwhelming terror of impending death.

And that sickening smile he'd given her when they'd escorted him out of the courtroom for his six-month stay in prison, his thin lips forming his promise: *I will come for you.*

Yesterday, she'd gotten the call from the Los Angeles County District Attorney's Office. Jimmy Ramsey was out on parole. She'd known he would be getting out. She'd been preparing for it by taking a leave of absence so she could get out of town, but nothing had prepared her for the shock of knowing he'd been released. Free to pursue her. And he was coming for her. She knew it.

"Stop it!" She hugged her pillow to her chest. He was probably three thousand miles away, stalking her in L.A., clueless that she was hidden away in the Maine woods, right? Her best friend, Alan Haywood, was watching her apartment and he'd call her as soon as Jimmy was spotted.

Everything was under control.

Besides, Jimmy wouldn't travel across the country just to stalk her.

No, but he'd travel that far to kill her.

If he realized she wasn't in L.A., he might remember hearing about the family resort in Maine and decide to see if she was out here. He'd pull out his credit card, mosey on over to the airport, grab a last-minute ticket and then he'd be here...

Argh! She closed her eyes and pressed her palms to her eyelids, trying to expel the thought from her head. *Deep breaths. Inhale for five counts. Exhale for eight counts.*

A distinct thump sounded above her head and she lurched off the bed. She landed on her feet, her fists balled and her breath heaving, dread paralyzing her for an instant. Then she shook it off and raced for the open windows. She yanked them shut, locked them and jumped back. Her hands shook, her skull ached where Jimmy had smashed it and her legs threatened to give out.

The scrabbling on the roof continued. Little thuds and scratches, faster now.

Dammit. She wasn't ready to die. She hadn't been before and she wasn't now.

She grabbed the phone, but her fingers were shaking too much to hold on to it. It clattered to the floor. She dove for the handset and dialed 911. The operator answered, her calm, detached voice so wrong for the intensity of the situation.

"1370 Birch Road. There's an intruder! Please send someone. Hurry!"

Kim jumped away as the wall nearest her began to shake. He was climbing down the side of her house! She heard a thud on the ground and fresh panic surged over her. Was he planning to break a window and come in the ground floor?

"There's an officer in the area. He should be there in about three minutes."

"Thanks." Kim hung up just as the operator was telling her to stay on the line. As if that would help if Jimmy came through her window wielding a knife. *Stay away from me or this operator will kill you.* Uh-huh. Yeah, that'd work.

The phone rang and she jumped.

The operator calling back?

Or was it Jimmy phoning from her front step? Laughing at her fear? Mocking her? Counting down the seconds she had left to live? No, thanks.

She let it ring.

The police would be there in three minutes.

That was all the time she needed to buy herself.

She kicked her bedroom door shut.

No lock.

A scrambling noise from outdoors spurred her into motion. She ran to the end of her dresser, wedged her back against it and pushed with all the strength her trembling limbs could provide. With a protesting shriek that made her own hackles rise, the bureau screeched its way across the wood floor, a mournful sound that made cold fingers of fear close around her spine.

The creepy wail didn't end until she had the dresser jammed safely in front of the door. The taut silence was barely a respite as she stepped back to inspect her work.

Not enough. He could still get through.

She ducked into the attached bathroom, grabbed the lid off the back of the toilet and hoisted it over her shoulder, taking up a post by the side of the door. If he stuck his head in there, she'd brain him with the porcelain. It wasn't a gun, but it was heavy and hard. She wasn't going down without a fight.

Kim strained, listening for the sound of breaking glass or splintering wood. Or the ominous thud of footsteps on the stairs.

Silence. Not even a noise from the side of the house anymore. She took a deep breath. Maybe it hadn't been Jimmy. Maybe it was a really fat raccoon. Or even a bear.

Or maybe she was deluding herself right now. Maybe she'd been yards away from the man who wanted her dead.

But the silence stretched. Even if it had been him, maybe he was gone.

But what did it matter if Jimmy had left tonight? If it had been Jimmy on her roof, if he had found her…he'd be back again.

And again.

Until he was through with her.

So what was she supposed to do?

Be like Cheryl, her beloved sister, who had changed her name and disappeared? If Kim ran, she would endanger Cheryl as well as herself because her sister was safe only so long as Jimmy pursued Kim. Though after tonight, she really wasn't enjoying this plan too much, either.

Her goal had been to set him up to violate his parole, either by getting caught stalking her apartment or by following her out of state. Of course, the original plan had been to take a short leave of absence and set herself up in a very secure hotel, one that he'd never be able to penetrate, but her dad's accident had changed all that. Now she was still acting as bait, but in a remote and unprotected location.

Not good.

Bright lights glared and her room began flashing in blue, like a disco invading rural Maine.

The police.

Kim snuck over to the window, peering cautiously through the corner of the glass. A cruiser was sitting in her driveway and there was a uniformed officer walking up the front steps toward her door.

For now, she was safe.

But she was certain the danger was only beginning.

SHE FLUNG THE front door open, where a cop stood in the shadows. She'd made it. Oh, God. She'd made it. She wasn't going to die tonight. Her knees suddenly gave way and she went down.

"Whoa!" The man jumped out of the shadows and grabbed her, pulling her back to her feet. "You okay?"

Something caught in Kim's chest at that voice. That husky timbre… She looked up, then felt her world spin into a black abyss. "Sean?"

His grip tightened on her arms, and he pulled her into the light. "Kim?"

It was *him.* His eyes were tired, his face more bony and lined, his hair shorter than it had been ten years ago, but it was *him.* "Sean!" She threw her arms around him. "I thought you were dead!" He smelled the same as always. That musky scent that had made a sixteen-year-old girl fall in love, and it seized her gut and tugged.

For an instant, his arms tightened and he crushed her against him and it was as if the past ten years had never happened. They were both eighteen again and the world hadn't betrayed them.

Then he pulled back and set her to the side and a rift of cold air settled in her chest. "What's wrong?" he asked.

Wrong? She blinked. Wrong was the cold shadow in his eyes, the rigid set to his jaw that said he wanted nothing to do with her anymore. But what could she expect? It was what she'd wished for.

"Kim? You called the cops?"

Sweat broke out on her forehead again and she hugged herself. "He's going to kill me." Her voice was no more than a whisper, but Sean must have heard her because the lines on his face deepened and his expression became harsher.

"What are you talking about?" His hand went to his gun. His eyes became vigilant. He looked all cop, and something else. Something more. Someone who knew how to handle a weapon and who thrived on the threat of death.

Where was the gangly kid she'd almost married? The boy whose only goal in life had been to run the Loon's Nest alongside her parents? Gone, apparently, replaced by a hard man she didn't even know.

A man who was here to protect her from Jimmy.

"Who's going to kill you?" He shifted her slightly, putting himself between her and the doorway, his gaze boring deep into the interior of the house. Searching for the threat.

"Jimmy Ramsey." Just saying his name made her legs start to shake again.

"Who's he? Is he inside?"

She was freezing, even though it was a hot, muggy night. Guess fear of death would do that to a person. "I heard him outside."

"Outside?" Sean grabbed her, shoved her inside the house and slammed the door shut behind them. "Who? Your husband?"

Was it her imagination or did he stumble over that word? She shook her head and clutched her arms to her chest, the old T-shirt hanging loosely off her. "My sister's ex-husband."

"Cheryl's husband?" He frowned. "What's going on?"

She pressed her back against the door, afraid of the house and its cavernous interior with so many hiding places. "He was in prison and he got out and I heard something on the roof and then he climbed down the side of the building and then you came and I don't know if he's still here or…"

Something flickered in his eyes, but he offered no comforting words. Not as he would have ten years ago. "Lock yourself in the bathroom while I check things out." He opened the powder room door, old instincts apparently directing him to the right place without a second thought. "I'll be back in a minute."

She grabbed his arm before he could get away. "Be careful. He's a cop."

Sean stopped, surprise flickering on his face. "A cop?"

She nodded. "He'll kill you."

"No chance." He disengaged her grip and guided her into the room, then pulled the door shut. "Lock it."

His footsteps didn't take him away until she'd engaged the lock with an audible click.

And then, all she could do was wait.

KIM LEANED AGAINST the door, trying to catch her breath. Her chest was so tight, her hands cold, her forehead hot.

Sean. He was here. At her house. Alive.

And Jimmy was here. At her house. And he wanted her dead.

She groaned and slid down the door to the floor. Her hands were shaking so badly she dropped them to the tiles and let her head flop back against the wood.

What was Sean doing in town? She never would have agreed to come back if she'd known he was around. Even for her sister, she couldn't have done it. Cheryl had begged her to return to Maine when they'd found out about their dad's accident because Cheryl was still trapped in hiding and couldn't come home. For her sister, Kim could endure anything.

Except Sean.

And Jimmy again.

She had no strength left to cope with either of them, not even for Cheryl. She was exhausted, so unbearably tired.

A knock on the door sent her leaping to her feet. Kim smashed herself up against the opposite wall. Was it Sean, or had Jimmy killed Sean? What if Jimmy had come back to finish her off at a leisurely pace?

"It's me. Open up."

She nearly collapsed with relief at Sean's voice. "Is it safe?"

"Yeah."

Kim inched toward the door and flicked the lock, but the doorknob turned before she could open it. Sean stuck his head into the room, his dark eyebrows knitting when he saw her. She had no doubt that he'd be able to see through her facade and know that she was terrified. For an instant, his face softened and she thought he was going to give her the reassurance she craved, but then his expression hardened. "Come on out. We need to talk."

An agonizing need to have his arms around her again jolted her into moving toward him, but he turned away before she could reach him.

Nothing. No comfort. No special look. No touch of support, even though he had to know how much she needed it. Regret made her energy sag. Had she done that to him?

Changed him from a sweet, doting guy into someone who wouldn't even touch her arm in comfort? She couldn't ask. Couldn't apologize. Where would she start after a decade of silence? Should she try?

He held the door for her and stepped back when she reached him, his eyes cold and distant. Pushing her away. He didn't want to hear about their past. She could read it in the tight set to his mouth, the way he held his arm so she couldn't brush against it.

They were strangers now.

Strangers who had to discuss the man who'd almost killed her once and wouldn't let her escape next time.

Chapter Two

Sean grabbed a soda from the fridge, pulled out a chair with his foot and sat down at the kitchen table. "Talk."

Talk. God, there were so many things to discuss. And nothing to say.

Nothing except for Jimmy.

Kim sat down across from Sean and tried not to think about how much she wanted him to hold her. Just for a minute, so she could feel secure and loved and warm. Which was stupid. That was the reason she hadn't wanted to come back. Falling into the trap of the familiar and the safe already, just like her mom had warned her.

A lump came to her throat at the thought of Joyce Collins, as it always did.

Sean fixed his gaze on her. "Jimmy Ramsey. A cop who wants to kill you. Tell me."

Right. She could focus. She could think. With Sean sitting across from her, his gun on his hip, she wasn't scared.

For the first time in eighteen months, she wasn't afraid.

Exhausted to the point of numbness. Freaking out to be sitting across from the man she'd been thirty minutes from marrying. Saddened by the chasm between them and the fact that she'd caused it. But not fearing for her life. It was a start.

"Jimmy is…or was…a cop in L.A. Cheryl met him

when he was working at one of the events I brought her to." What a night that had been. Cheryl had been so excited at the chance to meet a Hollywood star, yet from the moment she'd seen Jimmy, she'd cared about nothing else. "He's incredibly good-looking, and she was hooked immediately."

He pulled out a notepad and jotted something down. "Keep going."

His index finger on his left hand was crooked now, as if it had been broken and healed wrong. What had his life been like in the ten years since she'd left?

"Kim." His voice was devoid of warmth or familiarity. He was nothing but a cop to her anymore.

As it should be. As she'd wanted. So why did she feel as though a black cloak had suddenly been wrapped around her soul? "Jimmy pursued Cheryl hard, and they were married two months after they met."

"Two months? That's not like Cheryl."

"He was manipulating her, but I couldn't talk her out of it." How she'd tried. "It nearly ruined our relationship." After more than six years of estrangement between her and Cheryl, she'd been too afraid to risk their tentative new friendship by lobbying against the marriage. "So I backed off." What an awful, horrible mistake that had been.

"And then?" His eyes were intent on hers, but they were devoid of emotion. Empty of warmth. She didn't recognize them.

She sighed. "Then Jimmy started beating Cheryl up."

"*Damn.*"

Exactly how she'd felt the first time she'd seen the bruises on Cheryl's arm. "After he put her in the emergency room, I talked her into leaving him. The women's shelter slipped her out of the hospital before he even knew what happened."

His pen was motionless, suspended above the paper with the stillness of death. Oh, nice analogy. How about the stillness of a snowman on a subzero day? That was much cheerier. No death analogies needed.

"And then he came after you?"

Kim shrugged, but she couldn't stop the shiver that raced through her body. "He thought he could convince me to tell him where she'd gone." Plus, he'd been pissed. Really, really pissed.

He set the pen down and leaned forward, his voice no longer quite as detached and clinical as before. "How did he try to persuade you?"

It took two deep breaths and supreme effort to block the image from her mind before she could answer. "A knife."

He cursed, then shoved back his chair and yanked her to her feet. "Let me see the scars." His eyes were no longer empty of emotion. They were hot and angry, and something buried deep inside her quivered in recognition of his passion.

She tried to pull away. "Forget it. It's over."

"I have to know what I'm dealing with." But he released her arm. "If he was on your roof, it's not over."

Oh, God. Right. It wasn't over. "So you do think…you think he was here?" Her voice sounded so weak and pathetic she hated herself. Why couldn't Sean tell her that it had been some four-legged creature and that she'd been a paranoid fool? She lifted her chin and cleared her throat. She would *not* be Jimmy's victim anymore. "Did you find tracks?"

Sean hesitated. "It could have been an animal. There are indications of a bear around the house and on the deck near the grill."

"But you're not sure?" Why couldn't he be certain? Why couldn't he say Jimmy had never been near the house? Dammit. Even a bear with rabies would be better than Jimmy.

"No, I'm not sure." He cracked his jaw, the pop loud in the silent house. He still hadn't regained his aloofness, his fingers twitching restlessly by his sides. "So do you have scars or not?"

She shrugged and didn't answer. Her scars were her own private hell, thank you very much.

He slammed his fist into a cabinet as he turned away, leaving a raw dent in the wood from the high-school class ring he still wore on his finger. He rested his hands on the counter and dropped his head. She could see his shoulders rise and fall with his breath. Guess he figured out the answer to his question on his own. Bully for him.

After a long moment, he turned toward her. His face was reserved again, though he was struggling to contain the emotion rumbling in his eyes. "You didn't tell him where Cheryl was, did you?" His tone assumed the answer she gave him.

"No. I didn't."

He nodded and she thought she saw a flash of respect cross his features. "Did he try to kill you?"

She swallowed. "Yes." It was when she knew he was going to kill her that she realized she would never be like her mother and accept death as the easy answer. It was sort of difficult to get excited about finding the will to live, given the circumstances at the time, but a part of her was grateful that she'd discovered her strength.

A muscle ticked in his neck, but the rest of him was immobile. "Prison?"

"I testified against him. I put him away."

Sean swore again and she shoved her trembling hands under her legs. How much did she not want to relive this nightmare? But she had to. She had to make sure that Sean understood the threat. Not Sean specifically, but the police in general. Because Sean wasn't hers anymore. She'd made sure of that when she left. Apparently, she'd done a damn good job of it, too. Wasn't she talented? Hah. She didn't feel so good about her long-ago actions right now. All the more reason to get out of town and back to L.A. as soon as possible. "He got out on bail right away, and for the twelve months before the trial, he followed me around. Called me. Sent me e-mails. Befriended the guards in my building."

Her mouth was too dry to swallow and she took Sean's soda and drank from it. "His strategy was to scare me. Make me wonder when he would come back to kill me. It gave him power to know I was looking over my shoulder. To realize I was afraid to answer the phone at night or walk to my car after work." She flexed her hands, making fists. "He got only six months in jail because of all the cops who testified as character witnesses. When they led him out of the courtroom, he looked right at me and mouthed the words 'I will come for you.'" She raised her gaze to Sean. "He got out on parole yesterday."

Deep terror settled in her bones and she knew Sean saw it by the anger vibrating in his eyes. Anger on her behalf? A tremble of something alive sparked inside her, but he averted his face and gazed out at the dark lake. "Where can you go tonight?"

Go? "What are you talking about?"

"If he's back, you can't stay here." He gestured around the house. "Look at all these windows and doors. No alarm. You won't be safe."

She glanced at the windows and a cold chill settled in her belly at the thought that Jimmy could be sitting a few yards away, watching her while he hid in the darkness. "Where am I supposed to go?"

"A hotel? A friend's?" As if he didn't care. Anywhere that would take her off his worry list.

And suddenly, she felt outrage roil up inside of her. She'd been quaking in fear for the past eighteen months. She'd given up the life she loved and traveled across the country to escape Jimmy, braving the memories of her childhood home, and now he was going to steal this last bit of independence from her by making her move into a hotel? Dammit! It was enough!

She smacked her palms on the table and glared at Sean. "I'm not running away again. I'm tired of changing my life because I'm so afraid. He's been manipulating me for months and I've had it!" She sat straighter now, empowered by Sean's presence and the fact that he'd found no signs of attempted forced entry or human footprints. "He probably wasn't even here, or if he was, he had no intention of hurting me. He's trying to twist my mind again and I'm sick of it!"

"Fine. Be sick of it. But you're not staying here. Not until you get an alarm." He frowned. "What about Max's place? Why don't you stay there?"

Stay at her dad's house? Something twisted inside her. Something that felt like grief but was actually hate. She could tell the difference and it was hatred she felt for her father. "You didn't hear about my dad?"

The lines around his mouth tightened. "I know about Max. I've been to see him in the hospital five times. I thought you could stay with Helen and the kids."

"Stay with his wife? Are you kidding?" No way. No way. *No way.* Kim might have never met Helen, but she despised her. When Helen had married Kim's dad three weeks after Joyce was buried, Helen lost the right to a fair trial. Guilty by association.

Disgust and betrayal snapped in Sean's face. "You haven't changed, have you? Destroyed everything ten years ago and you're still doing it."

What? He was blaming her? "I didn't destroy anything. Max did." The man didn't even deserve to be called her father anymore. *Max* was impersonal and fitting.

Sean's upper lip curled in disdain. "Max did nothing wrong." Then he narrowed his eyes. "No one at the hospital mentioned you were in town. You haven't even been to see him, have you?" The accusation was deep in his voice and she flinched.

Guilt flared up and she threw it back on him. "I just got

here a couple days ago, so back off." The excuse sounded weak, even to her. But what was she supposed to do? Admit how guilty she felt that she hadn't rushed over there to get answers for Cheryl? So what if Kim didn't want to see her dad? She had planned to check with the doctors without going to the hospital, but they wouldn't give out information over the phone, even though she'd grown up here and should fall under the category of "trusted local." She hadn't been able to bring herself to meet with the doctors in person. What if Helen and her kids were at the hospital? What if Max woke up while Kim was in his room? What if she simply couldn't handle the memories?

Dammit. She had to get over it. Go over to the hospital. Talk to the doctors. Cheryl deserved information.

"So you haven't visited him." He leaned back and shook his head in disgust. "What's wrong with you? Your family used to be so close and now you won't go see your own dad while he's in a coma?"

Naked anguish wrenched in her chest. Okay, that wasn't simple hatred. Definitely some emotional baggage in there. Crud. Being back in town was ripping through her defenses. "Don't judge me." Yeah, so what if she'd always been the first to hug her parents and used to drag Sean to Sunday dinner with the family every weekend? That was long gone now.

"Don't judge you? You, the woman who took off on me without so much as a note. The woman who didn't come back for her own mother's funeral. You don't even care that your dad's in a coma. What the hell have you become?"

Emotions bubbled and raged inside her and she knew she would explode. Too much to cope with. She closed her eyes and took a deep breath. She refused to care enough to explode. This wasn't her life anymore. After a moment, she opened her eyes. "I think you should leave now." She strengthened her trembling voice by giving Sean a hard stare.

"I agree." He shoved back his chair and stood. "Lock your doors." His jaw flexed and a tendon bulged in his neck. "I'll make sure there's a drive-by every hour, but I doubt he'll come back tonight."

"Fine." She followed him to the door. "Assign someone else to this case."

"Believe me, I'm going to try."

"Good." That was what she wanted: Sean not in her house or her life or her dreams. Sean, with his cold, judging eyes. Sean, who was her history, not her present. "See you around."

He shut the door behind him with extra force and she snapped the locks shut on her past.

KIM AWOKE WITH a start when she heard someone holler her name. Her heart leaping, she lurched to her feet and cracked her head against the bathroom sink. Oy, that hurt.

She pressed her hand to her throbbing skull. The bathroom had been the safest place in the house, with no windows and a good lock on the door, so that's where she'd slept after Sean had left. Along with all the fireplace implements. Wrought iron, heavy and sharp, she'd lined them up next to her, ready for Jimmy.

Who had never come.

Someone shouted her name again and she glanced at her watch. Almost nine in the morning.

Daylight was good.

She stretched, feeling increasingly foolish as she recalled last night's fiasco. How stupid had she been last night? As if Jimmy had made it all the way across the country to find her. If he really was after her, he'd spend time lurking around her work and her apartment in L.A. trying to locate her. It would take him a while to figure out that she wasn't there. By that time, she'd have heard from Alan that Jimmy was stalking her and the restraining order would land Jimmy back in prison. Then she could return and all would be good.

Darkness always made the nightmares worse. You'd think she'd learn to control them. But no, she hadn't and, thanks to her overactive imagination, she'd ended up dragging Sean to her house. All because Jimmy had managed to mess up her brain at the same time that he'd shoved that knife into her thigh. Throw in the guilt from avoiding the hospital when Cheryl was waiting for an update on their dad and it had made Kim even more of an emotional disaster, freaking out at the slightest sound.

Screw Jimmy. She was never going to be his victim again—not physically, not emotionally.

This morning, she was going to call the police station and tell Sean that the whole thing was a false alarm and to forget it. Because Jimmy wasn't in Maine. At worst, he was still in L.A., stalking her empty apartment.

She would *not* live in terror anymore, and the first step was to admit that her fears were irrational.

The doorbell rang, and she almost smiled at the sound. How weird to hear that familiar tune after ten years. Last night, she'd been so obsessed with being murdered she hadn't even noticed it, but today it struck her.

She kicked the fireplace implements aside and stepped into the hall. No one jumped out at her, but she still peered through the window before opening the front door, just to make sure Jimmy hadn't marched up to the house. An elderly man with gray hair, leathery wrinkles and a faded Red Sox cap grinned at her.

Relief and happiness cascaded through her and she tugged the door open. "Eddie!"

He held out wiry, ancient arms and she accepted, hugging the man who'd been in charge of the boats at the Loon's Nest for forty-three years.

The Loon's Nest was the official name for the rustic vacation resort-slash-camp that had been in her dad's family for over a hundred years. The ninety-two cabins lining the shores of Birch Tree Lake were rented out every summer. With no kitchens or any sort of utility room, all the families ate at a central dining hall three times a day, and there were plenty of programs to keep the guests entertained: picnics on the islands, hikes in the mountains, softball games and more. Kim's childhood home was on the outskirts of the camp, giving the family some privacy from the guests.

Her dad had moved out when he remarried, but he'd kept this house while he and Helen set up their cozy love nest a few miles away. The old home had sat fully furnished and empty, sustained by Max's hopes that one of his wayward daughters would someday return to run the place.

And here she was. Back in the house. But it wasn't on Max's terms, and she wasn't here to stay.

"Kimmy!" Eddie kissed her cheek. "I can't believe you're back."

"It's so good to see you." She gave him a big hug, the scent of his pipe tobacco cascading back to her, a memory long forgotten. It made her want to curl up in his lap and listen to stories about the old days.

As a kid, she'd spent thousands of hours following Eddie around, sucking up all his knowledge about the lake and boats and nature. She adored him. God, it was good to see him.

Okay, so there was one good thing about being back in town.

"Come in." She held the door open. "I want to hear all about everything." As Eddie stepped inside, she stuck her head out and peered around. The woods were quiet, the underbrush jiggling from chipmunks. Birds were chirping, and a squirrel was running around with a pinecone in his mouth. No Jimmy.

Still, she bolted the door behind them. Yeah, he was probably hanging around her apartment in L.A., but it didn't hurt to be careful.

"How did you know I was back?" She steered Eddie toward the kitchen table he'd sat at many times, then pulled a pitcher of lemonade out of the fridge.

"I've been watching the house. Figured you might come back when your dad got in the accident."

Oh, crap. "Does everyone know I'm back?"

He shook his head. "This house is too far away from the rest of the camp. No one comes out here. I've been driving by on the lake, keeping an eye on the place."

Phew. She wasn't up to facing people yet.

"Thanks for stopping by." And she meant it. Eddie was dear to her, the only vestige of her past that wasn't tainted.

"We're real sorry about your dad."

She managed a civil nod. "Thanks."

"That boat was okay. It wasn't my fault."

Surprised at his response, she touched his hand. "Of course it wasn't your fault, Eddie. It was an accident." Wasn't it? Hadn't Cheryl told her it was an accident? Cheryl had been Kim's conduit for all the town news since they'd left.

Not that she cared about the details of what had happened to her dad. But Cheryl cared, so she had to ask. "What exactly happened? No one has told me."

Eddie frowned. "Some kids were camping on Big Moon Island about a week ago. They heard a boat motor roaring and then a crash just before midnight, so they went down there and checked it out. The moon was out, so they were able to see your dad unconscious under the water, the boat cracked up on the rocks. Smashed his head on a rock, apparently. Kids hauled him out and gave him CPR while their buddies got help from the marina. Kept him alive, but he never woke up." Eddie blinked several times. "Best friend a man could have. Should never have happened."

No kidding. Her dad was the guru of boating safety and could navigate the lake blindfolded, even at night. He'd never, ever run aground, let alone smashed a boat full speed into one of the islands. The darkness wouldn't have made a difference to him. He didn't need daylight to navigate the lake. No one who had lived on it for fifty years did. The moon and stars were more than enough.

"The gearshift was locked down, so people figure that it got stuck," Eddie said.

So what? That wasn't enough to cause her dad to crash into an island. "What about the propeller? Couldn't he have turned?"

"Jammed, too." Eddie shook his head. "Weirdest damn thing. Makes no sense. I take care of that boat, and it was fine. Sure, it's twenty years old, but it's in perfect shape. I didn't screw up."

"Of course you didn't—"

He interrupted her, anger resonating in his voice. "The cops won't listen to me, but you will. I know what happened."

"What?" For an instant, Jimmy flashed through her mind. Would he target her entire family? Except that he'd still been in prison when the accident happened. Thank God for that. One less thing for her to be paranoid about.

"It was that new wife of his. *She* tried to kill him."

Chapter Three

"Helen's trying to murder him?" How ironic if his new beloved *did* kill Max, after he'd taken the life of his first wife. Poetic justice, although there would never be justice for the loss of Kim's mother.

Then Kim sighed. This wasn't the movies. Wives didn't go around offing their husbands. Especially by cracking a boat up on some rocks. A very bad way to try to kill someone because the chances of death were minimal. Only a total idiot around the water would think that might work.

Eddie grabbed her arm, his gnarly fingers digging into her skin. "Helen despises the camp. She hates everything about his past life. She's been trying to get him to sell the place for years and he won't. Saving it for you girls, and she don't care."

A second wife who hated the lake? Her dad sure could pick his women. But Helen apparently spoke up. Joyce had kept quiet and suffered until a bottle of antidepressants became her only solution for escape from the man who had destroyed her. Damn him!

But Eddie wasn't finished and wouldn't leave Kim to suffer the memories of her past. "That's why I came over here today. You gotta save the camp."

Um, hello? No chance of that. "What are you talking about?"

"Helen's destroying it. You gotta take over until your dad can come back."

"No." She pushed back from the table. "I can't. I'm only out here to check on Max. I have to go back to L.A. in a few days. My job." Not precisely true. Her leave of absence from her job as an editor at *the* Hollywood insider magazine would last a month, but she would be on the first plane back to L.A. as soon as it was safe.

She and Alan had figured it would take only a couple of weeks for Jimmy to come after her, so she could be back at work shortly. She had a gorgeous apartment, lots of friends, and invites to all the best parties so she could keep tabs on celebrity gossip. Everything that made life complete. Most of the time.

Unfortunately, in order to stay hidden from Jimmy, she'd had to go MIA from work entirely. No calls, no e-mails. She was going insane, wondering how much her replacement was screwing up. But she and Alan had decided it was too risky to have any contact with the office. Someone would need to mail her something, her address would be released and then she'd be in trouble. Total silence was the only way, and she was going through definite withdrawal. L.A. was her home now, not the lake.

Besides, there was no way she could reinvest herself in this place. Not with Sean here. Not with Helen lurking around. She had to leave, not dig herself deeper. "Eddie, I can't help with the camp."

Hope faded from Eddie's eyes. "I understand."

Could she feel guiltier about the despair on his face? "Eddie…"

He let go of her arm. "I gotta get back. July's a busy time. Boats are going in and out and my assistant don't know a propeller from a life jacket."

She bit her lip as he trudged to the door, his shoulders

stooped and his gait shuffling. He'd gotten so old since she'd last been here.

Who was she kidding? He'd gotten old in the five minutes since she'd turned him down. "Um…Eddie? How bad is it?"

"We'll be bankrupt by the end of the summer."

Oh, no. "Are you sure?"

"Yeah."

"But then the place will be sold." And Cheryl would have nowhere to come home to when she was finally able to resume her life.

There was no way Kim could let her little sister down. It would take her a lifetime to repay Cheryl for the two times she'd already betrayed her.

The first time was when Kim had left ten years ago, abandoning her little sister to a suicidal mother and a clueless father.

Yeah, sure, Kim had left because her mom had talked her into it with her whispered confessions while she and Kim were huddled in the alcove of the church, Sean waiting at the altar. Heck, Joyce had helped her pack, so desperate she was that Kim not make the same mistakes she'd made. Giving up dreams, being stuck in a dead-end marriage with a man she didn't love, being trapped in Ridgeport forever, miserable beyond anything she could endure—all because of teenage love that hadn't been real. The stark anguish in her mother's eyes had terrified Kim, and she'd realized that if she stayed in town, she'd never be able to resist the lure of Sean, his safe and familiar arms, things that would destroy her the way they'd devastated her mother.

Of course, Kim would never have left if she'd truly understood how desperate her mom was. Joyce had sworn that she'd follow Kim soon after with Cheryl and they would all be happy. But her mom had killed herself six months later, driven to it by her husband, the man who refused to let her go. Never would Kim forgive Max for destroying her family. Ever. Not after she'd received the letter.

Kim should have realized how bad the situation was when she'd left or, at the very least, come back for Cheryl after Joyce killed herself. Instead, Cheryl had tried to take her own life, and Kim still had nightmares about it. Convincing Cheryl to come to California for school, then paying for her expenses didn't begin to make up for the fact that she'd almost lost her sister.

The second time Kim had let Cheryl down was with Jimmy. When Kim had known it was wrong for Cheryl to marry him, but hadn't stopped her.

Mistakes that had nearly killed her sister—twice.

No way would she let Cheryl lose her legacy, as well. Sweet, innocent Cheryl, who had never realized how bad their dad was, keeping in touch with him even after all that had happened. "Give me five minutes to change and I'll follow you up to the office."

Eddie's face lit up with hope, hope that wrenched Kim's stomach. "I'm not a business expert, Eddie. I don't know if I'll be able to do anything."

"You will." He beamed at her and Kim felt her gut sink. How could she save the camp?

SEAN HAD HIS BOOTS up on the desk and his eyes closed when the door banged open, jerking him awake.

Chief Bill Vega knocked Sean's feet off the desk and they thudded on the floor. "It's almost eleven in the morning. What are you still doing here?"

"Waiting for an e-mail." Sean stretched and glanced over at his empty in-box. He was waiting for the police report on Jimmy Ramsey's attacks on Kim and Cheryl. And he had a call in to Jimmy's parole officer to check on his whereabouts.

"How was last night?" Bill casually poured himself a mug of cold coffee. "Any interesting calls?"

Sean eyed the man who'd given him his start in law enforcement so many years ago. "No."

"How's she doing?"

"Who?"

"Kim Collins, that's who." Bill sat down on the edge of Sean's desk. "I heard she's looking fine."

"Screw you." He shot Bill a hostile glare, but he laughed and didn't budge. The man obviously didn't give a rip that his question made Sean recall how Kim looked last night. How she'd felt when he'd held her for that one moment. It had felt like coming home. It had been right, so absolutely perfect. And then he'd remembered that everything about her was wrong. Everything about *them* was wrong.

Unfortunately, recalling that fact hadn't made her look any less appealing in her oversize T-shirt and sweats. Her casual outfit reminded him of the innocent teenager he'd loved. Last night, she'd looked so young and vulnerable he'd wanted to sweep her up in his arms and take her home to protect her. Except she wasn't innocent, and she'd made it damned clear what she thought of being in his arms when she'd left ten years ago.

"Did she throw herself at you?" Bill grinned. "Let me guess. It was a trumped-up phone call to get you over there, wasn't it? No sign of a prowler. Did she have you check her bedroom?"

"Don't you have work to do?"

"Nope. That's why I hired you, so I don't have to work."

It was weird to have someone teasing him. Sean didn't joke anymore. Hadn't for a long time. He wasn't interested in striking up a friendship with Bill or anyone else. "Well, I have work to do."

"You're off duty and you've been here for a month. What could you possibly have to do?"

"Stuff." Not that it should surprise him that Bill was giving him a hard time. After all, they'd been friends when he worked here before, even though Bill was about five years older than Sean. Back then, Sean had called him Billy and talked about things that mattered. Bill hadn't respected his privacy back then and apparently, he still didn't. Difference was, now Sean didn't want that kind of relationship. Watching your best friend die could have that effect on a man.

Bill nodded. "Yeah, stuff like finding a place to live. You still living at the motel?"

"No." Just yesterday, he'd finally rented a cottage. He'd stayed at the hotel his first four weeks to avoid obligations in case he decided he couldn't deal with being back in town. But it hadn't been so bad, and he'd spent some time with Kim's dad and his new family. Yeah, it wasn't the same as it had been, but his bond with Max was still there. Once Max had had the accident, that had sealed it for Sean. He'd stay around for as long as the man might need him—and maybe longer. For the first time in ten years, he felt as though he might find a place for himself again. With Max, he had hope for the first time in a long time.

And then Kim had shown up and changed everything. It made him want to pack up and leave, the way he'd done before. But he wasn't going to. This was *his* town, and he'd come back to claim it. All he had to do was stay away from her while she was around. Especially since all he wanted to do was haul his sorry behind right back over to her house and strip away the past ten years to find out what had happened that night.

But he had too much pride for that.

"Glad to hear you've finally decided to stay awhile." Bill grinned. "So? Did she get a boob job while she was living in L.A.? I hear that all the chicks out there have boob jobs."

"For God's sake, Billy, back off." He picked up a pencil and drummed it on the desk.

Bill lifted an eyebrow. "So there are still some feelings there, huh?"

"No." He tapped the pencil harder. Faster.

"Liar." Bill dropped into a nearby chair and pulled it

closer. Tossed his hat on a desk and ran his hands through his spiky red hair. "Listen, sorry about sending you over there last night. I didn't realize it would mess you up. I mean, it's been ten years and all. Kinda figured you might be over it by now."

Sean snapped the pencil between his thumb and index finger. He let it drop to the ground, then gave Bill his most hostile glare. "I don't give a rip about her anymore, so drop it."

Bill stared back for a long moment. "What happened to you in the Army, man? You've turned into a major SOB."

It wasn't what had happened to him in the military. It had started in this town, at the merciless hands of Kim Collins when she'd ripped away the innocence of a young kid. "Kim might have a stalker."

"You?"

"Shut up."

Bill grinned. "Just checking. What's up?"

"Cheryl's ex-husband, Jimmy Ramsey. Wife beater that Kim put in jail. He's out on parole and he swore he'd come after her." Just saying it made his blood pressure escalate again.

"What do you have so far?" Bill settled into his cop persona, so much easier for Sean to take. He'd counted on their friendship to get him the job, and now he was regretting it. Friends demanded more than he was willing to give.

"I have a call in to his PO to see if he's checked in." The message from Kim on his phone that morning had aggravated him. She'd been so flippant and dismissive that Jimmy was after her, telling Sean to drop the case.

Not that he had any intention of listening to her. He was a cop, and his job was to protect and serve, even if the civilian in question happened to be the woman who had left him standing at the altar with two gold rings in his tux pocket. Yeah, sure he hadn't been able to turn up any evidence of a prowler outside her home, but when he'd stood there in the dark, he'd been certain something had been disturbed. The night sounds of the forest had been too quiet. Until he was convinced no one was after her, he wasn't going to back off.

"What about Cheryl? You talk to her?"

"She's in hiding."

Billy gave a low whistle. "It's serious stuff then, huh?"

"Kim helped her disappear and took the heat after Cheryl left." Impressive as hell that Kim had stuck around and faced Jimmy when she knew what he was capable of.

Billy grinned. "That's our Kimmy. She always protected that little sister of hers."

Sean tossed the thin file he'd created at Billy. "You take the case."

Billy handed the folder back. "It's yours."

"I don't want it." He set the papers on the desk. "Find someone else."

"We're understaffed, even with you here. With all these summer folk causing trouble, no one's got time to be following up on some psycho from California."

Sean folded his arms. "I'll switch duties with someone. I don't want it." Just because he couldn't drop the case didn't mean he was the one who had to be her shadow. Already tried that ten years ago and it wasn't his gig. Not anymore.

"I got a bunch of rookies on staff here. All our experienced guys went off to Portland when they got the funding for more positions. Not one of these guys knows how to do an investigation. All they can do is write up traffic tickets and OUIs. That's why I wanted you back. I need some hardened badass for these boys to follow."

"This case is a good opportunity for someone to learn." He didn't want to get involved with Kim. But putting Kim's life in the hands of a rookie? "You can provide oversight. Train the kid." His computer beeped that he had new mail and Sean nodded at it, even as he stood up and walked away from his desk. "That's the info from L.A. It's yours."

Bill swung to his feet and lumbered his large frame across the small office that looked as if it hadn't had a face-lift in thirty years. Stained ceiling tiles, warped wood paneling on the walls, battered desks shoved against one another to make room in a too-small space.

Luxury compared to Sean's life in the Middle East, where he'd been for the past few years.

While Bill opened the e-mail, Sean picked up his car keys. Time to get away. He'd go visit Max. Remind himself why he wanted to stay in town. "I'm taking off."

Bill waved absently as he studied the screen. "Yeah, go shower. You need it." He spun the monitor toward Sean, a color image filling the screen. "Before you go, take a look at this."

He didn't want to know. Didn't want to see it.

But he looked. It was a photo of Kim in a hospital bed, wearing a gown that had been pulled to the side. Her eyes were closed and she looked tiny and wan. She was covered in bruises, and there were gashes across her stomach and ribs.

Then he looked closer and his stomach heaved. Her entire thigh had been torn open, practically from hip to knee.

He swore. Death was far too good for Jimmy Ramsey.

"Look at the one of her sister."

Bill opened another image that showed Cheryl in a similar position with her arm at an unnatural angle and one side of her face so puffy she was almost unrecognizable.

Sean cursed again and clicked on the picture of Kim again. She'd endured all that to protect her sister. Half the guys in his Special Forces unit would have spilled their guts for less.

"You still want to hand this off to one of the rookies?"

Sean leaned back and closed his eyes, trying to quiet his

stomach. He, of the cast-iron gut, who'd seen more blood and body parts than he could count, getting nauseous because of a couple of photos? He was going soft. "The guy got six months."

Bill whistled. "Six months? That's it?"

"He's a cop."

"A cop. How many years of service?"

"Fifteen before he was suspended." The situation was ugly. "He's been investigated three times for excessive violence against female suspects but never disciplined. He has connections. Influence."

"Damn."

Yeah, no kidding. A cop with fifteen years' experience knew what he was doing. Ramsey would take down a rookie cop in a heartbeat. And rookies were all Bill had working for him.

Hell.

Sean picked up his phone and called the parole officer again. It was almost eight in the morning Pacific time, so he should be in by now.

A raspy voice answered on the first ring. "Vin here."

"Officer Sean Templeton here calling from the Ridgeport Police Department in Maine."

"Yeah, I just got done listening to your message. Ramsey hasn't checked in."

"Will you call me when he does?" *If* he does.

"Yeah. Later." Vin hung up.

Chatty guy.

"So?"

Sean hung up the phone. "He hasn't checked in." So Jimmy *could* be in Maine.

"I don't want him in my town." Bill actually looked a little stressed.

"You and me both." Sean dug his fingers into his forehead. Miserable friggin' headache. He had to think.

Needed to figure this out. "You have to take this case. A rookie is no match for Ramsey."

"Can't do it. I'm already overloaded. It's you or a rookie."

Sean narrowed his eyes at the man he'd once called his friend. "Do it for me."

"Do it for yourself."

He cursed. "The woman is my ex-fiancée. Don't you have rules against taking a case that you're personally involved in?"

"Not in this department. We're too small." Billy lifted an eyebrow. "Besides, you said you don't care about her."

"I don't."

Billy grinned. "Seems to me, the only reason I'd have for taking you off this case is if you were so screwed up by her that you were incapable of performing your duties. She got you that bad, Templeton?"

"Of course not. I can do my job."

Billy tossed him the folder. "Then I guess it's yours."

Sean caught the file. He was trapped, and they both knew it.

"Welcome back, Sean. Enjoy your first case."

"You're too damned cheery."

All he got was a bigger grin. "And *you're* too damned ornery. Go take a shower and we'll see you back here tonight. You're in charge of the night shift. I'm gonna stick to days now that you're around."

"I'm in charge? No way, Billy." The deal had been that he'd be a patrol officer with a beat, about as far from his Special Forces experience as possible. He didn't want responsibility for anyone anymore. All he wanted was a paycheck.

"It's Chief Vega to you. Remember that or I'll have to write you up for insubordination. The nights are yours. Enjoy."

Sean groaned. He had to get out of here. He couldn't deal with someone trying to be friends with him.

He might be off duty, but he wasn't going to be off the clock until he finished this deal with Jimmy Ramsey and got Kim out of his life.

Right now, he was going to find Kim.

He needed some answers.

EDDIE WAVED KIM off as he turned toward the docks, leaving Kim on her own to head into the office. As she clomped up the wooden steps, she could almost hear her dad on the phone, or her mom laughing at the reception desk.

Almost, but not quite. Joyce wasn't there, Max was in a coma and Kim had a psychopath stalking her.

Not exactly the utopia of her youth. That utopia was a mirage she'd never fall for again. Behind those moments of laughter, Joyce had been suffering and no one had realized it. Even now, Kim was the only one who really knew why her mom had killed herself, thanks to the letter Joyce had mailed right before she ended her life.

A letter that would haunt Kim forever.

She nodded at one of the maintenance guys on his way out of the office, the logo on his shirt identifying him. A giggle caught her attention and she turned in time to see one of the female employees latch on to his beefy arm and guide him in the direction of the laundry facilities.

Yeah, when Kim had been young, she'd lusted after the maintenance guys, too. Today, she only noticed their muscles and assessed how hard they'd be able to hit their wives.

Was she messed up or what?

She stepped inside the screened porch foyer and saw two strangers working the front desk. That was where her mom had spent her days, enjoying the contact with the guests and the outside world they represented.

Now it was a guy in his late twenties wearing a tight, black T-shirt that showed off his well-developed upper body, and a slightly older woman with blond hair pulled into two pigtails. They were arguing about something, and the woman seemed to be winning.

Kim was all in favor of avoiding both of them, but her dad's office was behind the reception desk. She cleared her throat, trying not to feel like a stranger in the place that had been her home. "Hello."

They ignored her and kept bickering.

"Hey!" What was up with this? For all they knew, she was a guest. Having the staff arguing in front of her was hardly what her parents would have allowed. It was as if anarchy had taken over now that Max wasn't around.

The woman spun toward her, plastering a cheery smile on her face in an amazing metamorphosis. "Good morning and welcome to the Loon's Nest. May I help you?"

"I'm…Max Collins's daughter, Kim."

The woman's eyes snapped wide open and she clapped a hand to her mouth. "Oh!" Then she dropped her hand. "I'm so sorry about your dad. Such a nice man."

"Yeah, I know." *And no, I haven't visited him yet, so don't ask.* Gee, think she was getting a little testy? She tried to smile and put on a friendly voice. "And you are?"

"Didi Smith. I work here year-round, helping out your dad in the winter." Didi was supermodel-skinny, but her eyes were sharp and intelligent. Maybe a fraction too much makeup for working the front desk at the Loon's Nest, but she knew how to maximize it to enhance her looks. Didi was a woman who wasn't afraid to admit her femininity. She'd fit in perfectly in L.A. Kim shook her hand, then nodded at the man, who stuck out his hand, as well.

"Will Ambrose. This is my first summer. Welcome." He gave her a nice smile that she could see would have a good effect on guests. It made her want to smile back, so she did. Felt weird to grin, but good, too. She should do it more often.

"I'm going to be in my dad's office for a bit, okay?"

"Sure." Didi fished a set of keys out of her back pocket. "I'll unlock it for you."

"He locks his office during the day now?" Since when did that happen? It wasn't as if he kept any money in there, and with Didi and Will running around out front, no one would be able to wander in unnoticed. Sure, she'd locked the door at the house, but that was because she had a homicidal maniac after her. Not too likely Max had landed one, as well.

Didi shrugged. "He started locking it in early June, maybe a month and a half ago."

"Did someone break in or something? Why the concern with security?"

"I don't know." Didi looked at Will, who shrugged.

"Never mind." The last thing she needed was to start thinking too much about her dad. "I'll be inside if you need me." She stepped inside and shut out Didi and Will, leaning back against the door while she looked at her dad's office for the first time in a decade. The room looked as if it belonged to a stranger.

Gone were all the family photos, except for a few of Cheryl and herself. Absolutely no sign of her mom, right down to the removal of the light fixtures Joyce had installed. The furniture was different, the curtains had changed and there was carpet on the beautiful old pine floor. It was as if someone had tried to transform it from a rustic camp office into something more suitable for suburban Boston.

Was this the handiwork of her dad's new concubine, or Max's attempt to erase the memory of his wife?

Not that it mattered. Kim was here to preserve a future for her sister, not dwell on the past. So she lifted her chin, walked to the desk and sat. She flicked on the computer and waited for it to boot up. Maybe she hadn't been to the hospital yet, but she could at least save this camp. No worries of running into her dad or his wife-from-hell.

This was good. Since she couldn't occupy herself with her own work, she could use the camp as a distraction from remembering that the last time she'd been in this town, her mother had been alive. A heaviness settled around her and Kim clamped down on the memories. See why she hadn't wanted to come back? Thinking about the past made it harder to deal with the present. Who needed that? Not her.

She shut off her emotions and opened that year's financial statements, which made absolutely no sense to her whatsoever.

She was a magazine editor, not a numbers person.

But Alan was. Maybe he could help. She picked up her cell phone and dialed his mobile. He answered on the second ring. "How's Maine?"

"It sucks. Any sign of Jimmy?"

"None. I've staked out your place and your work, and he hasn't turned up. No hang-up calls on your machine or at work. He'll show, though. I know he will."

Or maybe he's already in Maine.

No, dammit. She wasn't going to let him get to her. She was going to focus on Alan and how good it was to hear his voice. Alan. Safe and secure, her only real friend in L.A. It was amazing how close they'd gotten in the year and a half they'd known each other. Nothing like a couple of attempted murders to accelerate the bonding.

"How's the camp?" Alan asked.

"Just about in bankruptcy. Hey, can you tell me how to read financial statements?"

"Not in the five minutes I have until my next meeting. Why?"

"Apparently, the camp is in bad shape, so I promised an old friend I'd check it out."

"Seriously? You're actually looking at camp financial statements? I was joking when I asked you how it was. You said you weren't even going to set foot in the camp."

"Yeah, well, things changed. Can you help me? Where do I start looking to find out what's going on?"

He made a noise of exasperation. "I can't tell you how to audit a company in thirty seconds."

"Well, teach me something. I have work to do." She opened another file. Payroll. Will and Didi were on there. And Eddie. She didn't recognize any other names.

"I have extra vacation time. Why don't I fly out there and help you?" He hesitated. "I'm not sure I like you being out there alone when we don't know where Jimmy is."

She almost smiled. It felt good to have someone care about her. It was a shame that there was zero romantic interest between the two of them. Though if there had been any, they would have broken up by now. Between Jimmy and Sean, she wasn't exactly a poster child for healthy romantic relationships. Jimmy had made worse that which was already broken. "You can't come, Alan. You have to stay out there to watch for Jimmy. Remember the plan?"

"Yes, but the plan also entailed you hiding out in a secure hotel, not in a defenseless cabin in the middle of the woods."

Excellent point.

A loud rap sounded on the office door, startling her. It swung open before she could extend an invitation and she lurched back, grabbing a paperweight and aiming it at the intruder. Sean marched inside and her hand dropped in relief.

He was wearing jeans, boots and an old gray T-shirt that showed off the hard, lean body of a military warrior.

When she'd left ten years ago, he'd been a skinny eighteen-year-old who hadn't grown into his long limbs.

Not anymore.

He was all man, and he looked furious.

And for some stupid reason, she was glad to see him. Probably the fact that she had a stalker after her and Sean had a gun on his hip and looked ready to kill.

God help her if it was any other reason.

Chapter Four

"I gotta go. Bye." Tension rushed over him as Kim quickly hung up the phone.

Was she hiding something?

"Who was that?" Sean shut the door and leaned against it, taking a quick scan of the office. No threats, nothing out of place. Safe, for the moment.

"My friend. Alan Haywood. He's watching my apartment in L.A. to see if Jimmy shows up." Her cell phone rang again and she glanced down at it. "It's Alan."

He held out his hand. "Give it to me." Alan, huh? He didn't like the sound of a friend named Alan. Sounded fishy to him.

She glared at him. "No." She answered it. "What?"

She waited for a moment, then smiled. "No, I'm fine. The cops just arrived and I sort of panicked. But nothing has happened." She covered the mouthpiece and directed her next question to Sean. "*Has* anything happened? Did you find him?"

He shook his head and tried not to think about how the man on the other end of the phone had made her smile. Sean used to make her smile. Now all he did was make her panic. What had changed the night she'd decided to leave him? Not that he'd ever ask. She wasn't his problem anymore. Time had given him the distance he needed not to ask. Not to care. Not to obsess.

"I promise I'll call you every hour," she said into the phone. "Love you." She hung up and set the phone down. "Why are you here?"

"'Love you'?"

"He's a friend, Sean." She lifted an eyebrow. "Why do you care?"

"Just wanted to make sure it wasn't someone working for Jimmy trying to find out where you are."

Tension flickered in her eyes, but she quickly shoved it aside. "Didn't you get my message this morning? Jimmy isn't after me. I was being irrational and letting my imagination get to me. I'm fine."

Why did she have to be so stubborn? Anger roiled through him and he threw down the photos of her in the hospital. His ability to dismiss his concern about the case vanished the moment he'd seen those photos. Yeah, he'd tried to pawn the case off on Billy, but now that it was his, he was going to be haunted by those images until Jimmy Ramsey was back in jail—or dead. As a cop, he couldn't walk away. As Kim's ex-lover…well, that was something he had to get over. That wasn't why he was here. "He's no threat? I should drop the case? You'll be fine?"

"Where did you get those?" Her hand went to her thigh, where he knew a nasty scar had to be hidden.

He leaned against the desk, his hands flat on the surface. "Jimmy hasn't checked in for parole."

She caught her breath, her fingers curling around the arm of the chair. "It was a bear."

"Why are you shutting me out? I'm here to help you." Hard to imagine there was a time when he'd known every secret she had. She wouldn't even let him into her worst nightmare now.

Kim seemed to steady herself and threw him a challenging stare. "Why are you here? I thought you were going to assign someone else to the case."

He gritted his teeth. "It has to be me."

"Why? Do you think maybe you're too personally involved—"

He held up his hand. "It's been ten years, Kim."

"Believe me, I know how long it's been."

So she'd been counting the years as well? "What happened back then doesn't matter anymore."

Her eyebrows furrowed ever so slightly. "It doesn't?"

"No." It couldn't. He'd moved on, and he wasn't interested in revisiting their past. He simply wasn't. Instead, he nodded at the pictures. "That's what matters now."

She followed his gaze to the photos, and said nothing. He couldn't tell what she was thinking anymore. Oh, sure, he could sense her anxiety and fear, but nothing else. He sure couldn't see inside her mind. Didn't know why she'd left, why she hadn't visited her dad, why… The list was too long.

"Kim."

She looked at him. "What?"

"Let's make a deal. I'm here as a cop. That's my job, and let's not take it any further than that. The past is gone."

After a long moment, she nodded. "Fine. No past. It's better that way."

"Yeah." Then why did he so desperately want to find out what had happened? Why had she left? Dammit! Why couldn't he stop thinking about it? Was he so weak that one moment with her in his arms caused ten years of immunity to collapse?

"I'm getting an alarm installed today. I'm going to alert the staff to keep an eye out for him." She met his gaze. "He won't get me."

"It's my job to keep you safe. I'm not going away."

She groaned. "Why does it have to be you?"

"Because it does." He felt years of rage bubble up, bitterness he'd kept buried for so long. He couldn't contain it.

"I might not have been good enough to marry, but trust me, I'm good enough to keep you alive."

Her glittering eyes snapped to his face. He wished he could see pain and regret in them, but he saw nothing beyond the defensiveness. "I thought the past was off-limits."

"I won't let you use it to endanger yourself. Get over it and let me help."

"Sean—"

The door swung open and Sean was on his feet with his hand on his gun before Didi had even stepped inside. "You have a visitor," she said. She lifted her eyebrow at Sean in the same not-so-subtle flirtation she'd directed toward him when he'd first arrived.

As if he had time for that crap. "Who is it?"

Didi narrowed her eyes in the typical look of a woman who wasn't used to men being immune to her charm. "Tom Payton from the marina."

"I'll come out and meet him," he said.

"Me, too." Kim jumped up, ignoring his glare to stay in the office. "I have to run this place, Sean. I'm not going to let Jimmy rule my life."

"You're taking over the Loon's Nest?" Didi asked Kim as she trailed along after them. "Really?"

"Really." Kim walked into the reception area one step ahead of Sean, but he made sure she wasn't between his gun and their guest, who appeared to be a skinny kid wearing cutoffs and sneakers. He looked like he was eighteen, but something about his eyes said he was more likely to be in his mid-twenties. He was wearing a Yankees cap and his nose was sunburned. He blushed when Didi shot him a come-hither look. Guess the kid hadn't figured out that Didi probably gave that smile to anyone with a Y chromosome.

"I'm Kim Collins."

The kid nodded. "Tom Payton. Eddie sent me up here to

get you. He wants to show you something on Max's boat."
He looked nervously at Sean. "You're the cop?"

"Yeah."

"He saw your cruiser. Wants you to come, too."

Sean glanced at Kim as they followed Tom out the door.
Her face was shuttered and she wouldn't look at him. Was
she pissed at Sean or upset because they had to deal with her
dad? What had happened to make her hate Max so much?

No, that wasn't Sean's problem. It was so frustrating to
find himself falling into the old patterns: caring about her,
wanting to know what she was feeling, wishing he could take
away her anguish. He'd thought he hated her too much to
lapse into past behaviors. Habit. That's all his feelings were.
A bad habit it was time to break so he could focus on the
more important questions. For one, what was going on with
Max's boat?

Eddie met them at the door to the boathouse, where he
had Max's boat in dry dock. He wasted no time on pleasant-
ries. "You guys gotta see this." He walked them over to the
boat and pointed to the steering column. "Right there."

Sean could see some scratches on the casing. "What am
I looking for?"

Eddie pulled out a screwdriver and pointed to a small
piece of metal poking out. "That little piece wedged in
there?" He tugged on the steering wheel and it didn't turn.
"Jammed the steering column so it can't turn."

Sean squatted and pulled a flashlight off his belt. "You're
sure?"

"Yeah." Eddie leaned on the rim of the boat. "Told you
his wife was trying to kill him."

Sean had been treated to Eddie's murder theories during
their late nights at the hospital and he still didn't buy them.
In Sean's opinion, Eddie felt guilty and was trying to absolve
himself. Sean was certain Helen adored Max, even if she
didn't want to operate the Loon's Nest for the rest of her life.

"Assuming for a minute it wasn't Helen, how else could this have happened?"

Kim was standing back, her arms folded across her chest. She was acting as though she didn't care, but he couldn't believe it. He simply couldn't. He'd seen her love for her family too many times. It had been real and enduring. How had it come to this?

Eddie frowned. "I didn't do it."

"I know, Eddie. But could it have happened by mistake?"

He hesitated. "Well, Tom was working on the boat earlier in the day. He might have made an error, I guess."

Sean could hear Tom outside talking to one of the resort guests about renting a boat to go waterskiing.

He sat back on his heels. "If the piece got wedged in there before Max took the boat out, how could he have steered from the start? Or it is possible that it shifted?"

"It definitely shifted as he drove. Helen probably wedged it in there and knew the steering would freeze up at some point."

"But that could have been when he was going slow and was in no danger. It's not a very good way to kill someone."

Eddie frowned. "She's not real bright when it comes to lake things. Lucky for us."

Sean ground his teeth, trying to remain neutral. "Why are you so against Helen?"

Eddie's eyes narrowed. "How can you be on her side? She's the outsider."

"I'm not on anyone's side, Eddie. I'm just trying to get answers."

Eddie turned away and looked for Kim, who was standing even farther away, her arms hugged around her body. "You believe me, don't you, Kim? It was Helen trying to kill him."

She glanced at Sean and he saw such stark angst on her face he felt it slap him. He had to close his eyes for a moment to force himself not to reach out to her. Dammit! *Break the habit, Sean!* But at least he'd been right to doubt her claim that she didn't care about her dad at all.

"I don't know what to believe." Her voice was so pained that Eddie immediately softened.

"I'm sorry, Kimmy. I know it's hard for you to talk about it." He refocused on Sean. "But this is your job. You find a way to pin it on Helen before she destroys this place. I love this family and I'm not going to see it destroyed by some scheming outsider like Helen."

"I'll look into it. Keep the boat off-limits and I'll send someone to check it out." Sean inspected the rafters of the boathouse. There was a ledge around the ceiling where life jackets and some small boats were stored. Perfect hiding spot for someone who wanted to tamper with the boat and needed a place to wait until the opportunity arose.

This whole place was rife with opportunity for a stalker. It was a bunch of cabins in the woods. If Kim tried to run this place, she'd be walking on secluded trails all day long. He looked at her, and she was checking out the rafters as well. When she met his gaze, he knew she'd been thinking the same thing.

Good. Maybe she'd listen to him now.

KIM WAS TRUDGING back toward the office when Sean caught her arm. He nodded toward Tom. "Let's chat with him."

"About my dad's accident?" She swallowed hard.

"Yeah." He didn't let go, forcing her to accompany him. He wouldn't let her run away from her own father's fate. Not when she'd given him that glimpse of her hidden angst. He wasn't going to make it easy for her to reject Max. Because he loved Max. Not because he gave a rip about Kim's happiness anymore. Or at least he was trying not to. It was harder than he wanted it to be. "Tom. Got a sec?"

Tom turned away from the guest who was paddling away in a canoe. "Yeah. What's up?"

"You worked on Max's boat before he took it out?"

"Yeah."

"Did you inspect the steering column?"

"I did the normal maintenance. Everything was fine." But he wasn't making eye contact, and he was shifting restlessly on his feet.

"But did you check the steering column?"

Tom's hands settled on his hips. "I didn't look for things wedged in it." There was a defiant edge to his voice. A challenge.

Interesting. "Eddie showed you the steering column?"

"Uh-huh."

Yeah, Eddie would make a good investigator. "Any thoughts on how it got there?"

Tom shrugged. "It wasn't me. I didn't screw up."

Sean lifted his eyebrow. "No one says you did. I'm just trying to gather information."

"Well, it wasn't me." Tom picked at the edge of his T-shirt. "Is that it? I gotta get back to work."

Sean let him go.

Kim stared across the lake, her arms folded across her chest. "You think my dad's crash wasn't an accident?" Her voice was clipped and reserved.

He didn't buy her aloofness. "Do you?"

She pressed her lips together. Finally, she shrugged.

"Do you even care?" He had to ask. Had to know if she could even acknowledge that she felt something inside that frigid wall she'd erected around herself. Had to understand how the woman he'd loved had become the woman she was today.

After a long moment, she nodded once. Then she walked away.

SIX HOURS LATER, Kim waved the hunky maintenance guy away after she locked the door behind him and set the new alarm. Carl, the head of maintenance she'd seen flirting with one of the girls that morning, had driven her home and done a walk-through of her house before leaving.

She hadn't asked for his escort, but Sean had had a little chat with Carl before taking off for the day. After she'd refused Sean's bodyguard offer, he'd compromised by giving her someone else's assistance.

She leaned against the locked door and sighed. She couldn't live like this, but she couldn't deny that a small part of her felt better after Carl had inspected the place. Was Jimmy here? Was he in California? Was she losing her mind? He was making her so crazy she didn't know what to think.

Her cell phone rang. She flipped the phone open. "You don't need to call me every five minutes."

"Still no sign of him out here," Alan said. "I'm getting worried. He should have tried to find you by now."

She swallowed. "You know he's going to show up out there. He has to."

"Have you seen any sign of him yet?"

"No." She hadn't told Alan about the noise on the roof last night. Why would she? Growing up, she'd heard so many noises and they had never been a homicidal maniac. Until she had proof it was anything other than a bear, she wasn't going to let her paranoia rule her. "I got an alarm and the cops are on it."

"I think I should come out there. Stay with you."

She frowned and forced herself to walk into the kitchen to find something for dinner. "I'm fine. Really. We have to stick to the plan." Stay organized. Stay in control. It was the only way to win. "His goal is to get us to react emotionally and make a mistake. We can't let him win."

Alan was quiet for a moment. "I don't like it."

"Join the club." She paused. "Can you do me a favor?"

"Sure."

"Can you double-check the date Jimmy got out of prison? Find out for sure if he was still there a month ago?"

"Why?"

"There's been some stuff going on around here. Weird stuff. I just want to make sure that Jimmy didn't have anything to do with it."

"What's going on, Kim?" His words were rushed, almost panicky. "Talk to me."

"Just find out, okay?" She didn't want to talk about the possibility that Jimmy had tried to kill her dad. Talking about it gave the swirling innuendos validity, and she didn't want to do that. Not unless there was a reason. "I'm seeing ghosts where there are none and I need to remind myself of the facts, okay?"

"That's all it is?"

"Yes." Heaven help her, she hoped that was all it was.

He grunted. "I'll check. Call me in an hour, okay? To check in."

She couldn't keep the smile off her face. "Thanks for caring."

"See you later, Kim. Be careful."

She disconnected and shoved her phone in her pocket. No way was she leaving it in another room. Such a fine line between being paranoid and being careful. She'd been clinging to the right side of the line for the past eighteen months, but right now she was dangerously close to catapulting down the other side of it into an emotional hell that would destroy her the way it had killed her mother.

SEAN PULLED HIS cruiser into Kim's driveway later that evening. It was past midnight and the lights in the cabin were still on. Nerves getting to the woman who claimed to be so tough?

He parked outside her front door and climbed out, standing silently to listen to the woods. To feel the darkness.

Owls were hooting softly. Loons were calling. The sounds of night were active and right.

Then why was his skin prickling?

He turned slowly and stared into the woodsy hill above the driveway. It was too dark to see, but he didn't need his eyes. He could sense something. Someone.

Soundlessly, he unclipped his gun and slid it free, aiming it into the woods.

"Sean? Is that you?"

A window scraped open and he glanced up at Kim. "Quiet."

Her eyes widened and her mouth snapped shut.

He turned back to the woods, but whatever had been there was gone. He could sense nothing. Had it been his imagination? On edge because the woman he once loved might be in danger? Or an accurate cop instinct?

He wished he knew.

He holstered his gun and faced the window. "Any problems tonight?"

"Was someone out there?"

"I don't know."

Her eyes were huge and he wanted to grab her and hold her and chase those nightmares away. The past didn't matter, huh? What an idiot he'd been to think he could order it away. "I'll check out the rest of the property, then head on out."

She stared at him. "Do you want to come in?"

Hell, yes, he wanted to come in. She was leaning out of her old bedroom window. They'd stolen many a moment in that spot while her parents were out on the lake. Too many memories. "Um, no, I need to keep moving."

Her fingers gripped the window frame. "I could make some coffee, so you don't fall asleep."

"You want me to come in?"

Silence fell and he regretted his question. Kim was too

proud to acknowledge that she was scared. He shouldn't have forced her to admit that she wanted his company because she never would. Not anymore.

Despite everything, he wanted to be inside that house with her. It didn't matter what the circumstances were or that they were trying to pretend they were strangers. He simply wanted to be with her. To keep her safe, whether she could admit she needed help or not. "I'd like some coffee."

She hesitated, then nodded. "I'll be right down."

The slam of the window jarred through the night and Sean headed to the front step to meet her. Despite all his efforts to fight his attraction to her, to resist the lure of returning to her side, he was getting sucked in.

He stood on the doorstep and listened to her feet thudding on the stairs as she ran down to greet him. A sense of the inevitable settled heavily on his shoulders. He didn't want to be here, yet he couldn't stop it.

And it had nothing to do with the job.

They had ended badly before, and he'd seen enough to know it wouldn't be any different this time. For ten years, he'd buried the pain. But seeing her again was bringing it all back to the surface again, and it sucked.

Dammit. He was tired of the unanswered questions. Maybe it was time for the discussion they'd never had. Maybe that would finally free him from caring, because Lord knew, nothing else had worked.

Chapter Five

Kim punched the alarm code to disable it, then paused with her hand on the doorknob. She took a desperately needed moment to remind herself that Sean in her house meant nothing. Cop and civilian. No past. Just like last night, when he'd been there as a police officer.

He didn't want to talk about what had happened before. So what if she wasn't over it? It didn't matter that she hadn't been able to stop thinking about him since she'd seen him. She felt so ashamed she'd walked out on him that way, without a word. Without an explanation. Now that he was back in her life, she couldn't stop thinking about how he must have felt waiting for her.

Waiting. Wondering. She'd betrayed him.

It had been ten years ago. A lifetime had passed. Their relationship was over, and she had to remember that. She closed her eyes, took a deep breath and opened the door. Sean was standing on the step, looking frustrated and determined, and her heart jumped.

Did he look good in his uniform or what? He was so different from the boy she'd loved, but he was the same, too…maybe. "Come on in."

He stepped inside and stopped just over the threshold, acting like a guest. So different from the other night when he'd taken possession of her house as if he belonged there. The way he used to act when they were teenagers. Now? They were like strangers. Regret flooded through her and she tried to shut it off, even as a longing for the intimacy they used to share made her want to touch his shoulder. Lean against him. Feel his warmth strengthen her.

"You're sure the coffee is no trouble?" he asked. His voice was polite and even, and he was scanning the interior of the house. But there was an undercurrent to his tone that made her skin prickle. What wasn't he telling her?

"No problem at all." Coffee. Right. She'd invited him in for a caffeine boost. "You can wait in the family room. I'll start the pot."

"I'll go with you." He fell in behind her as she headed toward the kitchen.

Their feet echoed on the pine floors, his steps heavy and slightly uneven, hers soft in her sneakers. She glanced over her shoulder. "Do you have a leg injury or something?"

His gaze flicked to her face. "Why?"

"Your walk isn't the same as it used to be. It sounds different."

He lifted one eyebrow. "You remember what my walk sounded like?"

She felt her cheeks heat up and she turned away. "I guess so." How embarrassing. He probably hadn't thought about her once since she'd left, and here she was, admitting she could recall how he used to walk. So she'd spent the last decade thinking about him. So every man she'd dated had fallen short in comparison. So what?

She yanked open the fridge where she'd stashed her coffee beans and he leaned against the counter next to her, his arms folded loosely across his chest. "What else do you remember?" His voice was soft, with that same roughness it'd had when he used to whisper in her ear when they made love. The shift wasn't intentional; it was simply how he spoke when he was battling his emotions.

What was he thinking about that was making his voice gruff? She swallowed hard and shut the fridge. "Um…I think you broke your finger."

He glanced down at his crooked digit and flexed it. "Yeah, I did."

The churning of the coffee grinder startled them both and they looked at each other, then laughed at the same time. "Guess I'm a little on edge," she said.

His smile faded into something soft. "Yeah, me, too."

"Really?" The old Sean had always told her his feelings, but she hadn't thought this new, aloof Sean would.

He shrugged, his gaze fixed on her as she shoveled grounds into the machine. "I thought someone was out in the woods when I got here."

Her hand slipped and she dumped the grounds on the counter. "You did?"

He reached out and brushed his fingers over the back of her hand, his touch light and shockingly heavy at the same time. A gesture he'd made a thousand times before. Their unspoken language of support. Her gut lurched and she didn't know whether to pull away. She'd needed that touch so much, but could they really go back there?

"But I wasn't sure if anyone was out there or not," he said. "I'm not used to questioning myself." He looked down at his hand, still resting against hers, and then moved away.

For a moment, there was a tense silence, then he cleared his throat. "Coffee smells good." He busied himself sweeping up the spilled grounds off the counter and into his hand.

She nodded. Moment over.

Sean went to the sink and dumped the grounds, then washed his hands. The only sound in the room was the running water, then the drip of the faucet after he shut it off.

"I could stop by tomorrow and fix that if you want. Wastes water."

She met his gaze. "What's going on, Sean?"

He tossed the paper towel under the sink, knowing where the trash can was without even looking. "I don't know where Jimmy is and it worries me. He still hasn't turned up in California. From what I can figure, he's not the kind of guy to lie low now that he's free."

She shook her head. "No, about us."

He froze, then spoke carefully, as if choosing his words precisely. "What about us?"

"I...um..." She licked her lips, not sure what to say. After ten years of apologizing in her mind, it didn't make it any easier to do in person. "I'm sorry."

"About what?"

"Leaving you." She was so sorry. She'd loved him, and she'd hurt him. People didn't hurt those they loved.

"What about the rest of it?"

She frowned. "What are you talking about?"

"Leaving your family. Abandoning them. Hating them. What about that?"

Defensiveness made her voice sharp. "You don't understand."

He leaned against the counter again and folded his arms over his chest. "Then tell me. Tell me why you let your father sit alone in his hospital room every day without visiting him. Tell me why you didn't come home for your mom's funeral. Tell me why, Kim. Explain it to me so I can stop hating you."

Pain shot through her. "You hate me?"

"Yes."

"Oh, God." She sat down at the table and blinked hard. Her throat was tight. "You used to love me and now you hate me?" It hurt. So much.

Sean sighed and sat across from her. "I don't hate you."

"Liar." Why had she thought a simple apology would solve

everything? There was so much more between them. None of the emotions had gone away. They were all still there. Maybe even more now, because she'd had a decade to obsess over them.

The corner of his mouth curved up. "Okay, sometimes I thought I hated you."

She pressed her lips together and stared out through the glass doors at the lake. She could see the reflection of the moon on the water and some lights on the opposite shore. A boat went by the dock, its red light passing slowly on the water, close enough that the driver would be able to see in her windows. She shivered as it slipped out of sight into the blackness, the hum of its engine fading into the night. Other than the cry of the loons, there was silence.

"Why do you hate your dad?"

She looked at Sean. Maybe it was time to talk. He deserved that. "He killed my mother."

Sean's forehead furrowed. "What are you talking about? She killed herself."

Kim shook her head. "She sent me a letter before she did it. The reason she committed suicide was because she hated my father and being married to him and he wouldn't let her go. Death was the only way she could be free."

Sean's face darkened. "You're trying to tell me that she committed suicide because your dad drove her to it?"

"Yes." She let her breath out in a deep exhale. It felt so good to tell someone. She'd never had anyone to tell, had sat on that knowledge for so many years. Cheryl would have been the only one to tell, but she still loved their dad and Kim would never take that away from Cheryl. It had always been Kim's burden to carry alone. Until now. Sean could share it with her. Just like the old days, when he would lessen her pain merely by being by her side and understanding.

"You're wrong." Sean bit out the words with an intensity that shook her.

"What?" The fragile respite she'd found shattered instantly at his rejection.

He smacked his fist on the table and shoved his chair back. "You're wrong. Your dad is wonderful. He adored her, he worshipped all of you and he took me into the family as his own son. He tried to save her. It was your leaving that did her in. You're the one who destroyed the family, and I don't understand why."

She stared at him. "Every day I have to live with the fact that if I hadn't left, I might have been able to help her. To save her. You don't need to make me feel guilty. I've already got that covered."

Sean gripped the edge of the table and took a deep breath. "If you feel bad, why are you rejecting your dad? He needs you. His wife left him, and both his daughters. He has nothing without you."

Remorse surged through her. "Stop it! It's not my fault! I might not have been able to save my mom, but my dad was the reason she killed herself. It's my dad's fault, and he doesn't deserve to be happy. He ripped our family apart with his obsession about this lake and his inability to see that his wife was miserable. Don't blame me because your boyhood dreams of being my dad's son were lost! You could have stayed here for him and you chose to leave, too. So back off!"

They were both on their feet now, chests heaving with deep breaths. Moisture filled her eyes, but she fought it off. No way would she shed another tear for these men. Never!

The coffeemaker beeped that the brew was ready, but neither of them moved.

"Why did you leave me, Kim?" His voice was so soft, but it slid through her like a dagger.

"Because I was afraid that if I married you, I'd end up like my mother." The words tumbled out, desperate to be spoken after years of suppression. "Please understand, Sean. I can't deal with it alone anymore. You have to know that I didn't hurt you on purpose. I loved you and—"

"You thought that you'd end up killing yourself if you were married to me?" He retreated, his face crumpled with the blow of her words. "That I would make you so miserable the only way out would be to die?" He looked as if he'd been punched in the gut, over and over and over again, as if he was in so much pain he could never live again.

What had she done? "No, that's not what I meant…" She reached for him, but he stepped out of her reach. She hadn't realized how much those words could hurt until they tumbled out of her mouth. "Sean, come back. It's not like that. It wasn't you. That came out wrong." She'd tried to take away his pain, but she'd hurt him more. So much more. Her stomach blistered with her mistake. "Sean—"

He waved her off. "I gotta get out of here."

She grabbed his arm as he headed for the door. "Sean! Don't leave. I was eighteen! I didn't know—"

He spun around and wrapped his fingers around her upper arms, holding her close to him. His face was so near she could feel his breath on her lips. "I would have died for you. I loved you more than life. And you throw that crap in my face?"

She couldn't fight the tears this time. "I loved you, too. I really did. But my mom…she was so convincing when she told me I couldn't marry you and that I had to leave town. I was confused and didn't know what to do. Then my mom died and I got so scared and my dad was losing it and Cheryl tried to kill herself and all I could do was read the letter from my mom and I didn't know—"

"Shut up."

She bit her lower lip and stared at him. How could she ever make this right? Why did she have to keep hurting him like this?

"Go see your dad, Kim. I don't know what your mom said to you, but she's wrong. He's been dying a slow death ever since she killed herself. He loved her the way I loved you."

"I'm so sorry I hurt you."

"If you're sorry, then go see your dad. He's the one you need to save. I'm over you."

"Are you?" God help her, she didn't want him to be over her. She wanted him back. She laid her hand on his cheek. "Are you really over me?"

He pulled her hand away. "Don't even go there, Kim. I might have been able to forgive you for leaving me, but I'll never be able to forgive you for what you did to your family."

"Dammit, Sean! Why don't you take off your blinders and see that my dad's the bad guy? Not me. Just because I left you doesn't mean I'm guilty of all the wrongs in the world!"

"You destroyed your family. Your dad didn't. He tried to save it." The conviction in his voice blew through her and she realized that he fully believed his words.

She pulled away. She knew Sean had idolized her family, but come on! How could he not see the truth? "You're so angry at me that you'll try to blame me for everything?"

"Believe me, I wish it was that simple."

Before she could ask what that meant, he walked out the front door and slammed it behind him.

THE NEXT EVENING, Kim pulled her sweatshirt over her hands as she walked up to the nurses' station. She could do this. She'd spent all day in her dad's office at the Loon's Nest working up the courage to go to the hospital. Now it was almost eight at night and she was finally here. What if she threw up? That would be totally embarrassing. "Hi."

A nurse looked up. "Good evening. Can I help you?"

She swallowed. "Um, I'm Kim Collins. My dad is in the hospital here. His name is Max Collins. I'd like to talk to his doctors."

"Of course. I'll let them know you're here." The nurse pointed down the hall. "He's in room 302. I'll have the doctor meet you there. It could be a while before he's available." She turned away before Kim could request another meeting spot.

She didn't have to go into the room. She could wait outside. In the hall.

For her sister. She was doing this for her sister.

She made it as far as a bench next to his room and sank into the seat, pulling her feet up in front of her and hugging her knees. Who was she kidding? She was here because of what Sean had said last night. After he'd left, the hours had dragged by as she lay in bed, staring at the ceiling and thinking about things she hadn't thought about for a long time. She'd even begun to doubt her own view of the situation—until she'd gotten up and reread her mom's letter.

The words were unassailable. There was no room for Sean's interpretation. Her dad was no saint. But she still felt horrible about the expression on Sean's face when she told him why she'd left him. She hadn't meant it the way it sounded, but wasn't that exactly why she had left? On the other hand, it didn't make any sense anymore, thinking that Sean would destroy her.

"What are you doing here?"

She winced at Sean's hostile voice, but she didn't look up. "Waiting for the doctors."

"You been in to see him?"

"No." She stared at the floor and watched his feet come into view. Faded black boots and blue jeans. Apparently, he was off duty. Did the man ever sleep?

Oh, great. So now she was worrying that he wasn't taking care of himself? Her mom had been right. You stay around a man like Sean and you'll never be able to resist him, even if he won't make you happy. The only chance to find herself had been to leave.

She'd found herself. So why did he still have this effect on her?

His feet moved out of her sight and she had to bite her

lower lip to keep from asking him to stay. She did *not* need him. And even if she did, what right did she have to ask? It wouldn't be fair to reach out to him and then leave again.

She couldn't change the past, but she could stop herself from repeating it.

Then the bench sagged and she glanced up to see Sean sitting beside her. He looked tired. More tired than she'd ever seen him. "You're not sleeping."

"Are you?"

She shook her head, wishing she knew what to say to bridge the chasm between them. Another apology would be so inadequate.

"Ms. Collins?"

She stood, and Sean rose next to her as a doctor approached. He had gray hair, glasses and a kind face. "I'm Dr. Weiss." He nodded at Sean. "Will you excuse us?"

Sean's face tightened and he stepped away. He wasn't family and had no right to hear. For all she knew, he hadn't even been able to talk to the doctors about the man he considered his own father. Kim touched his arm and he stopped. "He can stay."

Dr. Weiss nodded and Sean returned to her side, his shoulder brushing against hers in a silent thanks. "Your father had a serious head injury. He was unconscious underwater for almost too long. He hasn't woken up yet, and we have no way of knowing if he ever will. If he does, we can't predict the amount of brain damage he has sustained. He may wake up and be fine, or he may never be the person he was before the accident."

To her horror, tears welled up before she even knew they were coming. What was up with that?

Sean's arm slipped over her shoulders, his fingers twisting in her hair. "But he could wake up and be as good as new, right?" His voice was tight, clipped.

It felt so good to be held by him. She couldn't keep

herself from leaning into him as she wiped her cheeks, even though she knew she had no right to do so.

The doctor nodded. "It's possible he could be fine, but I wouldn't get my hopes up if I were you."

"You aren't us," Sean said quietly. "Is there anything else you can share?"

"No. I do recommend you spend time with him. Sometimes that can make a difference." The doctor gave them a brief smile. "I have to run, but if you have any questions, have the nurses' station page me."

"Thank you," Sean said.

Kim managed to mutter something appreciative and the doctor rushed off.

The second he left, she turned toward Sean at the same instant he lifted his other arm around her. She pressed herself against his chest and he buried his face in her hair. They said nothing, just clung to each other, holding on to the one thing they could touch.

It was Sean who spoke first, his voice muffled against her hair. "Will you come see him? Please?"

She released him and stepped back. "I can't."

"Dammit, Kim. Why not?"

"This is why." She pulled her mom's letter out of her pocket and handed it to him. "I received it three days after she died. Don't read it now, and I want it back when you're done with it."

He started to unfold it and she grabbed it from his hand, folded it and shoved it into his front pocket. "Later, Sean." She gave her head a little shake to clear it. "Any leads on my dad's accident? Or on Jimmy?"

He drew his shoulders back in a visible effort to gather himself. "Helen let me check your dad's personal files. For the past two months, he's been withdrawing fairly large sums of money on a regular basis, but we couldn't find any evidence of what he was spending it on."

Kim frowned. "What does that show?"

"I don't know."

"If Helen was the one who tried to kill him, do you really think it's smart to tell her you don't think his crash was an accident?"

He lifted an eyebrow. "You don't trust me to be circumspect?"

She had no energy for a fight. "I don't know. I'm too tired to think. What can I help with?"

"Is there a place in the house that your dad used to hide stuff?"

She frowned. "He had a hidden safe in his office, but I don't know if it's still there."

"Let's go check."

"Now?"

"Unless you have other plans? Maybe with that friend of yours? Alan, you said his name was?"

Was she imagining the annoyance in his voice? "Alan is in California. And no, I have no other plans."

"Fine. I'll follow you in my car."

"Fine." Just what she needed. More alone time with Sean.

"THE DOOR'S LOCKED." Kim sighed and leaned her head against her dad's office door. "I forgot, he locks it now. I don't have a key."

She looked so exhausted that Sean started to raise his hand to touch her hair the way he used to, but he dropped his arm instead. Why did he still want to touch her? Hadn't he seen all he needed to know that their past was over? Last night, she'd eviscerated him with her statement that she'd been afraid that she'd end up killing herself if she married him. He closed his eyes for a moment and tried to shove away the ache. Why couldn't he hate her? That comment alone should have done it.

But he couldn't hate her. He shoved his hands deep into

his pockets and his fingers hit the letter she'd put there. What was in that letter? Would it answer some of his questions? God, he wanted to read it. It couldn't have been as bad as she said.

Kim pushed herself off the door. "Someone should be around here somewhere. They never leave the reception desk unattended at this hour."

Right. Focus, Sean. "How about the mailroom? Maybe someone's in there sorting." He turned away and walked to the other side of the reception desk, shoving open the door to discover Didi, the flirty receptionist, going at it with Will, the guy who had been working the desk when Sean had stopped by the other day. He stifled a grin and flicked the light switch. "Good evening."

Kim walked in just as Didi shrieked and flung Will off her. They hadn't quite managed to fully compromise themselves, but Sean had no doubt that he and Kim would have gotten an eyeful if they'd arrived five minutes later.

Didi grabbed her shirt from the floor and darted out of the room, stammering an embarrassed apology. Will's face was bright red and he was fastening his pants as fast as possible. "I'm so sorry, Ms. Collins. I really am. We didn't mean for this to happen and I know we shouldn't have done it here…" He stuttered when he zipped some skin and abandoned his nervous stammering to focus on the apparently complicated task of getting dressed. He hustled out of the room, tucking in his shirt.

Sean grinned and leaned against the doorjamb, recalling the days he'd done that speed-dressing thing when Kim's parents had returned home unexpectedly. Kim caught his expression and looked surprised. Then her cheeks flushed and she started to laugh.

"Been there, done that, huh?"

She nodded, her eyes dancing. "You remember that time you fell on the glass of iced tea that was on the floor by the bed?"

He grinned. "I was bleeding all over the place and trying to get dressed before your dad made it to the top of the stairs." It felt good to laugh with her. Maybe this was what they both needed, a break from worrying about her dad, their past and everything else. Sometimes you just had to let it go.

"And then when you stood up, there was blood seeping through your jeans and my dad totally busted us." She was laughing now and it made him realize that he hadn't seen her smile since she'd been back.

"You're beautiful when you smile."

Her smile broadened. "Thanks. You don't look half-bad, either."

"Not half-bad?" He grinned at that. "In the old days, you used to swoon over me."

She lifted her eyebrows. "In the old days, you couldn't keep your hands off me. You made me believe I was the sexiest girl on the planet."

"You were. Still are."

"Then how come you aren't trying to bed me constantly?" She put her hands on her hips and tried to look offended.

He levered himself away from the door frame and sauntered toward her, giving her his most devilish look. "Is that an invitation? Because you know I'd never turn down a chance to spend the night in your bed."

She gave him her best come-hither look, spoiled by her laughter, as it always was. She'd never been any good at playing the serious seductress. Not that it mattered. Laughter had always been their aphrodisiac. From the way he noticed the curve of her body under her T-shirt, it still was. "Since when do you wait for an invitation?" she asked.

"Didn't realize the invite was still open." He hooked his index fingers in the belt loops on either side of her hips and tugged, the way he'd done so many times before. The action came so naturally to him, he didn't even have to think about it.

And, as she'd done on countless occasions, Kim let him pull her toward him, her hips swaying in rhythm with each movement of his hands, her fingers resting on his forearms. At the last second, the laughter faded from her eyes and she looked uncertain. "You really want to kiss me?"

"Hell, yes." He didn't give himself permission to think about it. He simply did what he wanted to do.

Chapter Six

Kim tasted the same way Sean had remembered in his dreams. Vanilla and toothpaste, and something else he'd never quite been able to place. Her lips were soft under his, a perfect match for him.

He could kiss her forever. Stand in that mailroom and kiss her until the world was gone.

Then she made a small sound in the back of her throat that he recognized and she slid her hands up his arms, linking her fingers behind his neck.

Okay, forget kissing. It would never be enough. He needed more. He needed all of her, every bit as badly as he'd needed her a decade ago. He let go of her belt loops and flattened his hands on her back, crushing her against him while he dove into her mouth. He couldn't get enough. She was everything to him, and she'd never left his soul. He'd been a fool to think he was over her, to think he didn't care.

He dropped his hands and cupped her buttocks, pressing her hips against his front. Closer. He needed her closer. He needed to touch her, taste her, inhale her. Every inch of her. The mole on her left little toe, the scar on her right hip from the fishing-hook mishap when they were in tenth grade, all of her. She was his, and she'd never stopped being his.

Her fingers in his hair, her breath hot in his mouth, her

body lashed against his as if she was afraid someone would try to tear them apart. He knew the feeling. Desperation rushed over him as he slipped his hands under her shirt. The feel of her bare skin against his hands rocked his knees and he had to take a step to keep their balance. Had it been this way when they were teenagers? The power was so intense, familiar yet shockingly unexpected. Imbued with an intensity he didn't recognize.

Someone cleared her throat and tapped lightly on the door.

Kim and Sean released each other at the same time and stepped apart. Kim's cheeks were flushed and her eyes were bright, her lips red from the effects of their kiss. Out of habit, he rubbed his jaw to check whisker length. "I guess I should have shaved."

She lifted one shoulder. "It's okay." Her gaze slid away from him to the door, where Didi was standing, now fully clothed.

Okay? It was a hell of a lot more than okay, but what was he supposed to say? They had an audience, and before the kiss, he'd still been trying to convince himself he'd be better off hating her. He had no idea what he was thinking. Or what she was thinking, for that matter. She looked somewhat overwhelmed, though. He knew the feeling.

"So, um, I wanted to apologize," Didi said. "It won't happen again." She began to turn away. "We'll just get back to work."

Kim held up her hand. "Hang on."

He grinned. His sweet Kim would never stay confused for long.

"No sex in the office," Kim said.

Didi's eyes flashed, but she nodded. "No problem."

"Good." Kim took a deep breath. "I'll consider it over, then."

She caught Sean's eye and he wondered how far he and

Kim would have gone if Didi hadn't interrupted. He swallowed hard at the thought.

What was he doing? He couldn't afford to fall for her again. For God's sake, she thought marriage to him would make her suicidal. And she was leaving town. Did he need any more signs than that? No. So why couldn't he stop thinking about how she'd felt in his arms? He was a fool. A damned fool.

"I need a set of keys to this place," she said to Didi, "including my dad's office."

Didi frowned. "Sure. I'll get a set made up for you tomorrow."

"Can I get my dad's office key now? I need to get in there." Kim held out her hand.

Didi whipped out her key ring and pulled a key off it. "Here. Leave it in the register when you leave and I'll get a duplicate made tomorrow so I still have my set."

"Thanks." Kim walked out of the mailroom, looking back over her shoulder. "You have your shirt on backward, Didi. You might want to fix that before you come out."

KIM REMOVED THE books from the second shelf of the bookcase, pulled out the shelf backing and sat back on her heels. "It's still there."

Sean squatted beside her. "Do you know the combination?"

"It used to be my birthday, my mom's birthday and then Cheryl's birthday." She was so aware of his shoulder brushing up against hers, yet neither of them had mentioned the kiss in the mailroom.

How could she bring it up? She had no idea what to say. Yes, a part of her was thrilled that Sean had responded with such intensity, but she was equally terrified that she'd responded in kind. After ten years, she still had no immunity to him, exactly as her mother had warned. What Kim didn't understand was why being with him felt right. And that made her feel as scared and unsure as she had felt ten years ago, only this time she had a decade of guilt and over-analysis to add to the equation.

Sean reached for the combination and began spinning it.

"You still remember all our birthdays?" she asked.

The safe popped open, answering her question. Of course he remembered. She'd thought about him every year on his birthday. Wondered where he was. If he was okay. If he was thinking about her.

He looked frustrated. "I guess I wasn't as close to your family as I thought if I didn't know this safe existed."

She didn't know what to say to that, so she settled for resting her hand on his shoulder as they leaned forward to inspect the contents. There was a spiral notebook and some envelopes that looked as though they might have cash in them.

And a gun.

Kim stared at the black metal. "Did you know he had a gun?"

"No." Sean frowned as he pulled the notebook out. "He never mentioned it to me."

"Me, either. He doesn't seem like the gun type."

"I agree. He'd be more likely to shoot himself in the foot than nail a bad guy."

She smiled and Sean gave her a small grin as he flipped open the notebook. "You remember when I told him I wanted to be a cop and he told me that good boys don't play with guns?"

"You were eight at the time and he'd just caught you trying to shoot acorns with a squirt gun." She eyed him. "And when he startled you, you nailed me instead of the acorn."

Sean grinned. "Just gave your dad more fuel for his claim that guns were dangerous."

Her smile faded. "So why would he have one?"

"The better question is, why is he paying money to a private investigator?" He pointed to some writing. "I recognize that name. He's one of the more reputable P.I.s in Portland."

"A P.I.?" Tension slipped around her heart and squeezed gently. "And a gun?" She looked at Sean. "Jimmy?"

Sean eyed her. "He really scares you, doesn't he?"

She met his gaze. "I won't let him."

"Maybe you should."

"No." She stood up and walked across the room. "You don't understand. He likes to play psychological games with me. Get in my head so I freak even when he's not around. The way to beat him is to stay rational." She gestured at the notebook. "Not by imagining my dad's problems were caused by Jimmy when he was in prison at the time."

"People in prison know people on the outside."

She clenched her fists at the articulation of the thought she'd refused to acknowledge until now. "Like I need to hear that."

"I think you do. You're so focused on being tough that you're going to get yourself killed." He stood up and his face was tight. "Is that what you want? To end up like your mom?"

"No! That's my point! She lost it mentally and look what happened. I refuse to go down that path."

He stopped in front of her, the notebook clutched in his hand. "You aren't your mother, and you don't have her life. Don't get yourself killed because you're trying so hard to prove it."

She stared at him. "What are you talking about?"

"Never mind." He sat at her dad's desk and picked up the phone. "Templeton here. Can you look up a name for me? Pete Gibbs. He's a P.I. in Portland. I think I ran across his name recently and I don't remember why."

Kim sat down and slipped her hands under her thighs. "Who are you calling?"

"The station." He held up his hand to indicate that someone had come back on the line. "You're sure? When?" He tightened his mouth as he listened. "Has it been investigated?" He glanced at Kim. "Yeah, leave the report on my desk. I'll get it when I come in." He hung up.

"Well?"

He met her gaze. "Pete Gibbs has been missing for three weeks. His wife filed a missing persons report and the Portland cops have been on it, but they can't find any trace of him."

Kim swallowed hard. "I take it he doesn't usually go missing?"

"He's a family man. Checks in with his wife hourly." Sean met her gaze. "His admin inspected his files and reported only one file missing."

"My dad's?"

"A file titled Loony Bin. Pete didn't believe in keeping records that could identify his clients."

She slumped in her seat. "The Loon's Nest. The camp."

"Not a very good disguise if you knew what you were looking for. If you didn't, it wouldn't mean anything. There are loons and lunatics all over the state."

She sighed. "You know, I really don't have room in my life for *two* lunatics stalking members of my family."

He didn't respond to her attempt to lighten the tension. "If the attack on your dad had anything to do with the Loon's Nest, you're running the place now, so both trails lead back to you."

"Well, gee, thanks for that."

"You need to know the dangers."

"I have an alarm." She nodded at the notebook. "Are there any notes from my dad that tell what the meetings were about?"

"Nope. They only list the payments." Sean was drumming his fingers on the desk. "I need to get to the station and read the report on Gibbs."

She took a deep breath. "I'll be fine by myself."

"I'd feel better if you stayed at my place. I moved in only a couple days ago and it's unlisted, so no one would find you there. I have an alarm and everything." He held up his hand when she started to protest. "This isn't personal. It's business, and it's my job to keep you safe."

"No."

"Dammit, Kim, don't let our past put you in danger. Get over it and come to my house."

"Get over it? You just about knocked me out with that kiss in the mailroom twenty minutes ago. How am I supposed to forget that? Or was it nothing to you? Because it sure felt like something to me." She gulped when she finished, realizing she didn't want to know if it was nothing to him. She was so confused. In one minute, she wanted their relationship to mean nothing, and in the same breath, she wanted desperately to know that their connection hadn't been severed.

Sean took a deep breath and ran his fingers through his hair. "Maybe you're right. Maybe living at my place isn't the best idea." He stood up. "Come on. I'll follow you home and check everything out. You lock the doors, put the alarm on and answer the phone whenever I call you to check in. Got it?"

"Got it." So it *had* meant something to him.

KIM STOOD IN HER living room and stared out at the dark water of the lake. It was almost one in the morning and she still hadn't gone to bed. She was agitated and felt as though she wasn't alone. Was it her nerves or was she actually sensing someone?

Maybe she should have gone to Sean's place. It wasn't as if he'd be there anyway.

Her cell phone buzzed and she flipped it open without looking at it. "Hi, Sean."

"Who's Sean?"

She smiled. "Hi, Alan. What's up?"

"Who's Sean?"

"A cop. You'd like him. He calls me every forty-five minutes to make sure I'm still alive."

"You sure you can trust him?"

"Of course I'm sure. He's a cop."

"So is Jimmy. You think he wouldn't be able to concoct a story that would get a Maine cop to help him out?"

She was suddenly very glad it was Sean who was on her case and not some policeman she didn't know. "I know I can trust Sean."

"I told you not to trust anyone and you're doing it already? He's a cop!"

"If you must know, I was once engaged to him. I know him."

"You dump him or did he dump you?"

That was far too crass and simplistic to describe what had happened. "I ended it."

"So he could be pissed and looking for a chance to get back at you." Alan cursed. "I don't like it. I'm coming out there."

"What about our plan to catch Jimmy?"

"He's not showing up around here, Kim! Don't you get it? He's planning something and you're out there in the woods trusting some guy who has a grudge against you."

She scowled. "Why are you getting so upset? You're the one who's always been the one with a plan. Mr. Calm and Organized."

Alan's deep breath was audible over the phone. "I know Jimmy. He's going to do something, and soon. I want to be with you when it happens."

"What do you mean, you *know* him?"

"What kind of question is that? I've been by your side for the past year and a half, listening to the messages he leaves on your answering machine and watching him lurking outside your apartment building when I drop you off at night. Hell, I was the one who picked you up from the hospital. How can you ask me that?"

"Then stop freaking out on me because you're scaring me."

"Good! Either get on a plane and get home, or I'm coming out there. Call me in the morning and let me know." He hung up before she could respond.

What was up with him? He was acting as if he was her husband or something…. Was he jealous of Sean? Or was the waiting chipping away at his self-control?

Jimmy was working his sinister magic without doing a thing. Tearing away at the careful trap they'd woven for him, letting them disintegrate on their own until they were too fragmented to protect themselves against him. He hadn't touched her since the attack a year and a half ago, yet he'd been haunting her with her anticipation of what he was going to do next.

He'd been messing with her mind, and now he was getting to Alan. One by one, Jimmy was wearing them down until they'd be defenseless to his attack. He was already winning the mind games.

Screw him. She was going to bed, and when she woke up in the morning, she was going to be rested and focused on finding out what had happened to her dad. No way was she going to let Jimmy twist her mind.

ON THE OTHER SIDE of town at the police station, Sean studied his notes. Still no word on Jimmy, though police departments across the country had been put on the alert for him. The Gibbs investigation had been thorough—the man had simply disappeared without a trace. And no one had investigated Max's boat crash. It had been deemed an accident and that was that. The officer who had responded to the scene hadn't considered it odd that a seasoned boater like Max had crashed.

The officer in question was currently out on patrol. They'd be having a little chat when the man returned to the station in the morning.

TEETH BRUSHED, pajamas on, face washed, Kim walked from the bathroom into the bedroom. The closets were empty of psychotic maniacs, the windows locked, and there was nothing under the bed but dust. So she slid the dead bolt on her bedroom door—no more dressers to drag across the floor—and turned to face the room.

The gun from her dad's safe was on her nightstand and her cell phone was on the waistband of her pajamas. She'd never shot a gun and didn't have a permit for it, but Sean had shown her how to use it anyway. Better to shoot herself by accident and have a chance to live than let Jimmy cut her up piece by piece. Not that Jimmy was here, but her dad was in a coma and even her most rational side couldn't quite explain that one away as an accident.

SEAN CALLED HELEN to see if she'd heard of Pete Gibbs, but she hadn't. She didn't mind being woken up at two in the morning, not when the welfare of the man she loved was at stake. Then he rang the hospital to see if Max had shown signs of waking up. He hadn't.

Next, he phoned Billy to get his okay to put a uniform on Max's room. When Billy gave him the green light, the feeling in his gut was confirmed. Billy wouldn't have agreed if Sean's instinct about the suspicious nature of Max's accident was wrong.

He wished it was. The man was like his father. How could Kim hate him?

He remembered the letter from Kim's mom. Would he find the answers in there?

He unfolded the letter from his pocket and laid it on his desk. It was crumpled and the creases were starting to tear at the edges. How many times had Kim read it?

My dearest Kimmy,

Through you, I taste freedom. It is a wonderful feeling, and I live for each breath you take.

While I sit here in this dark place, my wonderful daughter lives in the light. Away from here, away from a love that would have destroyed you and your dreams. When you ask if any of us have heard from Sean, I can hear in your voice that you still love him. My wonderful Kim, never doubt your decision. You're eighteen and love seems so pure and so right, but it isn't. That's what I thought, and I was wrong. You need to grow and find yourself, not marry a man who would use your love to condemn you to a life you don't want. I won't always be here to remind you that you made the right choice. I wanted to put it in writing, so you could look at it again and again.

Remember the night of your wedding? You were so young, so innocent, so filled with grand ideas and plans for a life with Sean. But I heard him talking to Dad. He was going to take over the Loon's Nest, trapping both of you in this town forever. I saw the light in his eyes. He loves the camp. He idolizes your father. He was marrying you for the life he wanted, and he didn't care if you suffered for it. And you would have. You're like me, Kimmy. You are more than this town, more than this lake, more than that man. If you'd married him, you would have ended up like me, and I could never have lived with myself if I'd let my daughter make the same mistakes I made. You have found freedom. Never take it for granted, and never let anyone steal it from you.

Someday you may see Sean again and your old feelings will probably rise up again. First love never dies, and that's why you had to leave. You never would have broken free of him if you'd continued to see him around town. So don't come back. Not ever. To do so, you run the risk of losing everything you have fought so hard to get. I tried to leave your father before we got married, going off to college out of state. But he came after me, took advantage of my love and took me back to the life I'd tried to escape. As women, we're never immune to our first loves, but always remember that it's not real love. It's not the kind of love that will bring you happiness and sustain you when life gets hard. Trust me, I know. Love with your brain, not your heart.

I know you love me, and I know your heart is always here with me, even though you're far away. But know that your being away from here and being safe gives me more pleasure and joy than you could ever imagine. If you come back and let yourself fall into the trap, I will have failed as your mother. And more than anything, I couldn't live with that.

When Cheryl gets old enough, take her away, too. I wanted to wait long enough to help her make the right choice, but I'm out of time. I'm exhausted and I can't do it anymore. And I don't need to. You're safe, and you're strong enough to save Cheryl as well.

I'll always love you, Kimmy. I'm so proud of you.
Love,
Mom

Sean let the letter drop to the desk and closed his eyes. It was exactly what Kim said it was. Worse even. Joyce had thought him worthless. She'd thought he was a trap that would destroy Kim.

He'd thought she loved him like a son. Instead, she'd seen him as poison. He felt so utterly empty. Hopeless. Betrayed. Stupid.

Total and complete rejection from the family he'd considered his own. He'd thought it was horrible when Kim had left him. But this… He felt as if everything he'd ever believed had spun around and sliced him open.

How could he have been wrong? He'd loved Kim. He'd loved her mother. He'd loved the whole perfect family. How could Joyce have felt like that? About him, about Max, about the town, about life? He didn't understand. He knew Max loved Joyce. He loved Kim. How could love have destroyed a family?

He slammed his fists on the desk. "Dammit!"

Did Max know about this? Did Cheryl? Kim did. She'd known for ten years and dealt with it by herself. He couldn't even deal with it now. How could she have managed it ten years ago? She'd been just a kid.

He needed to talk to Kim. But what would he say? That Joyce was wrong? That Kim shouldn't have listened to her? That the letter was a mistake? Would he have walked away ten years ago if Max had given him the same speech?

He didn't know what to think. Or say. He felt as though he didn't know anything anymore. He dropped his face to his hands and wept.

KIM STARED AT the bed. She needed to rest. But she was too wired. Jimmy was stealing even the ability to sleep away from her.

She scowled. "You will not win, Jimmy Ramsey!" She smacked her hands down on the mattress and pain shot up her right hand. "Ow!" She yanked her hand back but saw nothing on the mattress other than the comforter. Something slithered down her palm and she flipped her hand over. Blood was oozing from her palm, running down her wrist.

Fear raced through her and she yanked back the comforter. Nothing but the pale pink blankets she'd had as a teenager.

She ripped off the blankets and something glittered at her in the middle of the bed. Something small and shiny.

She began to tremble.

Slowly this time, she pulled the sheets and mattress pad back, the blood from her hand leaving bright-red streaks on the flowered cotton.

Now she could see it.

The tip of a shiny metal blade sticking up from her mattress. Pointed and sharp, the rest of the knife was hidden from view, buried deep inside the mattress.

But she didn't have to look. She knew what the knife would look like. She knew the blade would match the scar on her thigh.

She dropped to her knees, staring at the steel tip. Then she yanked her cell phone off her waistband, hit Send and grabbed the gun off the nightstand. She would be a victim no longer.

SEAN JERKED UP when his cell phone rang, so caught up in the past. He lifted his head and wiped his cheeks. Dammit. He was too old to cry. Too old to feel this way.

The phone rang again and he picked it up to check the caller. Kim. What was he supposed to say about the letter? He didn't even know what to say to himself. Or Max. Or Helen.

Everything his world had been based on was trembling on its foundation.

He punched Send. "Hi."

"Oh, God, Sean. He's been in my bedroom."

Chills ricocheted down his spine and he jumped to his feet. "Where are you?"

"In my room. I think he's gone." Her voice wavered, then grew strong. "Dammit, Sean! He was in my bedroom."

He heard the click of her cocking the gun and was glad he'd shown her how to use it. He paused to call in the location to dispatch and request all available officers, then ran for the door. "I'll be there in ten minutes."

"Yell before you come in or I'll shoot you."

Chapter Seven

Kim tensed when she heard the knock on the bedroom door. "Who is it?" Yeah, she'd seen the flashing lights arrive and had thrown the house key to Sean out the bedroom window. She still wasn't taking any chances.

"It's Sean."

"Hold on." She unlocked the dead bolt, then moved across the room, raising the gun and leveling it at the door. "Come in."

She aimed as the doorknob turned and the door opened. Then Sean stuck his head in, freezing when he saw the gun pointed at him. "Easy with the gun."

"You alone?"

"No Jimmy."

"Okay, then." She let the gun drop and sank onto the edge of the bed.

"You okay?"

"No." She held up her hand, wrapped with a bloody washcloth. "I hate him."

He was across the floor in two long strides. "Let me see." His voice was gruff as he wrapped his fingers around the wrist of her injured hand.

"It's not deep."

He ignored her and unwrapped it. "Did you clean it?"

"Yes, but it keeps bleeding."

"You need to go to the hospital."

She pulled her hand free and pointed behind her. "The knife."

The shiny tip was sticking out of the bed, right where her body would have been if she'd climbed under the covers. Not enough to kill. Enough to hurt. And scare. Bastard.

Sean took a couple of pictures of the knife, then slipped on a pair of latex gloves and tugged it free. She couldn't help but flinch when he pulled it out.

"Is this the same type of knife he had when he attacked you?"

"Looks like it." She backed up. Stupid to run away, but she couldn't help it. Seeing the knife like that, in her bed... She swallowed.

Sean dropped the knife and reached out to steady her. "Kim? You don't look so good."

"He was in my room. My bed. I had an alarm and he still got in." She gripped Sean's arms, feeling her pulse begin to skyrocket. "Any night I go to sleep, I could wake up with him here. You realize that, don't you? That's what this is all about." God, she was cold. So cold. Shivering. Sweating. Shaking. "Making me realize there's no place safe from him."

Sean grabbed a blanket from the floor and wrapped it around her, then pulled her over to the bed and sat them both down. He surrounded her with his arms. "He won't get you."

"I'm freezing."

"It's shock." He tugged the blanket closer around her neck, then began rubbing her shoulders, his fingers digging deep. It was the first time since he'd arrived that he'd given her the comfort she needed, like the old days. She took it in greedily, knowing it might never come again.

"He's gone," Sean said. The heat from his body surged through her, easing the trembling. As a teenager, she'd loved him, but she'd never thought of him as someone who could keep her safe. It had been the other way around: he'd been the lost boy who needed a family to love. But right now, he was saving her. And she was going to let him. Just for now. Just for this moment.

"Right. Gone." She took a deep breath. "Gone." She felt like sobbing. How could this nightmare be starting all over again? No rationalization could convince her that she was imagining things now.

He continued to rub her shoulders. "When he attacked you before, it was in your bedroom, right?"

"Uh-huh." He must have read the police reports.

"Same knife, same room. Anything else the same?"

She turned her head to look at him, not wanting him to stop touching her. His touch was grounding her, sending warmth into her stripped soul. "Like what?"

He looked at his watch. "It's July twenty-fifth today. What day did he beat up Cheryl the last time?"

She stared at him. "On Christmas."

He nodded, as if she'd confirmed what he'd already been thinking. "And when did he come after you? It was only a few days later, right?"

"January third." The date was entrenched in her memory, that was for sure.

He said nothing else. His grim expression spoke for him.

She did the math. "So we have eight days until he tries to kill me."

"Maybe." His grip on her was a little tighter now than it had been.

"How can you be so calm?" Why wasn't he freaking? It was all she could do to keep from jumping to her feet and screaming until her voice broke, and then screaming some more. She felt so terrified, so angry and so horribly helpless. She hugged herself even tighter and tried to curl into a tiny ball. She couldn't deal with this.

He turned his head toward her. "You think I'm calm?"

That's when she saw the expression in his eyes. They were burning with such a violent hatred and dangerous aggression that she shivered. It was as if she could see the rage bubbling up inside and it was milliseconds from spilling free and turning him into a crazed, revenge-seeking killer. Maybe he wasn't touching her to calm her. Maybe he was touching her to keep himself under control.

Seeing his humanity instantly summoned her own strength and she uncurled her arms enough to set her hand on his leg. He immediately covered it with his free hand. "You're coming home with me tonight."

She met his gaze. "I know."

HOURS LATER, SEAN sat back in his chair and watched Kim sleeping on the couch in the police station. She was using her duffel bag as a pillow and Sean's sweatshirt as a blanket. Dealing with the knife incident and its aftermath had kept him at the station, and neither of them had suggested that Kim head off to his house without him.

Her hand had been fixed up by the paramedics. The puncture wound hadn't been too deep, but it had been enough to remind them both about what was at stake.

Billy walked over to his desk and sat, keeping his voice low. "I followed up on the Gibbs investigation. According to his wife, he got a call at dinnertime and headed out right after that. She didn't think anything of it because he was always getting phone calls and taking off without an explanation. They traced the call and it came from a pay phone about three blocks from his house."

Sean rubbed his eyes. "So he got lured out of his house and someone picked him off? Where's the body? Where's the sign of a struggle?"

"Could've been having an affair," Billy said. "Went AWOL with his lover."

"You believe that?"

"No."

The men fell silent for a moment, then Sean spoke. "About Max's accident…"

"Yeah?"

"How come it was never looked into at all? The man was a veteran boater. The mere fact that he crashed into an island was so out of the norm that someone should have picked up on it."

Billy lifted an eyebrow. "You didn't pick up on it, either."

"Yeah, I know." Sean had been so caught up in the potential loss of Max that he'd abandoned all cop duties and left them in the hands of his colleagues.

"Seemed like an accident, a good case to give to one of the rookies. His report didn't turn up anything suspicious, so I didn't worry about it." Billy rubbed his forehead.

"You think your officer could have been influenced by Jimmy?" Sean asked. With all the paperwork after the knife incident, Sean hadn't been able to catch the officer in question before he went off duty.

Bill frowned. "No."

"You sure?" It was uncomfortable questioning Bill about his staff, but Sean had no choice.

"If he missed a clue, it was because of inexperience, not because of bribery. I have total faith in my team." Bill's face had lost all trace of its easy humor.

Sean held up his hands in a defusing gesture. "Hey, I'm not on your case. I know I missed it, and I'm pissed about that. I just have to know who I can trust."

Bill nodded. "Fine."

Sean sighed. "I find it hard to believe that this accident with Max has nothing to do with Jimmy. The timing is too coincidental, and I don't buy it. If Jimmy had something to do with Max's crash, then he needed a partner because he was still in prison at the time. A cop would be an easy choice."

"I hired these guys. They're green, but they're honest." Billy stood up. "But I'll check everyone out again, just to be sure. Do me a favor and don't start spreading rumors that'll cause the entire town to stop trusting its police force. The town's too small, and they need to feel safe."

"I won't say anything," he agreed. "Let me know what you find. And…thanks. I appreciate it."

The chief nodded and walked out. Sean felt like dirt for questioning Billy's judgment. But they had to know for sure, no matter how unlikely it was.

Sean leaned back in his chair and pressed his palms into his eyes. It was past ten in the morning, his shift was over and it was time to go home. He hadn't slept much in the past couple of days, and he was fried. He picked up his keys and shoved back from the desk when his cell phone rang. He glanced at the display. It was Helen.

His heart jumped. Had Max woken up? He turned away so Kim wouldn't hear him and answered softly. "Hi."

"Sean? I heard that Kim got attacked last night. Is it true? What happened?"

Small towns. And Kim thought Helen was some frigid, calculating woman. Ridiculous. She was worried about Kim because she knew her husband would be concerned. "She's fine. An intruder is all. How's Max?"

"Nothing has changed." There was a pause. "I was thinking about all your questions, about the night of the accident. I remembered that he got a call saying that he was needed for some crisis at the office. That's why he was at the camp that night."

Sean sat up. Two missing and/or injured men. Two calls. A pattern or a random coincidence? He didn't believe in coincidence. His heart hammered. The first possible sign to validate Sean's gut feeling about the "accident." "What time did the call come in?"

"Around dinnertime. Maybe six or seven. Something like that."

"Did the call come from the office?"

"I don't know."

"Did he say who called?"

Helen's voice lost some of its energy. "No. I guess I'm not being too useful, am I?"

"You're very helpful, actually. Let me know if you think of anything else." He paused. "How are you holding up?"

"Fine. We'll get through this. It's the kids I'm worried about."

Helen's kids were still pretty young, and they'd adored Max from the start. To them, he was Dad. "I'm sorry. I'll try to swing by later today and see them."

"No. You find out what happened to him. We'll be okay." Helen hesitated. "Can you do me a favor?"

"Anything. You name it."

"Can you ask Kim to stop by the house tonight for dinner? I need to speak to her about Max."

He grimaced. "I don't think that's a good idea. Kim's not really in the right frame of mind for that at the moment."

Helen sighed. "Will you try?"

"Maybe." He heard some stirring behind him and turned around. Kim was sitting up, her eyebrows furrowed in sleepy confusion as she watched him. "I have to go. Thanks for calling."

He disconnected. "Ready to head out?"

"I'm not in the right frame of mind for what?"

"Having dinner with Helen and the kids."

"Oh." She didn't argue and he sighed, realizing that a part of him had been hoping she'd change her mind. Thanks to the letter, he understood why she felt the way she did about her father, but it didn't mean he thought she was right.

"Give me a second." He looked up the number for the phone company and ordered a report of all incoming calls to Max's house on the night of the accident. He gave them his personal fax number, then hung up. "Let's go. I'll fill you in on the way home."

Home. Interesting choice of words. He didn't even know what home was anymore.

He grabbed her duffel bag, swung it over his shoulder and settled his hand under her elbow. She didn't pull away, and they headed out of the station.

BY THE TIME Kim got to Sean's, she was too wired to sleep. It was almost noon, the sun was out and she couldn't stop thinking about the pain in her palm. "I can't believe you think Jimmy had something to do with my dad's accident. He was in jail." Yeah, okay, so he knew people on the outside, but really! She didn't have space in her coping capacity to think of a band of loyal Jimmy followers.

"I'm guessing." He grabbed her bag from the backseat. "Come on in. We both need some sleep."

She followed Sean up the walkway. He lived in a log cabin all alone in the woods. Not a neighbor in sight. If no one knew they were there, the isolation was good because there were no nosy people to notice her. If Jimmy found them, then the isolation merely meant that she could scream all night and no one would hear her. No one would come to her aid.

Cut it out, Kim! She had to find a way to stop freaking herself out.

Sean opened the door and punched the code to disarm the alarm. It was at least ten digits long. "I changed it when I moved in," he said. "No one knows it." He let Kim in, then shut the door and reset the alarm again. "Welcome to my palace."

The cabin was charming. Logs made up the exterior walls, there was a huge stone fireplace, a homey open-concept kitchen with a rag carpet and gorgeous pine cabinets. The overstuffed denim couches had red plaid pillows, and the recessed lighting cast a warm glow on the rooms. It was the cutest place she'd ever been in. "You decorated this?"

"No way. It came like this. It's the vacation retreat for some couple in Boston, but they're not using it this year." He headed toward a door at the rear of the family room. "Bedroom's in here. You can have it."

She followed him through to the bedroom. It was on the first floor and had a couple of big glass doors. "Hmm." How could she sleep open to the woods like that? So vulnerable and exposed.

He tossed the duffel bag on the bed. "You don't like it?"

"Anyone could come through those doors. Isn't there a loft or something?"

"You've seen the whole place."

She pressed her lips together. "Maybe we should stay at a hotel."

Sean came over to her and set his hands on her shoulders, kneading softly. "I'll be in the next room."

The next room seemed awfully far away with the puncture wound in her hand throbbing. She was so tired of being afraid. The only time she felt safe was when she was right next to Sean. She chewed her lower lip. "On the couch?"

"Yes."

She pulled away and walked over to the window, staring out at the trees. The sun was breaking through the branches, casting shadows on the deep woods. It could be totally creepy, with so many places for a killer to hide while he watched her, or it could be beautiful and romantic. With Sean beside her, she was almost tempted by the latter. "It's pretty." Appreciating its beauty wasn't like falling down a slippery slope of romantic yearnings, was it? A good compromise.

He came to stand beside her. "Yeah."

"I forgot how beautiful it was here." In her memories the

town and resort had been dark and dreary. Since she'd been back, all she could think about was how isolated she felt. But now, with Sean by her side with a gun in his holster, she felt safe enough to breathe, to notice things she hadn't noticed before.

"I never forgot," he said quietly.

It seemed so normal to be in a bedroom with Sean. Comfortable. She took a breath and let it out. "You don't need to sleep on the couch."

He said nothing.

"I mean, I don't think we should make love or anything, but I think we could manage to share the same bed without mauling each other, don't you?"

He looked at her. "You're serious?"

She turned away and grabbed her bag. "If Jimmy comes in through the window, you can't do me any good if you're on the other side of the bedroom door." She didn't wait for an answer, didn't give him a chance to say no. "Besides, I owe you after walking out on our wedding. I figure giving you the bed instead of forcing you to take the couch should make us even, don't you?" She kept her voice light, wanting to remind him of the tension between them, because heaven knew, if he kissed her as he had in the mailroom, she wouldn't have the willpower to stop him.

And she most definitely did not want to make love to Sean Templeton.

IT TOOK HER less than ten minutes to shower, leaving her hand stuck out of the shower curtain so she wouldn't get the bandage wet. She barely had the energy to throw on a T-shirt and boxers. She was so tired, she almost fell asleep leaning against the wall of the shower. Forget about drying her hair. Why bother? Sean had seen her looking hellacious plenty of times and had been planning to marry her anyway. It was way too late to try to impress him.

She paused for a moment before opening the door to the bathroom, trying to steel herself for the fact that he was probably in the living room putting sheets on the couch.

But when she opened it, he was in the bed, sleeping on his back. His upper body was bare, his arm thrown over his face to block out the sunlight. The thin, beige curtains were little protection against the noon rays. His gun was in its holster, slung over the headboard, and his body was relaxed in sleep.

Her stomach did a little flip and she sucked in her breath. He wasn't the teenager she'd almost married. Not by a long shot. Muscles ripped in his stomach, and hair curled on his chest. His biceps was flexed where it rested across his face, and there was a long scar on the back of his arm. He was all man, and she wanted him. And this didn't feel at all like the call of a lost first love. It felt like a woman wanting a man.

Maybe she should sleep on the couch, not him.

She walked over to the bed and lifted the covers, scooting in carefully so as not to shake the bed and wake him. He grunted but didn't move.

Kim curled up on her side so she could watch him, clutching her bandaged hand to her chin. His chest rose softly with each breath, his lips parted ever so slightly. He still hadn't shaved and the whiskers on his chin were long. She trailed her fingers over his jaw, remembering the first time he'd let her shave him. She'd cut him six times and he'd still let her try again a week later.

She sighed.

Then Sean jerked and moved his arm, his eyes at half mast as he peered sleepily at her.

She smiled.

He closed his eyes again and shifted his arm in that move he used to do when he wanted her to snuggle against him. She wiggled forward until her head was resting on the front of his shoulder. Then he curved his arm around her and pulled her close, his fingers buried in her hair.

She closed her eyes and fell asleep, breathing the familiar scent of the man who'd never left her heart.

Chapter Eight

Sean woke up wrapped around Kim's body. Her hair was draped across his face, her legs entwined with his. Her face was buried in the crook of his neck and her body was pressed against his. He inhaled, taking in her familiar scent, running his hand softly over her hip. She felt good.

Then her cell phone rang and he realized that was what had woken him. He cursed and slid out of the bed, diving for her mobile phone before it could wake her. "Hello?"

No one answered.

"Hello?" he repeated. A glance at Kim told him she was still asleep, so he took the phone into the other room.

"Who is this?" It was a man's voice and Sean tensed.

"Who are you?"

"My name is Alan Haywood. Who are you?"

Ah, her "friend." Something unfamiliar surged through Sean and he decided that the man had a wimpy voice. "Kim's sleeping right now and I'm not going to wake her up."

Silence. Sean grinned, knowing the things that Alan was imagining with Sean answering Kim's phone while she was asleep.

"Well, I'm at her house now and she's not here. Where is she?" Alan said.

Sean immediately frowned. "Her house in L.A.?"

"No, her house in Ridgeport."

"Is she expecting you? She didn't mention it."

"Listen, I don't know who you are, but if I don't hear from Kim in one minute, I'm going to assume she was abducted and call the cops."

Sean tensed. This man was taking responsibility for Kim's welfare? Forget it. The job was taken. "I'll have her call you when she wakes up. She was up all night and she needs her sleep." He frowned. "And why aren't you in L.A.? I thought your job was to watch the apartment for Ramsey and get him collared for parole violation."

"How did you know that?" Then there was a small sound of exasperation. "You're the ex-fiancé cop, aren't you?"

"Yep."

"How do I know you aren't dirty?"

"You don't, but if I was, that comment would be enough for me to disappear with Kim. Don't show your hand too soon or you'll lose."

"Who are you on the phone with?"

Sean turned to see Kim standing in the bedroom doorway. She was wearing boxers and a T-shirt, her hair was disheveled and she looked adorable. Then he looked down and saw the scar on her thigh and he felt the urge to smash the phone into the wall and kill Jimmy Ramsey. Too angry to talk, he strode across the room and lifted the leg of her shorts to the top of her scar. It went all the way to her hip.

He swore and Kim pulled away. "Don't." She shoved his hands away and turned to hide her leg from view. "Is the call for me?"

Damn Jimmy for making Kim ashamed of her own body. He remembered when she used to run around wearing a little bikini without a care in the world. He handed her the cell phone. "It's Alan. He's at your house on the lake."

She paused. "He's in town?"

"Uh-huh. He thinks I abducted you and he's threatening to call the cops. You might want to clarify that."

She gave him an apologetic smile. "He gets a little protective of me."

Sean couldn't keep the scowl off his face. "You sure you're just friends?"

Her cheeks turned pink. "Of course."

"You might want to make sure he knows that." Yeah, sure, it was none of his business what she was doing with Alan, but it sure felt like Sean's business.

"Thanks." She took her phone into the bedroom, shutting him out with a slam of the door.

Gone was the bonding of last night. Was it because of her leg or because the intimacy had reminded her that he was so vile that she'd kill herself to get away from him? Maybe last night's snuggling had been nothing more than residual tension from finding a knife in her bed. Vulnerability had sent her into his arms and he'd been stupid enough to think that maybe it meant something else.

Lesson learned. From now on, Kim was a civilian and he was a cop. Yeah, he'd read the letter, but it only explained *why* she'd left. It didn't change the fact that she simply hadn't loved him enough to stay.

That damn letter.

He wished he'd never read it. Had never seen Joyce condemn him in her own handwriting.

Sean gritted his teeth. As close as he was to Max, he'd thought he was close to Joyce, as well. But she'd hated him enough to turn her daughter against him.

For his whole life, he'd believed in that family and the love they had for one another and for him. One by one, each belief he had was being destroyed.

Alan could have Kim. Sean had had enough.

The fax machine beeped and Sean turned away, grateful for an excuse to think about anything else. When he pulled

the papers out of the machine, he nodded with grim satis-
faction. They were the phone records from Max's house.
Somewhere on that list was the call from the person who had
attacked him.

KIM PULLED ON her jeans, hiding her scars beneath the
denim. She was embarrassed that Sean had seen them. They
were awful and ugly. How could she have forgotten and
worn shorts to bed with him?

"Kim? What's wrong?" Alan asked. "Are you there?"

"Yeah, I'm here. Sorry. Nothing's wrong." She zipped up
her jeans and tried not to look at the bed, still rumpled from
their snuggling last night. "Why are you in Maine? Who's
watching my place in L.A.?"

"I had to come. I'm worried about you."

"For crying out loud, Alan, I have an ex-military cop
sleeping two inches from me. What do you think can happen
to me? If *he* can't save me, you certainly can't." She jammed
her feet into her sneakers and smashed a brush through her
hair.

"Nice mood you're in. And what do you mean, he's
sleeping two inches from you?"

"Oh, give it up, Alan. If I was having sex with him, which
I'm not, it would be none of your business." Was she in a
bad mood or what?

"Since when do you shut me out? I flew three thousand
miles to help you. I'm not the enemy."

Crap. He was right. "Listen. I'm sorry. I'm a little strung
out." While she changed the bandage on her hand—just a
little red mark on her palm that didn't do justice to the emotional damage it had wreaked—she told him about the knife
in her bed and the suspicions about Max's accident. By the
time she was finished, Alan was as cranky as she was and
glad he'd come out to protect her.

Maybe he couldn't save her from a psycho with a knife,

but there was one thing he could do. "Why don't we meet at the camp office in half an hour to go through my dad's financial files. Maybe if we can figure out what's up with him and the camp, we can determine whether this has anything to do with Jimmy." She gave him directions and hung up, then prepared herself to face the man she'd dreamed about all night.

She walked into the kitchen to find Sean sitting at the kitchen table with a granola bar, a sports drink and a fax. He was still wearing nothing but his boxers and he looked even better vertical than he had sprawled out in the bed last night. What was wrong with her? Why was she reacting this way to him? It had been ten years, for heaven's sake. She couldn't still be yearning after the man from her past, could she? She cleared her throat and opened the fridge. Anything to avoid being caught gawking at him. "What are you reading?"

"Your dad's phone records."

She found a yogurt and turned to find him watching her with a grim look on her face. "And?"

"And he got a call from the Loon's Nest at 7:30. It lasted about thirty seconds."

"So someone lured him there, then somehow got him into the boat and crashed it?"

"I think we're missing part of the story, but yes, I think that's the gist of it."

"Which number at the camp?"

He held the sheet out and she looked at it. "That's the guest phone in the lounge, which is open twenty-four hours a day. Any guest or staff person, or even anyone who wanders in, could use it." She frowned. "So it's not that helpful."

"Except now we know someone wanted him over there." He pointed to a second listing. "Another call from the camp, forty minutes later."

"That's my dad's office."

"I checked with Helen, and when I mentioned it, she said he had called her after he left to ask her what he was supposed to pick up at the grocery store. She didn't know what number it came from, but it looks like he made it into the office." He cracked his jaw, his eyes sharp and intense. "I want to have another look around his office."

"For what?"

"Signs of a struggle. Anything."

A struggle. "You think he got knocked out before he even got in the boat?"

"Maybe. Or maybe once he got down there. I don't know, but I want to look around." He rubbed his chin. "I want to check out the boathouse, too. Maybe have another chat with that kid who works there, Tom Payton."

"While we're doing that, Alan can go over the office files."

Sean narrowed his eyes. "Why is he going to do that?"

"Because he can look at the financials and maybe decipher what's going on with the camp that's making it fail. Maybe this whole thing with my dad has nothing to do with Jimmy."

Sean snorted. "And I suppose you're going to find another explanation for the knife in your bed, too? Maybe a bear broke in and left you a present?"

Kim glared at him. "Hey, I stayed here last night, didn't I? That should make you happy."

Sean lifted an eyebrow. "Since when do you do anything to make me happy?"

"What's that supposed to mean?"

"Nothing. Forget it." He threw his chair back from the table. "I'll be out in a minute."

She grabbed his arm as he went by. "Why are you mad at me? What did I do?"

He grabbed a paper off the counter and tossed it at her. "Here's your letter. I had no idea your mother hated me. First her, then you. What a fool I was to think I had a future with you and your family. I mourned your loss for years, then went off and joined the Army because I couldn't deal with staying in town. And you just gallivanted off to L.A. and made a great life for yourself without a care. I was a damned idiot not to see it."

She crushed the letter into her hand. "You read the letter?"

"Yeah." He walked past her into the bedroom, and she couldn't stop herself from shivering as he walked by. So good to know she still wasn't immune to Sean when he was half-naked.

"And? Do you understand why I left?" She walked to the door of the bedroom, where he was rifling through drawers.

"Oh, believe me. I understand." He tossed his jeans and a T-shirt over his shoulder, then shoved the drawer shut with his hip. "Like mother, like daughter. I wasn't good enough for either of you, was I?"

Oh, no. "Sean, that's not what the letter is about. It wasn't you. It was me. It wouldn't have mattered what man was in the picture. It was the town I had to leave."

He rolled his eyes as he walked past her into the bathroom and dropped his boxers.

She barely managed to avert her eyes…okay, fine. She *didn't* manage to avert her eyes at all, but Sean was too distracted to care. Guess he'd been naked around her so many times he didn't even notice. Well, she noticed.

"Give me a break, Kim. I read the letter. I heard your explanation. If it was simply the town, you could have asked me to leave with you. Ever think of that?"

She stared at him. No, she never had.

"See? That's all crap. You and your mom thought I'd destroy you. Not the town. Me."

How could she have thought this man would be the end of her? He was so real, so caring, so passionate. "Maybe we were wrong." The words slipped from her lips before she'd even realized she was thinking them.

He stared at her. "What?"

"I don't know. I just don't know anymore." She bit her lip. "My mother killed herself because of my dad. How do I forget about that and walk away? And should I even want to? I mean, she was my mother." She clutched her bandaged hand to her chest. "My mom is dead. My sister tried to kill herself. All I've done since is try to make sure I stay as far away from that trap as I can. And now you're in my life again and I have all the same feelings for you, just like she said I would. So how do I know what's right and what's wrong? God, Sean, I don't know what to do!"

"You need to see your father. Ask him what really happened with your mom."

Her gut knotted up. "He's not the perfect man you believe he is."

"He's not the scum you think he is."

"He married Helen three weeks after my mom was buried. Three weeks! You expect me to believe that he wasn't having an affair?"

Sean flinched as if she'd hit him in the face. "Why don't you ask him instead of judging him?"

"Have you asked him?"

He met her gaze. "No, I haven't."

"You don't want the truth."

His eyes flickered. "That letter has brought up some questions I want answers to. When he wakes up, I'm going to ask. Are you?"

"What if he doesn't wake up?"

"He will." He clenched his fist and smashed it into the door frame. "He *will*."

She was shocked by the raw pain in his eyes. "You love him, don't you? It's not just about the camp or about being a part of his family. You love him."

He grunted something unintelligible that she took as a confirmation.

"You love him like he's your own father."

He shrugged. "So?"

"So was my mom right? Did you want to marry me because of him and the camp? You get me, you get my family? Become my dad's son for real?"

"No! I…" His voice trailed off after his initial denial. He stared at her and the shocked look of self-awareness creeping over his face was enough of an answer.

He'd never loved her. Not really. Not the way she'd thought he had.

That hurt. Last night, she'd felt so close to him, remembering how special he'd made her feel when she was a teenager. She'd been wondering how love like that could die. Questioning whether it had.

But it hadn't been true love. Not for him. He'd confused romantic love with his yearning for a family. "All these years, I wondered if I did the right thing by leaving. I wondered if maybe, just maybe, she was wrong about us. About you." Kim shook her head. "And she wasn't, was she? God, Sean, I thought you really loved me."

"And I thought you loved me. Guess we were both wrong, huh?"

They stared at each other. No words seemed appropriate.

After a moment, he said, "We'll leave in ten minutes." Then he shut the door and turned on the shower.

A LEAN MAN WITH short blond hair was waiting for them when they drove up to the office. He was lounging against the porch railing, his California tan making his skin darker than his hair. The moment he saw the car he straightened, the lines of his body taut, his gaze sharp. He was fit and decent-looking, and Sean got a bad vibe from him even from a distance. The instant Kim stepped out of the car, the man grabbed her and hugged her. Sean was out of the car and beside them almost instantly. "I'm Sean Templeton."

Surfer dude released her and eyed Sean. "Alan Haywood. Kim's best friend."

Sean didn't like the possessive look in Alan's face at all, let alone how Kim had her arm tucked around his. He narrowed his eyes and took in the man's rumpled suit. "When did you get in?"

"Took the red-eye last night. I got in this morning and came straight out here. Haven't even found a hotel." He put his arm around Kim and squeezed. "I wanted to make sure you were okay."

"Got a ticket stub?"

Alan frowned at him and Kim smacked his arm. "Sean! What's your problem?"

"The knife appeared in your bed last night. I'd like to know exactly what time Alan arrived." Sean didn't like the look of Alan Haywood and his suit one bit.

Kim set her hands on her hips and glared at him. "He's my friend. Don't insult him."

Alan touched Kim's arm. "It's okay. I'm glad he's concerned." Alan felt around in his pant pocket and dug out a couple of ticket stubs. He handed them to Sean. "One for each leg of the trip. You can look them up to see what time I got in."

Oh, he'd be doing that. Sean shoved the tickets into his own pocket and studied the man. Alan narrowed his gaze and gave back everything Sean directed at him.

After a long moment, Alan stuck out his hand and Sean shook it. "Looks like we're on the same team," Alan said.

"Yeah." Maybe. "You leave anyone in charge of Kim's place?"

"Local cops are keeping an eye on it."

Sean raised an eyebrow. "You mean Jimmy's pals?"

Alan's gaze darkened. "I was going to pay a private investigator, but it was cost prohibitive. This was the best I could do." He looked at Kim. "Besides, I don't think

Jimmy's there. If he was going to hit your place, he'd have shown up by now. Somehow, he found out you weren't there."

"How would he have found out?" Sean asked. "Aren't you and Kim the only ones who know?"

"For God's sake, Sean. Back off! Alan's been helping me fight off Jimmy for the past eighteen months. He's *not* the bad guy." She set her hands on her hips again.

Sean scowled. As if she'd ever defend him the way she was defending Alan. Something pinged in his gut at the thought and he forced himself to shrug. What did he care what she thought? His job wasn't to make her happy. It was to keep her safe, to find Jimmy and to find out what happened to Max. After this morning, it was clear not only that there was nothing between them now, but also that there never had been. Had he really loved her dad more than her? He wanted to say no, but in his gut, he wasn't sure anymore. If Kim had asked him to leave with her, would he have gone? He didn't know.

So he ignored her and turned to Alan. "You're here to look at the files of the camp?"

"Sure, I can do that."

"Anything you find, you let me know."

Alan cocked an eyebrow. "Yes, sir." His tone was flippant and challenging, and Sean considered introducing him to the butt of his gun, just for fun.

Kim elbowed him. "Cut it out, Alan. He's doing his job."

"He's a cop and he could be on the take from Jimmy."

Kim stomped her foot then and glared at them both. "Would you guys stop with the pissing contest? You both want to get Jimmy, so quit trying to blame each other. You'll just be wasting time that could be spent getting somewhere. We only have seven days, remember?"

Alan flicked his gaze toward Kim. "Seven days until what?"

"He put Cheryl in the hospital on Christmas Day. Yesterday, the day of the knife incident, was the twenty-fifth of July."

Sean studied Alan's face while Kim explained the dates, looking for a clue. A flash of knowledge? A flicker of concern that they'd figure it out? Because there was something off about Alan, and Sean was going to find out what it was. He'd be filing a background check on Alan Haywood as soon as he got back to the office.

Chapter Nine

"Friendly guy," Alan said as he and Kim walked ahead of Sean toward the office. Alan's usually impeccable attire was a little wrinkled and he hadn't shaved recently. He looked like hell. But it was still so good to see him. A man she knew, without all sorts of baggage.

"Sean's a great guy," she said. "He's just a little cranky today." Yeah, major understatement. They were both in rotten moods. Funny how learning that he'd never really loved her had put *her* in a crappy state of mind. Good thing she hadn't married him. And as for all the attraction she'd been feeling since she returned to town? Residual first-love delusions, just as her mom had predicted.

On the plus side, Sean was finally out of Kim's soul and she could start over. She was free. So she lifted her chin, pasted a serene smile on her face and tucked her hand through Alan's arm as they strolled into the reception area, where Didi was busily sorting petty cash. Didi looked up as they walked in and Kim noticed that Didi's eyes were red-rimmed and puffy. Didi barely spared Alan a glance, even though he was male. What was wrong with her?

"Didi, this is my friend Alan Haywood. He'll be working in Max's office for the next few days." Kim looked at Alan. "How long are you staying?"

"As long as I need to." He held out his hand to Didi. "Nice to meet you."

She smiled absently at him and Kim was startled to see a faint flush rise in Alan's cheeks as he turned away.

She waited until they got into the office with the door shut. "What was that?"

"What?"

"You liked her."

He sat at the desk and flipped on the computer. "She's cute."

"You totally checked her out!" Alan wasn't the type of guy to ogle women on a regular basis. What was it about Didi that caught his eye?

He glared at her. "I'm here on business, not to date."

"Business, huh? Seems personal to me." Sean walked into the office and stood behind Alan, looking over his shoulder. "I'll be watching what you do for a while, if you don't mind."

Alan glowered at Sean. "I like my space."

"I'm sure you do." Sean shrugged. "As Kim said, I'm doing my job. I thought you wanted me to do my job. Change your mind?"

God help me. Kim walked out of the office, leaving Sean and Alan to their attitudes. They'd clearly hated each other from first sight. Whatever their problems with each other were, she wasn't in the mood to deal with it.

"Don't go too far," Sean shouted after her.

"I wouldn't dream of it."

Didi was sitting behind the reception desk and she still looked bummed. Anything to distract Kim from her life. "Didi? What's wrong?"

Didi immediately straightened and tried to wipe her eyes. "Nothing."

Kim glanced around. "Where's Will? Don't you two usually work this shift together?"

"Yes." The sniffles became louder and Kim peered more closely at her.

"Did you guys break up?"

Fresh tears spilled. "Yes."

Kim sighed and leaned on the desk next to Didi's. "Men suck, don't they?"

The corner of Didi's mouth curved up. "Sometimes, I guess."

"You love him?"

"Will? No." She sighed. "I just wanted a decent guy, you know? I thought he was nice."

Kim pulled up a stool and sat on it. Chatting with Didi about men reminded her of the days when she and Cheryl used to hang out. Swapping stories and secrets. Suddenly, she felt so lonely. "A nice guy doesn't seem like so much to ask," she said.

Didi raised her eyebrow. "How many nice guys do you know?"

She thought of the two men in her office. "I might know a couple." Alan she was sure of. Sean, well, he was too complicated to be described simply as a nice guy. He was so much more than that. Oh, who was she kidding? No one could describe Sean Templeton as a nice guy. Alan, yes. Sean, no way. Then she had an idea, an idea that rang of a past life in which she did normal things such as try to set her friends up. "My friend Alan, who just arrived, is single. Hasn't had a girlfriend in ages, actually."

"Why not? Is he gay?"

"No. He's…" Probably not a good idea to say that he'd been helping her evade a killer. "He's had some stuff going on. It's time for him to get out there again."

Didi studied her. "You're trying to set me up with him?"

"I'm trying to find you someone who will buy you dinner and won't be a jerk."

"Why do you care?"

Kim shrugged. "Alan's a great guy and he could use a friend while he's out here." She still wasn't sure why he'd come out to Maine. Yeah, he'd been her main supporter, but he'd gotten increasingly protective over the past couple of weeks. She was so unsettled by the situation with Sean, the last thing she wanted was to worry about entertaining Alan or deal with their bickering. If she could get Didi to come along for dinner, maybe her presence would alleviate some of the testosterone battles.

She looked at Didi. "Why don't I set something up for tonight? Join us for dinner. Are you free?"

Okay, fine, she also had an incentive to get Alan out of her hair: she wanted some time with Sean. The conversation they'd started this morning wasn't over. Maybe they hadn't loved each other the way they thought they had, but to dismiss their entire relationship wasn't logical. Nothing felt as though it made sense anymore.

Didi looked thoughtful. "I guess it would be okay."

"Great. I'll go talk to him." She patted Didi's shoulder. "Forget Will. He doesn't deserve you."

"Thanks, Kim." Didi cocked her head. "You're a lot nicer than I thought you'd be."

Kim frowned. "You thought I'd be a jerk? Why?"

"You're the boss's daughter."

"Oh." She hesitated. "Do people not like my dad?"

"Everyone loves him."

"Then why didn't you think you'd like me?"

Didi shrugged. "I don't know." A guest came in, inquiring about the hike up Owl Creek Mountain later on that day, so Didi turned away to help him.

Great. Kim's ego felt so much better now that she knew the staff at the camp had expected her to be a jerk.

She walked toward her dad's office to let the boys know she'd added Didi to the guest list for dinner.

SEAN STOOD IN the doorway to the boathouse, Kim by his side. He'd asked her to inspect the building with him on the pretense that she'd know better than him if anything was out of place, but really, he didn't want her alone with Alan. Maybe Alan was legit and wanted to keep Kim safe, but it was Sean's job not to trust anyone but himself. Besides, the guy was a city kid and he'd have no chance against Jimmy.

Yesterday, Sean's excuse would have been that he wanted to spend time with her. Now it was only business.

It had to be. There was no point in pursuing anything between them. But how did he cut off all the emotions he had wrapped up in her? He hadn't figured it out yet and it was frustrating the hell out of him, which was why he was trying to focus on his job. On the case. On Jimmy.

Nothing had turned up in Sean's search of the office, so he was hoping to find something on the boat. Tom Payton was inside the boathouse, working on a canoe. "Hi, Tom."

Tom jumped and looked up. "Oh, hi. I didn't hear you come in."

Sean leaned against the door frame. "Work on the boats a lot?"

"Yeah. It's my job."

He studied him. "How much experience do you have with boats?"

Tom settled back on his heels. "Enough."

"Enough? What does that mean?"

"It means I can do the job."

Something was definitely off with Tom. Sean would follow up with Eddie and see what was going on. "So does Eddie tell you what to fix or do you figure it out and do it yourself?"

The kid—okay, so he wasn't really a kid, but he looked like one at first glance—shifted restlessly. "Some of both. Why?"

"Did you work on Max's boat the day he crashed? Eddie said you were doing some work on it in the afternoon."

Tom glanced at Kim, then at Sean, then picked up his

sandpaper and applied it to the canoe. "That was my assignment, so obviously I did it, right? I mean, I do my job. I
already told you that. Why are you asking me again?"

Sean shot a look at Kim, then moved closer to Tom and
squatted next to him. "If you know something you aren't
telling us, you need to spill it. What's up?"

"Nothing. I worked on the engine like he told me. I was
around all afternoon like I was supposed to be and I didn't see
anything. I even stayed and did the evening shift because Eddie
wasn't feeling good and asked me to stay. I was here the whole
time and I saw nothing, okay?" The kid was sweating now.

Kim spoke from the doorway. "You won't lose your job,
Tom, so don't worry about that. Just tell the officer what you
know."

"Nothing. I don't know anything." He stood up. "I have
to go."

He walked out, brushing past Kim.

The kid was too dumb to realize he'd pretty much told
them he knew something. The question was, what did he
know? An invitation to the police station for an interview
might scare him into sharing.

"Aren't you going to follow him?"

Sean shook his head. "Let him stew for a few hours. I'll
call him in for an interview tonight when I'm on duty." He
turned to Max's boat, which was still sitting in the boathouse. "First, I want to check out the boat more thoroughly."

"What do you expect to find this time?"

He slipped on some latex gloves and climbed into the
boat. "Last time, we were looking for mechanical issues.
This time, I'm looking for signs of a struggle." He pulled
out another set of gloves and tossed them at Kim. "This is
the same boat he had when we were kids. You might notice
something out of place. But don't disturb anything."

Ten minutes later, Kim was down on her knees in the stern
when she called out his name. "Sean? Come look at this."

He dropped next to her. "What do you have?"

She pointed to some dark brown splatters on the side of the boat, tucked beside the bench seat in the back. "Mud?"

"Or not." Blood more likely.

"Did my dad have an open wound on his head?"

"Yep. Got stitches. That's what knocked him out."

Kim sat up and her face was pale. "Someone tried to kill him."

"Maybe. I'll call and have the guys come down and take a swab of it to see if it's blood."

"But even if it is my dad's blood, does it prove anything? I mean, he's been riding around in this boat for twenty years."

"In court, it means nothing. But to me, it does." He pulled her to her feet. "When I go into work tonight, be careful. If your dad was attacked, then Jimmy has at least one partner, which means there's more than one person we have to watch out for. Someone we haven't identified. Trust no one." He met her gaze. "I don't want even Alan knowing where you're staying."

"Why don't you believe Alan?"

"I don't trust anyone at this point. If I'm not with you, you need to be at my house." He saw her frown, and he knew she was rebelling. She'd never been the type to relish not being in control. Isn't that why she'd left? To take charge of her own life?

He scowled. Hadn't he resolved not to think about their past anymore?

Before she could argue with him, his phone rang. He pulled it out. The station. "Templeton here."

"It's Bill. Got a positive ID on your man."

He tensed. "Ramsey? Where is he?" Kim's head whipped toward him, but he resisted the urge to touch her. They'd gotten past that this morning. He settled for a reassuring nod instead.

"Got a body in Portland."

"A body?" At his question, Kim looked at him sharply.

"Yep. Found it in a Dumpster outside a bar this morning. Stinking up the joint something nasty."

Sean frowned. "If it smelled…"

"Then he'd been dead awhile. Want to go check it out?"

"You bet. I'll meet you at the station in ten minutes."

"Want me to send someone to stay with Kim while you're gone?"

He looked at Kim, waiting, her teeth chewing her lower lip while hope gleamed in her eyes. "Yeah, and make sure you trust him."

"You think I'd send someone I didn't trust?"

Sean grimaced. Of course Bill wouldn't. "Sorry."

"Where are you?"

"Camp office. I won't leave until he gets here." He hung up. "Got an ID on Ramsey. He's dead."

Kim felt her legs buckle and it was only Sean's quick move to grab her arm that kept her upright. "Dead? Really dead?"

"I'm going to go check it out." He guided her to the edge of the boat. "Sit here."

She sank down, her hands trembling, her legs quaking. "So it's over? It's all over?" Just like that, she had her life back? Oh, God, it was too much. She held out her hand. "Look at how much I'm shaking."

Sean squatted in front of her. He lifted his hands to place them on her legs, then shifted and put them on the boat on either side of her instead. "It sounds like he may have been dead for a few days."

"So?"

"So then someone else put the knife in your bed."

Kim closed her eyes against the pressure suddenly crushing against her temples. "It can't be." There couldn't be someone else out there, someone as bad as Jimmy, could there? Yeah, Sean had just finished telling her that Jimmy might have a partner, but the timing of his death would confirm it. Damn. "I can't go through this again."

"I'm going to go find out."

He shifted and she wondered if he was going to touch her. He didn't. She wanted him to.

"It makes sense. Jimmy had a partner, and that's who was after your dad while Jimmy was still in prison."

"No." She clutched the edge of the boat and opened her eyes. "No. Either my dad had an accident, or it had something to do with the camp. There isn't someone else out there after me. It's over, Sean. It's over."

"I'm sorry, Kim, but we both know that's not true."

"It has to be." Her voice was a raspy whisper. "I can't keep dealing with this."

"You have to."

His eyes were glittering and cold. He was all cop and he was treating her like a civilian who was making his job difficult. She immediately sat straighter and tossed aside her feelings of fear. He wasn't going to offer any comfort, and she'd never admit she needed it. Because she didn't. She lifted her chin. "I'm fine."

"Good. I'm going to arrange for another officer to guard you while I'm gone." He moved his hand as though he was going to ruffle her hair, but he dropped his arm before touching her.

They were like strangers again, not touching, not getting personal.

"I'll stay with Alan at the office until you get back."

"Fine. But I'm going to have another cop here, too." He stood up. "Billy trusts the man he's sending over, so I think you'll be okay with him."

"You *think?*"

"Someone is helping Jimmy and until we know who it is, the only person I trust with you is me. So stay in the office and keep as many people around you as possible until I get back."

"Okay." She pressed her lips together and tried not to gawk at the people milling around as they left the boathouse and went back up to the office. Was one of them Jimmy's accomplice? Was the sweet couple with the baby a front for a pair of killers?

Stop it! Jimmy was possibly dead and he was still ripping away at her sanity, at her feeling of safety, invading it until she cracked.

A part of her wanted to curl into a ball and give up.

Sean glanced at her and gave her a half smile.

And the other part of her was pissed. She was ready to take her life back. This was her home and she wasn't going to let Jimmy take it away from her.

NIGHT HAD FALLEN and the office felt too small for Alan, Kim and the cop who'd been sent to guard her. She and Alan had been going over the camp financials while the cop loitered in the shadows, playing up his bodyguard assignment.

Alan had been on her case all afternoon and evening about Sean, wanting to know all the details of their past together and why he had taken the case when he was personally involved. She was just about ready to throw Alan out of the room, and she threatened to do so three times. All that did was shut him up for about five minutes before he went off on Sean again.

They were both on edge, and the cramped office wasn't helping. Alan even scoffed at the notion that Jimmy's body was in Portland. He claimed it was a cover-up by dirty cops out to help a fellow officer.

Frankly, Kim was getting sick of him, regardless of how helpful he was being with the files.

The only one who didn't seem to be feeling the stress was her new bodyguard. His name was Garth McKeen, and he was pretty pumped about his assignment. He hadn't stopped moving since he'd arrived. Checking the window, the door, taking a stroll around the main lodge, watching who came and who went and which cars had sat too long in the parking lot. She'd report back to Sean about Garth's enthusiasm. She was pretty sure he was on her side.

Alan leaned back in the chair and stretched. "I'm fried, Kim. I can't read these financial documents anymore tonight."

Kim perched on the edge of the desk. He had dark circles under his eyes and he looked exhausted. "I can't believe we didn't find anything. We've been working on this for hours." She so wanted to uncover information that revealed that the dire state of the camp had nothing to do with Jimmy. Or that handed them the name of his accomplice. Either one would have been all right with her.

"No, but there's a lot more to go through." He glanced at Officer McKeen, who was peering out at the parking lot, shining his flashlight to augment the floodlights on the side of the building. "Why don't we get something to eat?"

She didn't want to eat with Alan. All she wanted was to get back to Sean's cabin with a pizza and forget all this crap. But how could she turn Alan down when he was out here to help her? She had no choice.

She was just about to accept when a light knock sounded at the door. Officer McKeen spun around, his hand on his holster. "I'll get that."

He sidestepped toward the door, leaning against it. "Who's there?"

"Didi Smith."

Officer McKeen looked at Kim. "You know her?"

"Yes. Tell her we'll be right out." Yahoo! She'd forgotten about Didi coming to dinner with them. It was the perfect excuse to ditch Alan and get some alone time. "Didi was supposed to come out with us tonight."

A glimmer of energy came into Alan's eyes. "I forgot about her."

"I'm too beat to go out. Why don't you two go?"

He shook his head. "I'll skip dinner with her. You need me."

"No. You need to go." She was sick of everyone coddling her. She simply needed a break. "I have Officer McKeen here and Sean will be back soon." But hopefully not too soon. She really needed some time to think about what had happened between them this morning.

"I don't want to leave you. It makes no sense, me going out with Didi while you're alone."

She caught his arm. "Listen, Alan. You'd be doing me a huge favor if you went with her. She was so bummed earlier, and if we ditch her, she'll be sad again. If you won't take her, then I'll have to go and I'm too tired. Please? For me?" She grinned. "Besides, you think she's cute."

He scowled, but he couldn't keep the hint of anticipation out of his eyes. "Fine, I'll go. But I'm not going to be out long."

She pulled a spare key from her pocket and handed it to Alan. "You can stay at my house tonight."

Alan took the key, still frowning. "I'll call before I come in so I don't scare you."

She hesitated. "I don't think I'll be staying there tonight."

"Where are you going to stay?"

With Sean? What would they say? Yes, they needed to talk, but not yet. First, she needed to figure out what she was feeling, what was going on. Besides, if Alan was at her house with her, would Jimmy, or whoever, really come after her? "I don't know. Maybe I'll stay at my place." Besides, she could always get Officer McKeen to stay there. Why did it have to be Sean protecting her anyway? It didn't. She looked at Officer McKeen. "You'll stay at my house tonight?"

"I'll be wherever you are until Sean gets back."

Between Alan, Officer McKeen and her alarm, her place

would be fine. Thank heavens. Somehow, now that she thought about it, hunkering down with Sean tonight didn't appeal to her. She was still reeling from his admission that he'd never loved her. *He'd never loved her.* He hadn't actually said it, but the look on his face had been enough.

But what about her? Had she loved him? How could she have been so miserable thinking about him for the past ten years if she hadn't? And last night at his house was the first time she'd felt at home since she left town a decade ago. Sure, L.A. was great, but that feeling of rightness deep in her soul had been missing. Was it Sean who made her feel that way? Was it simply being back in town? Or was it her need to seek out the familiar when being stalked by at least one violent psychopath?

She didn't know. And did it make a difference? It wasn't as if she could walk up to Sean, announce that she loved him and expect all to be well. His primary love was for her dad. For the camp.

She wanted more than leftover love.

Alan shut down the computer. "I hope Jimmy shows up tonight. I'd love for him to try to take us."

It took her a moment to recall what they'd been talking about, to remember that Alan was sitting across from her. "You really don't think that's Jimmy's body in Portland?"

"No way. He wouldn't make it that easy. Besides, who else would know about the knife?" Alan stood. "Cops protect one another. It's the way. He's not gone, Kim, and if Sean's any good, he'll realize that when he goes down there. It's not over."

She knew it wasn't over. The only question was, who was playing the game now?

Chapter Ten

Sean called while she was on her way back to her house, Officer McKeen following her in his cruiser. He wasted no time on preambles. "It was Jimmy. He's dead."

She gripped the steering wheel and felt relief wash over her. "You swear? He's dead?"

"Yep. It's him." He was quiet for a minute, the line humming. "He's been dead for four days."

Oh, *crud.* "You're certain?"

"Uh-huh. He didn't leave the knife in your bed."

Crap. "So what now?"

"We look into Jimmy's life and find out who he was close to. Family, friends, partners."

"You mean cops?"

"Everyone."

"That's a long list, isn't it?" She turned right onto the dirt road that wound up to her house. "That'll take forever."

"But we're also going to investigate everyone at the camp. With the stuff that happened to your dad, I'm betting that Jimmy's accomplice is working at the camp. If we cross-reference the lists, we'll have our man."

Kim frowned. "It would probably be someone who recently joined the staff. I'll go back to the office and pull up all the personnel files and document everyone who started working here eighteen months ago or less."

"Start with May, when the summer staff reported in. That's when your dad first met with Gibbs."

She pulled into her driveway and paused in front of the house. "I'm going back to the office to get the files. Where are you?"

"I'm still an hour and a half away. I'll meet you back at my place?"

She hesitated. "I was thinking of staying at my house tonight. Alan and Officer McKeen will be here, plus there's the alarm. It'll be safe enough." She shifted into reverse and began to turn around.

Sean was quiet for too long.

"Sean?"

"Maybe that's best. I need to go to the station anyway."

"Oh." Now how ridiculous was it that she was bummed that he hadn't argued with her? That he wasn't desperate for some alone time with her? Obviously, he hadn't spent the evening obsessing about their relationship the way she had. "Okay."

"Keep your cell phone on and let me know where you are at all times. Call me when you leave the office to head back to your place."

"Fine." She hung up and tossed the phone onto her seat. Then she rolled down the window and waved to Officer McKeen. "I have to go back to the office."

He nodded and turned around to follow her out of her driveway and back toward the camp.

HE SCOWLED AS he watched her drive away. *This was supposed to be his chance. The cop was out of the way and no one was around except that incompetent rookie. No one to stop him.*

But she'd left without getting out of the car. He knew he should have brought the gun. She'd be dead already.

He slammed the knife into the tree trunk, then wiped his

prints off it. Let her find it. Let her know how close she'd been tonight.

Because tonight wasn't his last chance.

He'd get what he wanted, and he wanted her.

His feet made no sound as he slipped through the woods, his black clothes disappearing into the night without a trace.

KIM CALLED ALAN on the way to the office. He answered on the third ring. "What's up?"

"Jimmy's dead. Sean confirmed it."

Alan was silent.

"Alan?"

"He's dead? Are you positive?"

Kim frowned. "What's wrong? You sound weird. Why aren't you excited?"

"I just can't believe it's over." Alan took a deep breath. "Do they need someone to go down there and identify the body?"

"I don't think so. They seem to have it covered." She hesitated. "Are you sure you're okay?"

"I'm fine. It's just…strange that after all this time, he's gone. Just like that, gone. I kinda had visions of being the one to kill him."

Typical guy. Wanting to be the hero. "Yeah, well, he died before the knife-in-the-bed incident, so don't get too comfortable. There's still a bad guy out there somewhere. I'm hoping it has nothing to do with Jimmy, but it might."

"So you want me to keep going through the files?"

"Uh-huh. I'm heading back there now to pick up some personnel files so we can check those out."

"Why do you need the personnel files at this hour?"

"Because we think maybe someone working at the camp is behind this. Sean thinks Jimmy had a partner on the outside."

Alan cursed and Kim smiled grimly. "Yeah, that's how I feel, too."

"Is this ever going to end?"

"It has to, Alan. I can't take much more."

"You and me both."

KIM FOUND THE FILES she needed and hit Print, then leaned back in her chair and waited for the documents. Officer McKeen was pacing the grounds, leaving her alone in the office for the moment.

The reception desk out front had been empty when they came in, with a sign posted indicating the attendant was unavailable and a number to call if help was needed. It was early for that sign to be out, seeing as it was only ten o'clock. They always tried to keep the desk attended until midnight. Kim checked the schedule and Will was supposed to be on tonight. Where was he? Just because he'd broken up with Didi didn't mean he could blow off work.

Not that it mattered. She had more important things to deal with, such as the fact that someone other than Jimmy had put a knife in her bed. Who could be after her other than Jimmy? Did it really have anything to do with him, or had someone merely tried to use the knife to throw them off? Yeah, sure, the knife had been an exact match, but the trial had been all over the news at the time. Well-decorated cop goes mental and tries to kill two women? It wouldn't have taken a huge amount of effort to guess that the weapon had been some big, badass knife.

So if the incident wasn't related to Jimmy, then what was it? Could Eddie be right? That it all came down to Helen and her desire to get away from this life?

Headlights flashed through the office and she started. Officer McKeen came racing into the office, his hand on his gun. "Are you expecting anyone?"

It had been almost two hours since Sean's call, proving that he'd done as he said and returned directly to the station. Why did that bother her? She had to accept that it was over between them. He hadn't loved her enough then, and he didn't love her at all now. That should make her happy. It was what she wanted. Instead, the thought left a gnawing emptiness inside her. "It could be Sean." She frowned at the wishful tone in her voice.

"It's not a cruiser."

"Maybe it's the front-desk attendant."

"Maybe." He stood next to the window, his gun held next to his shoulder, ready to fire.

The headlights shut off and Kim heard a car door close. "Who is it?"

"A woman."

She sidled over to the window and peered out through the glass. "I don't recognize her."

The front door opened and shut. Footsteps thudded across the wood floor and stopped outside the office door.

That's when Kim realized that the door wasn't locked.

A sharp rap made them both jump. "Kim? It's Helen Collins. Sean told me you'd be here."

Helen? She swallowed hard and the officer looked at her, his gun ready.

"You want to let her in?"

"I guess so, but don't leave."

"Wouldn't think of it." He kept his gun out and opened the door. "Come in."

It was the first time Kim had ever met her dad's wife and she wasn't anything like Kim had thought. No horns, no tail, no pitchfork. Her skin wasn't even red. She was wearing jeans, a long-sleeved T-shirt and hiking boots and she had her hair in a ponytail. In fact, she looked as though she belonged at the Loon's Nest. She stood in the doorway and studied Kim.

Kim shifted and couldn't figure out what to do with her hands.

"So we finally meet," Helen said.

"Yeah."

"You've been avoiding me. I asked Sean to bring you by the house."

"He mentioned it."

Helen nodded toward an empty chair. "May I?"

Kim shrugged. "It's your place."

"No, it isn't. It's yours." Helen sat down. "You and your sister are joint owners with your father. I have no interest in it at all."

"So I hear."

Helen lifted an eyebrow and Kim saw a strength in her that she'd never seen in her mom. "I'm not here to take grief from you. I'm here because I love your father. Personally, after seeing how you've torn out his heart for the past ten years, I'd prefer to send you back to the West Coast and pretend you don't exist."

Ouch. Such a warm and fuzzy woman.

"However," Helen continued, "your father loves you and he won't move on."

"Why should he? We're his real family."

Helen's eyes darkened as she leaned forward. "No, Kim. We are all his real family. You are his first family, we're his second. But whether you like it or not, we're all real."

Kim pressed her lips together and decided she hadn't spent enough energy hating Helen Collins over the past few years.

"Your father needs you, so I want you to get over to the hospital and talk to him. Visit him. Give him a reason to live."

Kim narrowed her eyes. "He didn't do that favor for my mother, did he?"

Helen looked shocked. "You blame him for your mother's death?"

"Of course I do. She was miserable married to him and he wouldn't let her go, so she killed herself. If he'd let her go, she would have lived."

Helen waved her hand over her eyes and looked shaken. "Have you ever talked to him about what happened with your mother?"

"No."

"Oh, wow." She leaned back in her chair. "I hadn't realized that." She shook her head. "I can't believe it."

"Believe what?"

Helen sat up again. "It's not my place to tell you. It'll have to be your dad when he wakes up."

"Tell me what? If you know something about my mom's death, you have to tell me." Her heart began to beat faster. "What don't I know?"

Helen hesitated. "There are circumstances around your mother's death that complicate things. It's…" She gave Kim an imploring look. "Listen, I really don't feel it's my place to tell you. Ask your dad when he wakes up." Her voice trembled slightly. "And if he doesn't, I'll tell you myself. You can't go home without learning the truth. But it would be better if you heard it from him."

Kim wet her lips, her head ringing. What was Helen talking about? "You married my dad three weeks after my mom killed herself. What's there to find out about? And I heard that you hate this camp and you're trying to destroy it. It's on the verge of bankruptcy and you don't care."

Helen jumped to her feet and slapped her hands down on the desk. "You're damn right I don't care if we lose this place. You want to know why? Because it's killing your father! He lives in the past, yearning for the daughters who rejected him, and it's destroying him! Until he comes to grips with his past, he'll never be able to live. I've been praying for years for something to set him free so he can live again, and if losing this camp will force him to look toward the future, then I'm all for it."

She drew in a ragged breath and, for the first time, Kim realized how exhausted she looked. Worn-out and haggard, but brimming with strength and courage. "You blame your father for killing your mother? Well, if you don't go visit him, then you'll kill him the same way. Can you live with that? Can you handle knowing that the man who loves you so much is dying without you?" Helen shoved off the desk, knocking a stapler and a stack of files to the floor. "Grow up, Kim, or get out."

Helen stalked out of the office and slammed the door behind her, making the picture next to it bounce on the wall.

Officer McKeen cleared his throat and moved to the window to watch her leave.

Holy cow. Kim raised her hand to brush her hair off her face and realized that her hand was trembling. She dropped it down to her lap.

Headlights filled the room and then disappeared as Helen drove away. Guess Kim had another person who might want her dead. And Helen certainly hated the camp.

Kim turned back to the computer and began a search for Helen. Then the door opened and Sean walked into the office. He walked in and slammed a huge knife into the desk so hard that the desk shook and a pencil rolled off it.

The three of them stared at it, stuck blade down into the wood, fingerprint powder all over it.

Kim began to shake again and sweat trickled down her temple. She pressed her hand to her scarred thigh and dragged her eyes off the knife to look at Sean.

She didn't even have time to form a question before he snapped out his terse statement. "You're staying with me." It wasn't an option.

"What happened?"

He walked over to the window. "That knife was in the trunk of the tree right outside your front door. He was waiting for you tonight." He turned to face her, his voice accusing. "And you were going to go home."

She stared at him. "I did go home. I was in the driveway

when you called and I decided to come back." She couldn't stop the trembling. What if she'd gotten out of the car? She looked at her bodyguard, who appeared rather shocked. What if Alan was right about cops on the take and Officer McKeen was one of them? What if he'd set her up? What if he was going to let her get out of the car and drive away? Or worse, what if he'd been planning to help kill her? She stared at his young face and felt terrified.

Who was she supposed to trust?

Sean glared at Officer McKeen. "You're relieved of this assignment. Take the knife back to the station for processing. It's already been fingerprinted."

"Yes, sir."

She could trust Sean. Maybe not with her heart but with her life. He was the one man who could keep her alive. Who *would* keep her alive. And maybe, just maybe, his anger meant something more than a cop being protective of a civilian.

Officer McKeen grabbed the weapon and ducked out of the office, leaving Sean and Kim alone. She stared at him, at the rage rolling off him. "Get your stuff," he said. "We're leaving. Now."

She took another glance at the gouge the knife had left in the desk and decided not to argue.

Chapter Eleven

Sean was too angry to talk on the ride home, and Kim didn't try to engage him. He kept waiting for her to demand more information about the knife or Jimmy, or to declare her independence and insist that she sleep at her house, but she said nothing. She simply sat with her feet up on the dashboard, her arms wrapped around her legs and her knees pulled up to her chest.

How close had it been tonight? Would it have been another warning or the end?

"You think Officer McKeen is dirty?" She was resting her chin on her knees, staring out the windshield.

"Why do you ask? Did he do something?" Sean was instantly alert.

"He didn't stop me from going to my house." Her voice was far calmer than he'd expected. "Alan thinks that cops might be willing to help out Jimmy, cop to cop." She didn't look at him. "He tried to convince me you might be dirty."

"I assume he wanted you to ditch me and let him protect you?"

She nodded.

"The best way to get to you is to get you away from me."

Kim slowly turned to look at him and he was chagrined by the emptiness in her gaze. The resignation that horror actually existed and she had to face it. "It's not Alan."

"When did you first meet him?"

"I met him at a party."

"Before or after Cheryl started dating Jimmy?"

Kim's eyes narrowed. "After."

"He approach you or you approach him?"

"We were seated next to each other at a dinner party."

A dinner party. Hah. When was the last time he'd been to a dinner party?

Kim frowned. "What's so funny?"

"Nothing." He swung into his driveway, certain they hadn't been tailed from the camp office. And he'd been looking. Nevertheless, he pulled out his gun and scanned the woods for a few minutes.

An unknown enemy was the toughest.

"Let's go in."

He let her into the cabin and set the alarm behind them. Last night, it seemed cozy. Tonight, it was claustrophobic. Too much tension between them. "I'll take the couch."

Kim didn't argue. Instead, she sank onto the sofa and hugged a pillow to her chest. It was then that he noticed that she was shivering. "Cold?"

She shook her head.

"Scared?"

"Mad."

He couldn't stop himself from smiling. "At me?" He pulled out a glass and stuck it under the faucet. "Want a drink?"

"No to both." She stared blankly at the empty fireplace. "I'm mad at all of this. At Jimmy for starting it. At whoever's playing the game now. Is it a friend of Jimmy's? Is it Helen posing as a cohort of Jimmy's to throw us off the trail? She could have gotten the details of the attack from Cheryl…." Kim frowned. "Of course she could have."

The glass overflowed, and he shut off the faucet. He couldn't believe what he'd just heard. "What did you say?"

"Helen." Kim was sitting up, her eyes bright. "I can't believe I didn't think of that. I know Cheryl told my dad about the attack. Helen would totally know what kind of a knife was used." She threw her fist into the pillow. "Don't you get it? She's trying to throw us off track by making us think it has something to do with Jimmy. Did you tell her he's dead? Of course, she doesn't know. You told her I was at the office, so she went to the house and stuck the knife in the tree." Her face paled. "Oh, my gosh. What if she came to the office to kill me tonight but couldn't do it because Officer McKeen was there? Did you tell her he was there? No wonder she was pissed." She jumped to her feet. "We have to get to the hospital to protect my dad. What if she tries to finish him off?" She sprinted toward the door, but Sean grabbed her wrist as she went by.

"Kim!"

"What?" She tried to twist free. "Don't you get it? When she finds out Jimmy is dead, she's out of time. She'll have to kill him. Let go!"

"There's an officer on your dad's room already."

She stilled, her breath panting. "There is? You knew it was Helen all along?" Her brow furrowed. "Then how could you send her to the office tonight?"

"Because she's not a killer. She loves your dad."

"She's crazy! Just ask Officer McKeen what happened at the office." Kim took another step toward the door.

"Kim. It's not Helen."

"How do you know?"

"Because I do."

She stared at him and some of the fear left her eyes. "You believe that?"

"Of course, I do." He studied her. "You trust my instincts, don't you?"

She sank onto the pillows again. "Honestly, Sean, I don't know what to think anymore. Finding out you were going to marry me for my dad is…well…it makes me wonder if I knew you at all. Even if I do believe in you, how do I know I'm right?"

He sat down on the couch next to her. "That's how I felt when you left."

"I guess I was right to leave if you didn't love me."

"Maybe."

"Wow. I never thought I'd hear that from you. Does that mean I can finally let go of the guilt I've been shouldering?"

"You felt guilty?"

"The whole time."

He smiled. Couldn't help it. "I thought you'd forgotten about me."

"I thought you'd forgotten about me." She fiddled with the edge of her T-shirt. "When you joined the Army, I worried about you, but no one ever had any news. I made Cheryl ask my dad every time she talked to him."

"I wanted to forget about my life here."

She frowned. "That's what I was trying to do as well, but I had to come back for my dad. Why did you come back?"

Trying? So she hadn't succeeded in forgetting about him or what they'd had? A glimmer of hope lit up in his chest. "I don't know why I came back. Nowhere else to go, I guess."

"That's sad."

"Or maybe it's good. Not everyone has a place to come back to when the world sucks."

"Are you going to stay?"

"For now. You?" He caught his breath, then let it out when she shook her head.

"Only until this nightmare is over. My life is in L.A. now, but until we catch whoever it is, I'm staying." She pursed her lips. "You're my best bet for staying alive."

"I can protect you only if you stay at my place and let me be your shadow." He'd said it before, but she had yet to accept it. Only a few hours ago, she'd been on her way back to her own house to stay.

But this time, she nodded.

His heart skipped a beat. She was accepting their intimacy and he wasn't sure if he was glad because it would make his job easier or for another reason.… "Then we're going to have to figure out how to deal with each other."

"Any suggestions?"

"Pretend we're strangers?"

She looked doubtful. "You really think that'll work? I mean, our history isn't exactly two dates and one drunken night of debauchery."

He smiled. If only it were that simple. "Maybe our relationship was so mixed up in your family that it was never about us."

"It still isn't about only us. I'm out here because of my dad. You hate me because I left my mom and dad. Jimmy was stalking me because of my sister. You want me to become best buddies with Helen while I think that she's trying to kill me and my father." She shrugged. "Who knows what's actually going on between us?"

"So there is something going on between us?"

She immediately shielded her face. "What do you mean?"

He shifted forward on the couch. "Last night, when we were in bed together—"

Heat tinged her cheeks, but she said, "It was something."

"What was it?"

"The past? Familiar turf that felt safe."

That's all she thought it was? He'd been thinking about a lot more.

They fell silent and he couldn't think of anything to say. Oh, there was plenty that he wanted to say, but nothing that he would say. Not after she'd just dismissed last night. He sure as hell wasn't going to be the one to open that door.

"Sean?"

"Hmm?"

"If you don't think the suspect is Helen, why did you put a cop on my dad's hospital room?"

"Because I think it's someone who knows him."

"Maybe you should look into Helen." Kim sat up. "You know, when my dad got the phone call to go to the camp that night, she could have followed him there. She knew all the details of the attack from Cheryl. And she had access to the safe in the office to find out that my dad was meeting with that private investigator."

Sean felt as if he'd been kicked in the gut. Kim was right. It could be Helen. Except… "But why? What about motive?"

Kim filled him in on the confrontation with Helen at the office and he felt sick. He dropped his head to his hands. "It could simply be that she loves your dad and his accident is stressing her out."

"Or it could be more."

Sean cursed. "It can't be her."

"Why not?"

He pressed his forehead into his hands. "Because your dad would never survive it. He loves her and her kids. He can't handle more loss. I wouldn't be able to save him."

The couch shifted and he knew Kim had moved next to him. "Is that why you came back? To save him?"

He didn't say anything. He couldn't.

"And now you're trying to save me?"

"Dammit, Kim. I can't fail anyone else. Don't you understand?" He ground his palms into his eyes and tried to will away the images flashing in his mind. Images of his best friend dying. Screaming for help.

"Who did you fail, Sean?" Her voice was quiet.

"Leave it alone."

The small sound of laughter was deep in her throat. "When did that ever work before? Have I ever backed off when you didn't want to talk?"

"I'm sick of referring to what we had in the past."

She was quiet then. "I'm sorry. You're right."

Silence.

"As a twenty-eight-year-old woman who does her best not to let men boss her around, I'm going to ignore your request for me to leave it alone as I would with any other man. Who did you fail, Sean?"

He couldn't help but smile. "You're a pain in the butt."

"That's what everyone tells me at work." The couch shifted again and he felt her lean against the pillows. Her hip was pressed to his, but neither of them moved apart. "Did I ever tell you what I do for a job now?"

He lifted his head and looked at her. "No, you didn't."

She raised her arms over her head and stretched. "I'm an editor for a dishy mag. We get all the inside scoop on celebrities and pay lots of money to paparazzi for pictures that invade the privacy of megastars. I go to all sorts of invitation-only functions and I'm expected to spend a fair amount of money on my wardrobe."

"Seriously?"

She grinned at him. "Surprised?"

"I guess. It doesn't seem like you."

"Sometimes it is. Sometimes it isn't. Who likes their job every day anyway?"

He shrugged. "Not many people, I guess."

"Exactly." She folded her arms across her stomach and stared at him. "I manage a staff of five. I had to fire an employee two months ago because she was harvesting celebrity e-mails from our files and selling them. She cried and told me how she had three kids and her husband had just left her and she needed the job." Some of the light went out of her eyes. "I fired her anyway. Found out later she didn't have any kids, but I felt terrible for that whole week until I learned the truth."

He studied her as she continued to ramble on about her

job and he realized that she really wasn't the eighteen-year-old girl he'd almost married. She was mature, confident and successful. A woman of her own mind and sensibilities. Would she have become this woman if she'd stayed in town and married him?

Maybe not.

He realized she'd stopped talking and was looking at him expectantly.

"What?"

She punched him softly. "You weren't even listening."

"I was thinking about how you're not the girl I once knew."

She smiled. "I've changed a lot."

"I can tell."

"And now it's your turn."

He was not so fond of the look on her face right now. "What do you mean?"

"I introduced you to the new Kim. Now it's your turn. All I know about you is what you were like ten years ago. What's new in your life?" She gave him an innocent smile. "How are we supposed to forget about our past if we don't build something new to lean on?"

He leaned back next to her so that their shoulders were touching. "I was in the Army for eight years. Weapons specialist. My main job was to get helicoptered into a zone, then hang out and direct incoming planes on their targets."

"You ever make a mistake and almost get a bomb dropped on you?"

"We were training the Marines one time and one of them had the aircraft approach from behind us. They dropped the bomb and that thing was coming straight down on us. Barely missed us." He shook his head at the memory. "Dumb fools."

"Is that how you hurt your leg?"

He frowned. "That was another time."

"What time?"

"Kim…"

She grabbed his arm as he started to get up. "Who did you fail, Sean? Tell me."

"My best friend, okay? Frank McCabe, father of two, got hit, and I didn't get him clear fast enough. He died. Dead. Happy?" He pulled free, walked into the bedroom and slammed the door.

He sat on the bed and dropped his face into his hands.

When the door clicked, he didn't move. "Go away."

Instead, the bed dipped and Kim slipped behind him, settling her legs on either side of his. She wrapped her arms around his waist and rested her cheek against his back.

He stiffened, knowing she was going to ask for details or tell him it wasn't his fault or order him to get over it.

But she didn't.

She simply held him.

Held him as no one had held him for a long time.

SEAN AWOKE TO the smell of fresh coffee. He opened his eyes to find Kim sitting at his feet on the couch, her legs tucked under her while she sifted through a stack of computer print-outs. Her nose was wrinkled in thought and her hair was shoved into a crooked ponytail. No makeup, still wearing her boxers and T-shirt from bed, she looked adorable. He could see the scar on her leg, but she didn't seem to be trying to hide it. It felt right, waking up with her close to him.

Then he grimaced, remembering last night. Kim had sat with him for a while and then they'd gone to bed. Him on the couch, her in the bedroom, neither of them even discussing their sleeping arrangements.

He still couldn't believe that he'd told her about Frank. Now she was going to treat him like some pathetic wimp who needed therapy. He scowled, and that's when Kim looked up and realized he was awake.

He braced himself for her reaction.

Instead, she smiled. "I decided that it would be foolish to assume Helen's guilt and not pursue any other leads, so I went ahead with searching the personnel files from the camp."

What? She wasn't going to bring up Frank? Insist he spill his guts? The old Kim would have demanded that he tell all, claiming true lovers didn't hold secrets from each other.

"Eleven people are new this summer. If we go back eighteen months to when the you-know-what hit the fan with Jimmy, there are twenty-three people who are new. I started making calls to check references and see if any of them lived in L.A., but it's going to take forever." She frowned. "Somehow, I don't think we have forever."

"August third is coming up."

"You still think that's relevant since Jimmy is dead?"

"He wasn't the one who put the knife in your bed on the twenty-fifth." He couldn't believe she really wasn't going to push. Maybe she was different from the girl he used to know.

Her energy faded and her face darkened. "Well, whoever it is, screw him. We're going to beat him."

God help him if he failed. He couldn't fail someone else. Especially not Kim.

She looked at him expectantly. "So what next? Do we split the list and make calls on these people?"

"Did you check the fax this morning?"

"No, why?"

"I asked Billy to fax me anything that came in at work." He kicked back the blankets and walked over to the machine. "I'm waiting for details on Jimmy." Sure enough, there were papers there. He picked them up and turned back, in time to catch Kim with a guilty look on her face. "What?"

"Can't you put some clothes on?"

He looked down, realizing he was wearing only his boxers. He liked that she'd noticed. "Sorry." He grabbed a T-shirt off a nearby chair and slung it on while he tossed the papers at Kim. "Take a look."

He was in the middle of zipping the fly on his jeans when Kim sucked in her breath. "Oh, my God."

He dropped next to her and leaned over her shoulder. "What did you find?"

She pointed. "Jimmy Ramsey has a brother."

Chapter Twelve

Kim was so aware of Sean as he leaned over her, reading the printout, conscious of him in a new way. He'd had his best friend die in his arms and he apparently felt that he could have saved him. To live with that knowledge?

No wonder he seemed colder and harder than the kid she'd known. He *had* changed. And so had she. What did that mean for the present? They hadn't loved each other as kids, not true love. How could they have? They'd been eighteen and mixed up in family dynamics.

But today? They were just beginning to get to know each other as adults. Was it too late?

"John Ramsey," Sean read, his breath tickling the side of her neck. "Born August 15, 1981."

"That makes him twenty-five." She didn't want to move away from him or encourage him to shift away, so she pulled the papers onto her lap and held them so he could see them. "If we cross-reference that information with the twenty-three names I came up with…" She fell silent as they studied the lists and looked up names.

When they were finished, they had three names: Tom Payton—despite looking as if he was eighteen, he was actually twenty-four—Will Ambrose, and Carl Andrews, the head maintenance guy who had driven her home that first day. They were around the right age and were new on the scene. Names and actual birthdates could be changed and employment records could be forged, and these three had sketchy backgrounds.

Will was MIA.

Tom was already acting strange.

And Carl was a huge, muscle-bound guy who could kick some serious butt.

She stared at the list. "You think one of these three is John Ramsey?"

"Makes sense." Sean shifted on the couch, but he didn't move away from her. "Did Jimmy or your sister ever mention a brother?"

"Not that I know of. Maybe they're estranged or something." She frowned. "But if they're estranged, then why would John Ramsey be after me?"

Sean leaned over Kim and grabbed the phone off the end table. He called the station and asked Billy to request a list of all visitors Jimmy had had while he was in prison. Then he hung up and tossed the phone on the coffee table.

He hadn't moved. His shoulder was still against hers, and so was his hip. Was he doing it intentionally, or was he too lazy to move? She didn't dare ask, didn't want to give him a reason to shift away from her.

She was so aware of his presence and his energy, in a whole different way than she ever had been before.

"I have an idea," he said.

"What?" She looked at him, realizing belatedly that his face was only inches from hers. She didn't turn away, and his gaze flicked to her lips.

"I think we should have Cheryl take a look at a staff photo and see if she recognizes any of those guys. Maybe John Ramsey showed up at some point while they were married. Maybe she's seen pictures."

Oh, wow, she didn't like that suggestion at all. "I don't

know. I don't want to endanger her by contacting her. Especially now, when someone might be watching. If Jimmy's brother really is after me, then he'd want to get to Cheryl, too." She'd almost given her life to save Cheryl once. She didn't want it to be in vain.

He nodded. "I understand."

But there was an element of frustration in his voice and she studied him. "You don't agree."

Sean leaned forward, resting his forearms on his thighs and shifting restlessly. "I don't want to endanger Cheryl, but I want this over. It's only a matter of time until this guy gets to you or her." He shoved off the couch and stood, pacing the room. Darn it! Why had he gotten up? "We could notify the police in her town and have them look out for her. We could ensure her safety."

Kim watched him prowl the room. "I thought we couldn't trust cops." Then she had a thought. "What about Officer McKeen? Do we know about him?"

Sean stopped mid-step and stared at her. "He's new. All of Billy's hires are new."

"What about the guard on my dad's room?"

"New. They're all new." He cursed and stalked across the room. "Come on."

"Where to?"

"We're going to go talk to Billy."

WHEN SEAN WALKED into the chief's office, he knew he was putting his friendship, his career and his future in law enforcement in Maine at stake. The state was too small for him to piss off someone as well respected as Billy.

Billy was sitting at his desk, arguing on the phone with someone. When he saw Sean and Kim arrive, he waved them in to have a seat. Sean shut the door behind them and they sat down.

And waited.

Billy finished his phone call and hung up. "They don't want to send the records of who visited Jimmy in prison. It's turning into a pissing contest between us and them and I'm sick of it." He scowled. "What did you come up with?"

Sean tossed the short list of names across the desk. "Folks new to the camp that are about the right age to be John Ramsey."

Billy studied the list. "Is this it?"

"Garth McKeen."

Chief Vega's friendly expression faded. "What about him?"

Sean replayed the events of last night, ending with the fact that the young man was the right age, hit the town at the right time and was a cop.

When he finished, Bill did not look friendly at all. "You're accusing me of hiring a guy whose goal is to murder one of the citizens in my town."

"Two of them, because of the accident with her dad. Plus the P.I. Any sign of him?"

Chief Vega leaned back in his chair, but Sean didn't buy it. "I did a background check on every one of these guys. Per your request, I questioned all of them again. Offended the lot of them, and I don't blame them. They're all clean." He looked at Kim. "Sounds to me like Officer McKeen's behavior last night was right on. He was actively patrolling and—"

"Maybe a little too actively."

Chief Vega eyed Sean. "What do you mean?"

"Trying to overcompensate for the fact that he was going to be setting Kim up. If he looks super-proactive, who would suspect?"

Bill stood up and banged his hands down on his desk. "Listen, Templeton, unless you can give me concrete evidence to suspect one of my officers, you need to leave. Merely stating that the guy is the right age and that he's new and that he happens to have a profession that fits your profile isn't enough. It's not even circumstantial." He gestured at the list. "And that's all you've got on these guys, too? Right age, new to town? Come on, Sean, you're better than this." He gathered himself and sat. "You know we have to build a case, have evidence, probable cause. What's this garbage you're bringing to my desk?"

Sean frowned. "My gut says I'm on the right track."

"Your gut isn't enough, not with this weak case. You have nothing. Nothing!" Chief Vega ran a hand through his red hair. "You have a boating accident involving someone who shouldn't crash a boat. A possible spot of his blood on the boat he's had for twenty years. It means nothing."

It meant something to Sean. He shot a glance at Kim. She was chewing her lower lip and watching the chief. Did she agree with Bill? Was she thinking that Sean was incompetent and that she would be better off not teaming up with him? He scowled at the idea. In the old days, she would have believed in him without a second thought, but what did that really mean anyway? They'd pretty much established that they'd been deluded teenagers. Today, she'd reserve judgment until she had a good reason. Better that way, but damn if a part of him didn't want her to trust him blindly anyway.

Chief Vega wasn't finished. "You show me a piece of metal stuck in the steering column and an eighty-year-old man who says he never messed up on his boats. And based on that, you want me to call it attempted murder?"

Sean frowned. "Don't you feel it, Billy? There's something off here."

"It's Chief Vega, and no, I don't. Kim was being stalked. The man who did it is dead. End of threat."

"What about the knife in her bed and in the tree?"

Chief Vega met his gaze. "A sick joke."

"Do you really believe that?"

He was silent for a long time.

That's okay. Sean could wait.

Finally, Chief Vega said, "As a cop, I can't afford to dismiss it. But until you bring me something concrete on your suspects, there's not a damn thing I can do about any of them." He met Sean's gaze. "And there's nothing you can do to them. You're a cop now, Sean. No vigilante justice. Play by the rules. I'm not questioning the integrity of my staff until you bring me something other than a gut feeling. The department would never survive it. You bring me evidence, I'll act. Without it, I can't and I won't."

"You used to go with your gut."

"Yeah, when we were teenagers. Now I have a job to do and a department to manage."

Sean cursed and stood. "Great rhetoric. Will it sound so good when you're at Kim's funeral?"

Kim's mouth tightened, but she said nothing.

Chief Vega looked at her. "You don't have to work with him, Kim. I can get someone else to watch you, or you can head back to L.A."

Sean tensed. He hadn't expected Bill to make the offer. If Sean were Kim, he'd be half tempted to take it. After this little discussion, how could she feel confident about him? "I request permission to go off duty and devote my full schedule to this case to provide protection for Kim."

The chief eyed him. "I hired you to help take some of the workload off me, not to go off on some personal vendetta."

"If I wasn't working this case, you'd have to do it." Sean knew he was right. As much as Billy might want to deny it, the details simply didn't add up.

Chief Vega turned to Kim. "It's up to you. You want him, you can have him. You don't, I'll find someone else."

She shot a glance at Sean. "I'll stick with Sean, thanks."

"You sure?"

"Yep."

Sean didn't realize how tense he'd been until he felt himself relax. He looked at Kim and she raised one eyebrow at him. She knew the facts. She knew he'd let his best friend die. She knew he was running on fumes and gut instinct on this case. She was smart and independent and able to stand on her own.

And she'd decided to throw in her lot with him.

For some reason, that show of confidence meant a hell of a lot more to him than her acceptance of his proposal all those years ago. She was putting her life—and her sister's—in his hands and he'd be damned if he'd let her down.

KIM'S CELL PHONE RANG as soon as they stepped outside the police station. "It's Alan," she told Sean as she answered it. "What's up?"

"I'm at the office working on your dad's files," Alan said.

"And?"

"Someone has been embezzling from the camp."

She sucked in her breath. "Are you sure?"

"Uh-huh. And in an attempt to hide his tracks, he's changed so many files and entries that there's no way this camp could run efficiently. It's impossible to track deliveries, payments to vendors, staff payroll—you name it. It's a disaster, but only if you're looking for it. Can you come by so I can show it to you?"

"You bet." She snapped the phone shut and frowned at Sean. "Embezzling isn't exactly in line with Jimmy Ramsey, is it?" So now they were back to two different crimes, or the attacks on her being a red herring. "What career did Helen have before she married my dad and started helping out at the Loon's Nest?"

"I knew you were going to bring that up."

"Show me someone else with an incentive to wreck the camp."

"She loves him."

"People have done far worse in the name of love."

He scowled. "She knows that losing the camp would ruin him."

"No, Sean. She believes that failing to let go of his past will kill him. If she has to rip the camp out of his hands to save him, she'll do it. She told me that, Sean. In front of Officer McKeen, if you don't believe me." She clenched her hands. "Or maybe the whole show was a lie and she actually wants the money and the inheritance. That's why the accident on top of the embezzlement. Did you know that she wouldn't get the camp if my dad died? Cheryl and I would get it. That means she had to siphon off the money before he died, so there was nothing left for us." She took a deep breath. It would shatter her father to lose the camp, if he wasn't dead already. Her throat began to tighten up and she sucked her lip between her teeth.

Sean yanked open the passenger door of his cruiser for Kim. "You want to get Helen thrown in jail, even if it'll devastate your father. You'll take any chance you have at destroying your dad and the family he loves."

She paused in front of him, one foot in the car. "Not anymore."

Before he could ask, she pulled the door shut, leaving him standing on the outside.

He climbed into his side and started driving. They were halfway to camp when he asked, "What changed?"

She sighed and stared out the window. *She* had changed. It hadn't occurred to her until Sean brought it up, but now that she was thinking about it, it was true.

"Kim?"

"I thought my dad was going to be killed last night. I thought someone was going to go to the hospital and finish the job. Remember when I tried to rush out of your cabin to go save him?"

He nodded.

"I didn't think about it. I just ran for the door. To rescue him." She bit her lower lip harder, but it wasn't working to ward off the emotions. "If I wanted him dead, I wouldn't have reacted that way."

"He's been in a coma since you got here and that didn't bother you."

She sighed and watched the trees go by. "I guess you were so certain he was going to wake up that I didn't really think he wouldn't. He's my dad. He'll be around for me to hate as long as I want." Hate. It seemed like such a strong word now. Too strong?

Sean managed to exercise enough control not to editorialize on that statement. The man was learning. Good for him.

"But when I thought someone was going to kill him...I got mad. And I got scared." Sean turned into the camp driveway, heading toward the parking lot. "I don't have a mom anymore and suddenly I realized I wasn't ready not to have a dad. Even if I don't talk to him, he's always there, you know?" As long as he was alive and she could hate him, there was still a foundation in her life. As long as she knew he still loved her and wanted her back, there was comfort in knowing that she belonged somewhere. If he died, then she had nothing. No home to come back to. No roots. No parents at all. No possibility of future reconciliation, if she ever decided she wanted it. "Dammit, Sean. I don't want him to die until I'm ready for him to die!"

He pulled into a parking spot and shut off the engine. He turned his head just enough to look at her. "You're crying."

"I am not." She immediately wiped her cheeks and turned to stare out the passenger window. No way was she going into the office looking this way. *Get it together, Kim.* She felt a light pressure on her shoulder, but she didn't look at him. "Go away."

"No."

"Please?"

His fingers trailed over her forearm and she finally turned in his direction. He smiled. "It's not easy to change your mind about something you've believed for so long."

"I haven't changed my mind. I still blame him for my mom's death. I just…well…I don't want him to die before I'm ready for him to die."

He nodded and ran his thumb over her lower lip. "I understand."

"Do you?"

"Over the past ten years, I haven't had a whole lot of kind thoughts about you," he said. "But when I showed up at your door a few nights ago to investigate the prowler and learned that you were in real danger, I was furious. Maybe I didn't want you in my life, but no way was anyone allowed to kill you."

She managed a smile. "You know, it must be a sign of my warped mental state that I actually think that's a really sweet thing for you to say."

He smiled back and she realized he'd moved even closer, his thumb trailing over her shoulder. "I think we may both be a little outside of the norm. Maybe that's okay."

"Maybe." She could feel his breath on her lips. Her heart was racing and all she could think about was how much she wanted him to kiss her. "Um, Sean?"

"Mmm?"

She wrapped her hand around his wrist and held tight. All she could think about was the feel of his bare skin under her fingers. "I forget what I was going to say," she whispered.

"Me, too." Then he leaned forward and kissed her.

Chapter Thirteen

This was nothing like the kiss they'd shared in the mailroom. That had been frantic and energetic and brought on by memories of their past.

This kiss was soft and sweet and perfect. It was about the present, about today, about *them* and only them.

He played with her lips, his touch gentle and almost unsure. Her heart rate was skyrocketing and all she wanted was for the kiss to last forever. She fisted the front of his T-shirt in her hand and pulled him closer. His breath mingled with hers. He tasted of toothpaste, and he smelled like soap and man.

More. She wanted more. When she parted her lips, he made a soft grunt and wrapped his hand around the back of her head, his fingers twisting in her hair, his other hand cupping the side of her face. How could his touch be so tender and yet infuse her with such incredible wanting?

His hand slipped down the side of her face, his fingers trailing over her neck as he kissed her deeper and deeper, his tongue playing in her mouth, warm and hot.

He pressed his fingers at the base of her neck and broke the kiss. His eyes were dark and smoky. "Your heart is racing."

His fingers were over her pulse, so she couldn't lie. And why would she want to? "I know."

A slow grin spread over his face and he leaned forward again.

Only this time when their lips met, it wasn't soft or gentle or tentative. It rocked with heat and passion and a need she felt to her core. She flung her arms around his neck and buried herself against him while he held her tight, so close she could barely breathe. Who needed to breathe, anyway? Breathing was overrated, especially when weighed against the feeling of his solid chest pressed up against her breasts. Their shirts did little to block the heat, and she felt his heart pounding against her chest. She leaned back. "Your heart is racing, too."

He grinned. "How about that? I've never had a kiss spike my heart rate before."

"Really? Not even when we were teenagers?" she teased.

He kissed her for a long time before answering. "It was never like this."

She felt the same way. This thing between them was different now. A hell of a lot more intense, for one. Almost scary. "I know what you mean."

He sighed. "Kim—"

The scream of a little kid startled her and she turned to see a family of four heading toward the boathouse with picnic supplies in hand. Two small girls were chasing each other, their voices shrill as they shrieked with excitement.

Sean's fingers tightened in her hair and she turned to look at him. "Not exactly the place for a make-out session, huh?"

He laced his fingers through hers and brought her hand to his lips. "Someday, we're going to have to get this right between us."

She swallowed. Was he talking about the kiss or their relationship? Had he not given up on them? Did he want to try again, or did he merely want a night of passion to toast their shared past?

She didn't dare ask.

Because she wasn't sure what she wanted him to say.

And she was desperately afraid of what her gut was telling her she was yearning to hear.

SEAN TOOK KIM'S HAND as they walked up the front steps into the office. He wasn't sure why he did it, but he did.

And she didn't pull away.

So they walked hand in hand into the office to find Didi and Alan huddled over the computer screen in a very cozy picture. Sean grinned at the sight. He couldn't drum up any regret if Alan got hung up on Didi and found another woman to call his best friend, because Alan being possessive of Kim was a pain in the butt for their investigation. No other reason.

"Hi, guys," Kim said, and the couple broke apart quickly, guilty looks on their faces. "Did we interrupt something?"

Alan's gaze flicked to their entwined fingers and Kim released Sean's hand immediately. But the soft look she gave Sean as she did it made Alan scowl. So Sean grinned and decided that he could be generous with Alan today. "What'd you find?"

Didi propped herself up against the windowsill behind Alan, as if she belonged there. Sean frowned. "Didi, would you mind giving us some privacy?"

Her lips pursed into a pout. "I've been helping him. I know what's going on. You might need me to explain some of the files."

Alan nodded immediately. "She needs to stay." Didi put her hand on his shoulder and he set his hand on top of hers. "She's been a huge help with this mess."

His respect for Alan dropped more than a couple of notches. Get a little sex and you start spilling confidential details to your bedmate? Always a good plan.

As Sean watched them exchange secret glances that made

him wonder whether they'd been rolling around on the floor before he and Kim arrived, he recalled the interlude with Will and Didi. Will, who fit the profile for John Ramsey and who had been missing for quite a few days. If one man would confess his secrets after a roll in the hay with Didi, would another one? "Didi, do you have a minute? I'd like to ask you some questions."

Didi nodded. "Of course. That's why I'm here."

Sean glanced at Alan. "It's about Will. Shall we go in the hall?"

Didi's fingers tightened on Alan's shoulder, then she nodded. "Sure."

"Kim, you can stay and go over the files with Alan. We'll be right back."

Kim nodded and walked over to the desk while Didi led Sean to the hallway.

There were two guests waiting for help, so she effectively took care of their issues, then turned to Sean. "Thanks for letting me take this out into the hall." She looked at the closed door. "I really like Alan and, well, who knows how he'd react if he knew I'd been dating someone else so recently."

"You mean having sex with."

Her eyes lost their softness. "What exactly is it that you need?"

"I'd like to know if Will ever talked about his past, his family, any activities he was involved in. Maybe he uttered a few names in his sleep?"

Didi frowned. "What are you talking about?"

Sean hesitated. If he didn't give her at least a hint about what he wanted to know, he might waste a lot of time. If he did give her info, well, it potentially compromised the investigation. What choice did he have? "I need to know if he ever mentioned a brother named Jimmy Ramsey."

Didi stared at him. "What?"

"A brother named Jimmy Ramsey."

"But his last name is Ambrose. Will Ambrose." Her eyebrows were knitted together in an effort to follow him and he decided at that moment that maybe Didi wasn't the brightest person he'd ever met.

"Names can be changed. Did he ever mention a brother?"

"No." But her tone was drawn out and thoughtful, indicative of truth more than a quick, vehement denial would have been.

"Did he ever accidentally refer to himself as John Ramsey? Not turn right away when you called him Will?"

Didi's eyes widened. "You think Will is actually someone named John Ramsey, who has a brother named Jimmy Ramsey?"

"Answer the question."

"No, I never noticed anything." She frowned. "Why?"

"Did Will ever show any familiarity with California? As if he'd been there?"

She shook her head, her expression mystified. "Why do you need to know this? What's happened?"

"What about Carl?"

"The maintenance chief?"

"Yes. Did he ever mention a brother or accidentally call himself John? Show any familiarity with California?"

"I didn't sleep with him." She folded her arms across her chest and looked offended. "Just because I made a mistake with Will doesn't mean I'm a slut."

"I didn't mean to imply that you did. But since you work at the same place, I figured you might have some knowledge of him."

Didi softened, mollified by his recant. "No to all of your questions, but I never spend much time talking to him."

Probably not by choice, given how she seemed interested in every guy who walked into the place. "What about Tom Payton?"

"The guy at the boathouse?"

"Yep. Same questions."

"No, but I don't talk to him much. He mostly flirts with the girls who are guests at the camp. Staff aren't good enough for him."

Interesting. Tom hadn't seemed to be the playboy type. He was due for an interview at the station anyway. "Thanks for your time, Didi." He hesitated, then added, "We don't know what John Ramsey looks like, but he's about twenty-five and we believe he may be in the area. He's potentially dangerous, so if you get any indication that he's around, call the police and stay away from him."

She frowned. "What about the other one you mentioned? His brother? Should I be watching out for a couple of guys who are hanging together?"

"No. Jimmy Ramsey is dead. It's only his brother we're concerned about."

Didi stared at him. "Dead? You mean, really dead?"

Sean nodded.

"How do you know?"

"We found his body."

She looked rather shocked. Pale. Her lower lip was trembling. "You think his brother killed him?"

"Seems like it was a bar fight in Portland. His brother may be trying to avenge his death, though, so be wary. He could be pretty desperate." Belatedly, he realized that Didi looked a little stressed. Too much info. "Listen, Didi, I'm sure you have nothing to worry about. His rage will be directed toward one target and that isn't you. I'm sure you're safe, so all I want is for you to report any suspicious folks, okay?"

She nodded, still looking stunned.

"How about I send Alan out to give you some comfort?"

"That's fine." She lifted her chin and seemed to shake it off. "I'm glad you told me. I'll keep watch." Her eyes widened suddenly. "You think that's who has been embezzling?" She pursed her lips. "All three of those guys spend time in the office. Of course, lots of staff come in and out of here, but those three definitely do. You think?"

Although he'd been thinking that John Ramsey was more likely going to go after Kim with a knife, who knew what his style was? Maybe he was more of the white-collar type than Jimmy was.

They needed to get more information on John Ramsey and fast.

"I'm working on getting a photo. Keep an eye on guests and everyone else. If I can get a picture, I'll make sure you get a copy."

She nodded, looking energized. "I'll totally be your spy."

At least she wasn't trembling in her shoes anymore. He decided not to tell her about his concerns with the knife. No need to frighten her. "If you see him, Didi, don't confront him. Just tell the police, okay?"

She nodded. "No problem. I'm all over it."

"Don't confront him," he said again, but she'd already turned away to help another guest. His gut wrenching in turmoil, he walked back into the office and shut the door. "Alan."

Alan and Kim were huddled over the computer and they both looked up. "What?"

"I asked Didi about Jimmy and John Ramsey and now she's on a mission to help find them. You need to make sure she doesn't go off on some vigilante thing." He hesitated. "If she gets herself hurt, I…"

Kim got a look in her eye that bugged him because he knew she was aware of what he was thinking. "It'll be fine," she said softly. "It isn't your fault."

He met her empathetic gaze and felt his throat tighten.

"Who is John Ramsey?" Alan appeared confused.

"We didn't tell you?" Kim looked at Sean, who shrugged. "I didn't tell him. We only found out this morning."

Kim filled Alan in on the John Ramsey discovery. By the time she finished, he was frowning. "You think this John Ramsey is the one who's been after Kim?"

"It's our only lead," Sean said.

Kim looked at him. "It could also be Helen, but Sean won't consider it."

He scowled. "I'm considering it." He had to. For the safety of Kim and her dad, he had to follow up. He might be haunted forever if Didi got hurt because she decided to play hero, but if Kim or her dad got hurt—or worse—because he refused to investigate a suspect, he'd—well, he couldn't let that happen. He just couldn't.

"You ever hear of a brother?" Kim asked.

Alan shook his head. "I'm not on personal terms with Jimmy, though. I only knew him through you." He leaned back in the chair and tapped his chin. "If Jimmy had a brother who was out for vengeance on Jimmy's behalf, I gotta think we would have heard from him over the past eighteen months. Where was he during the trial?" Alan shook his head. "My guess is that the brother probably took off on Jimmy and is doing his own thing. Probably disowned the scum."

Sean frowned. "Well, we can't find any evidence of him other than a birth certificate. He seems to have disappeared."

"Maybe Jimmy already killed him," Kim said.

Alan looked at her. "Probably."

Sean sat. "So if it's not the brother, then who? Who else has ties to Jimmy's past that are strong enough to want revenge for him?"

"A cop on his force?"

Sean shook his head. "Already checked. No cops that were close to him are on leave. They're all in L.A. Anything else?"

No one had any ideas.

Sean stood up. "I guess that means we pursue Helen and

John Ramsey and keep pressing L.A. for some more details that could help us find out what's going on." He nodded at Alan. "Didi's a little stressed out. I told her you'd go out and give her some TLC." He hesitated, then decided that a little violation of Didi's personal space was justified. "One of the guys we think could be John Ramsey is her old boyfriend. She's upset."

Alan stood up. "I'll go talk to her. Thanks for letting me know."

He strode out of the office, leaving the door open behind him.

Kim barely waited for Alan to leave before she looked at Sean. "You're really going to add Helen to your list of suspects?"

"Yes."

She lifted an eyebrow. "I admit I don't want my dad to die, and you acknowledge that Helen might not be perfect. Are we growing up?"

He gave a half smile. "Maybe." He nodded at the computer. "What did you find?"

They spent the next hour with Didi and Alan going over the documents that he had uncovered. Sure enough, almost all of the working capital for the Loon's Nest had been siphoned off. In another couple of weeks, there would be no money even to pay the staff.

By the time they finished, Sean was stunned. The Collins family's heritage and legacy were two weeks away from total loss. Didi, who had been explaining some of the files, excused herself, leaving the three of them alone. Sean still couldn't believe it. All the transfers had occurred after Max's accident. Coincidence? Yeah, right. Sean tapped the computer screen. "How do we find out who did this? Can we trace it?"

"I did find the account the money was being sent to." Alan held up a piece of paper. "A local bank. Here's the account number."

Sean took the note. "Let's go visit the bank."

"You think the embezzler would be stupid enough to actually send it to his own account?"

"Criminals make mistakes. That's how we find them." He stood up, hesitated and then said. "Good work, Alan."

Alan nodded. "What do you want me to do?"

"Find a way to save the camp," said Kim. "Stop the flow of money and see what we can do about shifting funds around." She glanced at Sean. "I'm going to go with Sean, but keep track of what you do so you can teach me. I'm going to take care of this place until my dad is back in the office."

Whoa. What did she just say?

"See ya, Alan. We'll be in touch." She marched out the door before Sean could follow up.

But he was definitely going to be pursuing that little remark. Was she actually thinking of staying around? For how long? How did he feel about it?

She and Sean walked through the front reception, where Didi was chatting with Carl, the maintenance guy. She gave Sean a sly look and continued to chat up Carl.

Sean felt sick as he followed Kim out of the office. He was now regretting having shared so much information with Didi. She was going to get herself killed trying to play crimestopper extraordinaire, and he couldn't let that happen. As if he needed one more person to be responsible for.

After Frank's death, he'd decided he didn't want anyone's life in his hands ever again. And here he was with three of them. And it was his own damn fault that Didi was involved. What if he screwed up again? What if he didn't see the real threat until it was too late? He couldn't live with anyone else's blood on his hands. Not Kim's, not Max's and not even Alan's. People he cared about. Caring too much made cops sloppy. Made them overlook things because they were scared.

And, yes, he was scared as hell.

Chapter Fourteen

"While you were talking to Didi, I scanned a staff photo and e-mailed it to Cheryl." Kim was already regretting her decision to compromise Cheryl's anonymity. And praying that it would pay off.

Sean rubbed her shoulder briefly as he pulled onto the main road into town. "We'll make sure she's safe. It was the right thing to do. We've got to get an ID on John Ramsey if he's in town."

"I told her to be careful." She bit her lower lip. "I'm so worried, Sean. I feel like we're missing something. And August third is coming up. Even if it's someone associated with the camp who is using the Jimmy angle as a decoy—" Did he note her restraint in not using Helen's name as the suspect? "—then he still might choose the third as the day to act. In fact, he probably would. Just to reinforce it." She hugged herself.

"We'll find whoever it is in time." He looked at her. "We need to deal with Didi. I could tell she was on a mission with Carl. I heard her mention L.A. to him." He shook his head. "I knew I shouldn't have told her. If she gets herself hurt…"

Kim touched his arm. "She won't. She's smart."

"But she doesn't understand the risks. I can't explain all the details to her because it's an open case."

She smiled. "Always the cop, aren't you?"

He shrugged. "I guess."

"Are you going to keep being a cop? Is that the career you want?"

Sean shrugged again. "It's okay."

"Okay isn't enough for a career."

"It's not bad, though." He shot her a sideways glance. "What about you? You going back to the magazine?"

Her heart stuttered at his question. Why was he asking? Did he want her to stay? Ridiculous. "Of course I am. Why do you ask?"

"When you were talking to Alan, you sounded like you were going to stay awhile. I just wondered how long you could stay before your job in L.A. disappeared."

Kim frowned. "I didn't mean I was going to stay forever. Just until my dad could run the camp."

"And how long will that be?"

She studied her entwined fingers. "I don't know. It could be for a while, I guess."

"My point exactly. I just wanted to know what your plans were."

"Why?"

"Because."

Not exactly informative, but what was she looking for? A declaration that he loved her and wanted her to stay? Heck, no! Then she'd have to break his heart twice by leaving.

Because she was leaving...wasn't she? Just because this place was starting to feel like home again didn't mean it was her future, did it? Sure, it felt like home in a way L.A. never had, no matter how hard she'd tried to fool herself. But L.A. didn't have pain. L.A. was easy. This place wasn't easy. She looked at Sean. *He* wasn't easy. But this place and this man reverberated in her soul and made her feel alive for the first time since she'd left. Did she really want to go back to feeling empty, even if that was a life without pain? Of course she did. It was so much easier, wasn't it? God, she was so confused.

"We're here," Sean said.

THE TELLER GAVE a little scream when they walked up. "Sean and Kim together again! I don't believe it!"

Yeah, gotta love small towns. He used a scowl to try to persuade Marilee Johnston to tone it down, but she was either oblivious or ignoring him. Guess when everyone remembers you as a skinny teenager, it's hard to intimidate. Besides, Marilee had known them well. She and her boyfriend Zach Turner had been part of Sean and Kim's circle of friends.

Kim was much more polite. "Hello, Marilee. You look wonderful. It's so good to see you."

The women exchanged hugs and chatted politely for a few moments while Sean fingered the paper with the bank-account number. He noticed that Kim didn't correct Marilee about the two of them being together.

He didn't clarify the facts, either.

After a few moments, Marilee gave them the opportunity to get to the point. "So are you two here to open a bank account? Are you finally going to get married?"

Sean handed her the paper. "Actually, we need to know who this account is registered to."

Marilee giggled. "You know I can't give that out." Before he had time to whip out his badge and try to get around a court order, she giggled again. "But for you guys, I totally will. It'll just take a second." She started typing on her computer, still chatting. "So it's great you both are back. There's hardly anyone from our year still living in town. Zach and I... You remember Zach, right? Anyway, Zach and I are always looking for fun couples to go out with. You guys ever take a road trip to Portland? There are some really neat restaurants there. You guys have kids yet? We don't but soon. If we have kids at the same time, then we could trade babysitting, and that would really be great because babysitting is expensive, you know?"

Whoa. Did Kim feel as dazed as he felt? All this banter about normal life things felt so odd. Babysitting? Going to Portland to eat? Ordinary things like those hadn't had a place in his life for a long time. Damn if he didn't suddenly wish they did. Anything was better than watching Kim nod and wondering whether he would fail her. Wondering whether she would die in his arms as Frank had.

She glanced at him and arched an eyebrow at the expression on his face. He scowled and clenched his fists against the urge to touch her, to make sure she was real. Alive. Breathing.

He didn't.

"So, anyway, where do you guys live now? We bought Zach's parents' house. You know where that is, right? Come on by sometime. Oh, and I'm so sorry about your dad, but I'm sure he'll be fine." Marilee frowned and peered at the screen. "This is your stepmom's bank account. You didn't know that? Of course you didn't. Why would you know the bank-account number for your stepmom? It's her personal account, the one she had before she got married. Did you know that she and your dad each have their own accounts as well as their joint one? It's so they don't lose the assets they brought into the marriage. It's a smart thing to do if you're older, you know? But Zach and I don't need to do that because we're young. Did you guys do that? Because if you did, I'm totally sorry. I didn't mean to offend you or anything." She stopped to inhale. "So are you two on for dinner at our house Friday night? It'll be totally fun. I'll invite some of the gang to welcome you guys back in town. Seven o'clock work okay? It'll be so great to have you!"

Someone yelled from the back and she glanced over her shoulder. "Gotta go. Friday at seven. Be there." She bolted for the back room, leaving a buzzing in Sean's ears.

Or maybe it was the news she'd given him.

Helen's bank account?

Helen's?

His gut clenched and he felt as if he was going to be sick. "I gotta get out of here."

SEAN WAS SITTING in the cruiser, his forehead pressed against the steering wheel when Kim left the bank. As she approached, he gently thumped his forehead against the wheel.

Then he did it again.

And her heart broke for him.

She opened his door and leaned in. "Sean?"

"I suppose you're happy. The woman you hate is everything you claimed she was."

She considered his words. Why wasn't she happy? This was her chance to drop-kick Helen out of her life. But she felt empty. Betrayed. Awful.

Sean's emotions were in her soul. How it happened, when it happened, she had no idea. And since when did they trump hers? She'd spent years cultivating her hatred for Helen and now she wanted the woman to be innocent? What was up with that? "I think we need to go talk to her."

Sean groaned and let his head flop back against the seat. "I can't believe she'd do that."

"Maybe she didn't."

He closed his eyes. "Give it up, Kim. I know you're glad. Don't insult me by trying to pretend you're not."

He was right. She should be glad. Glad, glad, glad. Why wasn't she? "I don't know how I feel."

He opened his eyes and studied her. "I thought you wanted him to suffer."

"Yeah, well, I should be the only one who makes him suffer. It's my prerogative. Handing off the dirty work to his wife isn't my style."

"So it's a control thing. Not that you're changing your mind?"

"Of course." Wasn't it? She'd spent ten years nurturing

her resentment and hatred. It couldn't be going away just because she was hanging out with Sean and his idealistic views, could it? Or maybe it was simply that she wanted a dad again. A family. Roots.

Is that what she wanted? Is that why L.A. seemed so far away now?

"Get in. We're going to go see her."

At least he wasn't going to leave her behind. "To her house?" She climbed in beside him, contemplating whether to put her hand on his arm. She wanted to touch him, to comfort him. Would he take comfort from her anymore?

"To the hospital. It's visiting hours, so that's where she'll be."

If Kim hadn't already been belted in, she would have dived out of the car. But it was too late, as the tires squealed on the pavement. She took a deep breath and let it out slowly. She was going to see her dad.

It was time.

HER HEART WAS racing, pounding as Sean pushed open the door to her dad's hospital room.

Ten years.

An entire decade since she'd seen him.

She followed Sean inside.

Helen wasn't there.

Her dad looked old. Vulnerable. Fragile. "Dad?"

He didn't move. Didn't open his eyes. The machines kept beeping their rhythm, the tubes doing their thing.

Kim dropped into the chair next to the bed and wrapped her fingers around her dad's hand. "Don't do this to me. I'm not ready to lose my last parent."

When Sean set his hands on her shoulders, she couldn't stop the tears. "He's so old."

"He's not old. It's the accident." His fingers dug deep, kneading and reassuring.

"But he has gray hair." She traced her dad's hairline, her fingers trembling violently. "He was supposed to stay young, to wait for me."

Nice time to realize she felt that way when it might be too late. She gripped his hand tighter. "No. It's not too late."

Sean pulled another chair next to her and sat down, closing his hands over hers. "He was waiting for you. Tell him you forgive him."

She blinked back her tears. "I love him. I don't know if I forgive him, but I still love him." How could her dad have gotten like this? In her mind, he was still the powerful man who'd hauled firewood when his guests ran out. Unstoppable. Fierce. "He's withered away." Had she caused this? Was this her fault? Was Sean right that her walking out on her father had been his undoing? His daughter took off, his wife killed herself and his other child left as well, leaving him with nothing except an old camp.

How awful for him.

She'd never thought of it from his point of view. "Did Helen…? Do you think she helped him through it?"

"Through what?"

"Everything."

"Yes, I do. I think he would have died of grief if it hadn't been for her and her kids." He tightened his grip on her hands. "If she really betrayed him…"

Kim put her finger over his lips and nodded at her dad. "If he can hear us…"

Sean nodded and leaned forward. "We're all here for you, Max. Kim, Helen, me. And as soon as we finish this deal with Jimmy, Cheryl will be back, as well. We need you."

Stupid tears wouldn't be stopped this time, but she didn't care. "I love you, Dad. Wake up so we can fight about what happened ten years ago, okay?"

Sean gave her a look. "That's the best you can do?"

She glared at him. "You're a pain in the butt. I just told him I loved him. I think I've come pretty far, personally."

"You can't apologize for abandoning him?"

"No, I can't. Not until I hear his side of the story." She turned her dad. "Hear that, Dad? If you want an apology from me, you're going to have to wake up." She leaned back. "There. That ought to provide an incentive for him to come around, the potential for having me grovel for his forgiveness."

Sean shook his head and she realized he was laughing quietly.

She gave him her best scowl, not that easy given that there were still a few tears on her cheeks. "What's your problem?"

"You. You're a piece of work." He caught the back of her head in his hand and pulled her close, giving her a soft kiss.

Oh, *wow*. This felt right, so right. Did her dad know they were kissing? Would he be pleased?

Oh, who cared? She was doing this for herself. It was only about them.

Wait a sec.

Was Sean doing this for her dad because kissing her was as close as he could get to bringing him back to life?

She pulled back and frowned at him.

He tucked a strand of hair behind her ear. "I'm not even going to ask what that look is for. I don't want to know." He kissed her again before she could argue.

Oh, what the heck. Kiss now, talk later. Instant gratification wasn't a bad thing, was it? She let go of her dad's hand and gripped Sean's wrists as he cupped her face. It was a tender kiss, relatively pristine on the surface, but the roar of emotions thundering through their intermingled breaths was appropriate only for the most private of encounters.

She sighed and let him take over the kiss. What was she doing? Falling in love with the man who hadn't truly loved her? No wonder she didn't want to go back to L.A. Should loving him feel wrong? Because it didn't. Not at all.

The sound of a throat being cleared pulled them apart. Helen was standing in the doorway, and she looked inordinately pleased. "So you came to see him."

"Um, yeah." Kim felt Sean's muscles contract at the sight of the woman who might have betrayed her dad, so she laid her hand over his and squeezed.

Helen smiled and walked in. She carried a vase of fresh flowers and a *Boston Globe*. "I'm going to read him the latest Red Sox news. He loves them, you know."

"I know." Kim watched Helen dump some barely wilted flowers into the trash, then refill the vase with the fresh ones. She knew those flowers. They were the same kind her father had planted outside the office at the camp. Helen had brought the camp to her dad.

Were these the actions of a woman who was trying to ruin the Loon's Nest or steal from her husband?

Helen pulled up a chair on the opposite side of the bed and took Max's hand in hers. "You two have gotten back together, I see. Max will be so glad." She smiled at Sean. "He has always loved you like a son."

Sean blinked a couple of times. "Until I drove his daughter away."

Where did that come from? Since when did he take responsibility for Kim leaving him? It had been her fault. Was he sharing the blame now? And if he was, what did that mean for today? For their present and their future?

Helen shook her head. "No, Sean. He never blamed you for that. It didn't matter whether you married Kim or not. You were always his son, regardless."

Sean's Adam's apple dipped as he swallowed, but he said nothing.

"Max doesn't always tell people that he cares." Helen stroked his hand. "I've been working on him, but old dogs don't like to change their ways." She looked at Kim. "He's always loved you, too, Kim. You being here… Well, I can't even tell you how much I appreciate it. He'll wake up for you."

This was the woman who wanted to destroy Max? The woman Kim had spent so many years hating? She looked at Sean and knew he was thinking the same thing. How could they accuse her of embezzling from the company her husband loved? Yet, the evidence was there.

"Helen," she said, "we need your help."

Sean raised an eyebrow at Kim, and she patted his hand. Helen nodded. "Of course. What do you need?"

"We discovered that the reason the camp is in trouble is because someone has been embezzling funds. There's only enough money to pay the operating expenses for the next two weeks."

Helen's face drained of all color. "Are you serious?"

"Yes."

Her grip tightened on Max's hand. "But who would do this?"

"You have to help us," Kim repeated. She didn't want Helen to take her next sentence the wrong way. "We traced it and the money is being funneled into your personal bank account to frame you."

Sean made a noise of protest, but she ignored him.

"Who would know your account number? Who would want to set you up for this?"

Helen looked shocked. "You would."

Oh, *well*. Hadn't been expecting that.

"You'd want to send me to jail or, at the very least, prove to your father that he should leave me." Helen's face regained some of its color and she began to look angry.

Better stop that slide. "Helen, I didn't do it. Yeah, okay, so there was a time when I would have been happy to see you, um, discredited." She ignored the condemning look on Helen's face. "But I'd never do something like this. And even if I would, I've changed my mind."

"You have?" Helen looked more than a little skeptical.

"You have?" Sean sounded startled.

"I have." Kim took her dad's hand in hers again. "If you make him happy, then he should have you."

"Since when do you want him to be happy? I thought you wanted him to suffer."

She sounded like a nice person, didn't she? "I haven't forgiven him, but I'm willing to hear his side of the story." She stroked his hand. "I guess seeing him here like this… Well, I'm not ready to lose the only parent I have left, you know? And if he needs you, then I guess that's okay with me."

Sean slipped an arm around her shoulder and squeezed. At least Sean didn't hate her.

She waited for Helen to answer, but the woman said nothing. Silence fell over the small room until Kim was just about ready to suggest to Sean that they leave.

Finally, Helen said, "If it's not you, then I don't know who it is. Do you?"

Sean hesitated, then filled Helen in on John Ramsey and the few suspects at the camp they had who matched his profile.

When he finished, Helen's forehead was wrinkled in thought. "I don't like that Tom Payton. He never seems to be working, and I don't think he knows much about boats. Eddie can't stand working with him."

Kim recalled Eddie's complaints that Tom didn't know a life jacket from an engine. "Why would they hire someone for the waterfront who wasn't experienced with boats?"

"He claimed he was. They didn't realize he'd lied until he'd been there a few weeks already. Max couldn't get another replacement at this late date or he would have fired him this summer." Helen rubbed Max's forehead. "Tom was pretty pissed when Max told him he wouldn't be invited back next year."

Kim frowned and looked at Sean. Had Tom been mad enough to set up the accident?

THEY STOPPED BY Will's house on the way to the station.

No car in the driveway.

Several days' worth of newspapers piled up on the front step.

Kim rapped on the door while Sean tried to peer through the windows. "Furniture is still here. There's a pizza box on the coffee table."

"Well, he's not answering the door." Kim set her hands on her hips and couldn't ignore her relief. It was a little unnerving to be marching up to the house of the man who could be John Ramsey. Yeah, sure, Sean was armed and had his gun ready, but still. It was wigging her out.

"I'll call and leave him a message to come to the station. Probably won't work, but it's easier than going through the courts for a warrant."

They walked back to the car and, as Kim was climbing in, she glanced back at the house. Then she frowned. "Sean? Was that blind in the second-floor corner room open before?"

Sean peered up at the house. "I don't remember."

"I could have sworn it was open." They stared at the window for a long moment, but nothing moved. "I guess not."

Sean pulled out his cell phone. "I'll call him right now."

They waited while the phone rang.

No sign of movement from inside.

"Hello, this is Officer Templeton from the Ridgeport Police Department. We need Will Ambrose to come down to the station for an interview. Please call the department and arrange a time." He left the number, then added, "Or you can open your front door and do the interview right now. I'm outside, and I saw you through the window."

Kim shot a glance at Sean. "You did?"

He pointed at the window in the room on the far left of the second floor. She looked up just in time to see a shadow move away from the window. A chill went over her. "He's watching us."

"Yep."

"Are you going to go in after him?"

"I don't have a warrant." Sean shoved his phone in his pocket and leaned across the roof of the car, watching the house. Waiting.

Waiting for the man who might want to avenge Jimmy's death. Was he watching her right now? Sharpening his knife as he studied her?

"Get in the car, Kim."

"Why?"

"Because he's watching you again. I don't like it."

Well, hell. Neither did she. After she got in the car, she hunched down. Stupid, yeah, because he already knew she was there, but it made her feel better.

Sean dug out his phone again and hit Redial. "You touch her and you die."

Then he hung up, climbed in the car and started the engine.

"Um, Sean?"

"Yeah?"

"Was that necessary?"

His gaze flicked to her. "I hope not."

Reassured, she wasn't. She was scared. Not only of dying, as she'd been for the past eighteen months. Now she was scared of dying before she had a chance to talk to her dad. Before she had the opportunity to figure out what was going on with her and Sean. For the first time in a decade, she was more afraid of what she'd lose if she died than she was of actually dying.

She reached across the front seat, pulled Sean's right

hand off the steering wheel and held on. He glanced at her in surprise but didn't say anything. Instead, he squeezed her fingers ever so slightly and gave her a small smile.

Chapter Fifteen

Sean had another officer pick up Tom and bring him to the station. It was time to put some serious pressure on the kid. Sean let Tom sit in the interrogation room for two hours before heading in there. By then it was dark and the youth was getting restless. And nervous.

Sean left Kim in the main office while he went in to talk to Tom. Sean sauntered in, threw one leg across the chair and leaned on the back of it. "Tom."

"Why am I here? Why are you keeping me here? Don't I have rights? Shouldn't I be allowed to leave? I didn't do anything. I swear, I didn't! Just tell me what you want and I'll explain and then let me go home!" He wiped his forehead, but the sheen of sweat remained.

As Sean had expected, Tom was going to be an easy one. "You ever been to California?"

Tom blinked, as if he hadn't expected the question. "What?"

"California. You ever been there?"

"No. Why? Should I?"

"Where were you born?"

"Madison, Wisconsin." Tom shifted. "Listen, I didn't do anything, I swear."

"What's the name on your birth certificate?"

He frowned. "Thomas Winfield Payton. But you must know that. Don't you have my birth certificate or something?"

"Why'd you hurt Max?"

Tom's face turned a blotchy red. "I didn't hurt him! I swear it! I didn't even touch the boat that day. Yeah, I know Eddie said I did and I was supposed to, but I wasn't even there."

"Where were you?" Sean kept his voice casual and friendly. Plenty of time to become intimidating if he needed to.

Tom clamped his lips shut. "I'll get fired."

"Haven't you already been fired?"

He cursed. "So what? I didn't need the job anyway. Who cares? Is that why you think I hurt him? Because he fired me? Give me a break. Would you hurt someone over a job working for some old guy on a bunch of ancient boats? No way."

Dumb kid. Didn't even appreciate the camp. "You're our number one suspect in Max's accident. Witnesses report that you became angry when Max told you not to return next summer. You work at the boathouse and were on duty the night Max got in the accident, yet you say you saw nothing. You have motive and opportunity. If Max dies, you're up for first-degree murder."

Tom's face did a slow morph into shock as he absorbed Sean's words. "M-m-murder?"

"Murder one. You feel like talking?" Sean saw the change come over Tom's face and knew the kid was going to spill. Spill what? That was the question. "I would have been really ticked if Max cut me off. Mad enough to go after him. Not to kill him, but accidents happen, you know?"

"No, I didn't!" Tom leaned forward. "This is the deal. I wasn't at the job that day because I took off with one of the guests."

"A guest? Who?"

"A girl. Underage."

"Name?"

He shook his head. "No way. I'm not pulling her into this. But I would have lost my job immediately if Max or Eddie found out. First, I'm not allowed to date the guests, and second, she was seventeen. I wasn't at work that night because we took a canoe out to one of the islands and spent the night."

"That's statutory rape."

"*If* I slept with her. I'm not saying I did." The defensiveness was back in Tom's voice. "Don't you see? I didn't kill Max. I wasn't even there. Eddie would've fired me himself if he knew I took off, but he's so out of it, he never notices if I'm not there."

"He trusts you. A novel concept for you, I'm sure."

"Hey, why should I bust my butt if I'm not coming back next summer?"

"Why did you get mad at Max if you don't care about the job?"

"Because *she* was right there and heard the whole thing! I had to do something to save my rep! Took me two days to convince her that I wasn't a loser. I don't need Max to screw up my social life, you know?"

Sean leaned back in his chair and studied Tom while he continued to spew about his underage girlfriend and male pride. That's what all that had been about? Sean shook his head. "I need the name of the girl who's providing your alibi for that night. And I want a copy of your birth certificate." He stood up and Tom didn't protest.

Much as Sean wanted this one to be easy, his gut bought Tom's story. He wasn't their guy.

But that still meant that John Ramsey was at large and someone was embezzling from the camp. If they didn't find out who it was, eventually the blame might land on Helen.

Crud.

* * *

SEAN WALKED INTO the main area of the station, feeling more than a little frustrated. Why the hell wouldn't the folks in L.A. come up with some info on John Ramsey? It couldn't be that hard, could it? He still hadn't gotten the list of who had come to visit Jimmy when he was in prison.

Then he stopped. Kim wasn't in sight.

He checked the bathroom.

No Kim.

His gut started to tighten and he grabbed a rookie doing paperwork. "Where's Kim Collins?"

"She left a few minutes ago."

"Left?" *Left?* "Where'd she go?"

"I don't know. I think she left a note on your desk, though."

He nearly threw the man aside and bolted for his desk. He recognized her writing on the folded sheet of paper with his name on it.

> I had to go. Alan called and said I'd better get over to my house. A break-in or something. Officer McKeen is going with me. Come over when you're done. Hope it went well with Tom.

Damn.

OH, MY GOD. Her house. Windows were smashed. Glass littered the ground. Flowers were ripped up. The front door was almost shattered. The bulb on the lamppost had been destroyed. Total destruction. The crime oozed anger. Uncontrollable, violent fury.

Kim tumbled out of Officer McKeen's cruiser the second he stopped it, his headlights illuminating the devastation. Alan was standing in the middle of the driveway, his hands on his hips, his face brutally angry.

"Alan? Are you okay?"

"Fine. I found it like this." His hands flexed and his face was red, a muscle in his jaw twitching. "Go inside. See what's there."

Um, not so high on that idea. "How do we know the person is gone?"

"I've been in there. There's no one here." He crashed his fist against the hood of the cruiser, swearing as she'd never heard him swear. "Come on." He grabbed her arm, his fingers digging in as he dragged her into the house. He shoved her into the living room and pointed to the wall. "Look."

Words were scrawled on the wall in what looked like black magic marker. *Jimmy's blood is on your hands. You die. Cheryl dies. Everyone dies. No one kills my brother.*

There was a knife stabbed into the wall at the end of the sentence, right through the center of a photo of Kim, Cheryl and her dad.

"John Ramsey didn't do that," Alan said, disgust dripping from his voice. "When I find the scum who's doing this, I'm going to—"

"How do you know he didn't do it?"

Kim spun around to find Sean standing behind her. "Sean!" Thank God he was there! Somehow, she didn't have faith in Alan's ability to protect her from a psycho. She believed in Sean, though. Totally and completely.

His eyes were bubbling with anger as he touched her arm gently. "You okay?"

Mentally or physically? Because they were completely different answers. "I guess."

He nodded, then turned to Alan, who was still muttering about his plans to annihilate the person impersonating John Ramsey.

"As I said, Alan, how do you know it's not John Ramsey?"

"Because he wouldn't be stupid enough to claim ownership! That's like asking the police to come arrest him after he kills his victims. Come on, Sean! Don't you see? Someone is trying to pin it on John so he can get away." Alan fisted his hands.

Officer McKeen appeared in the doorway. "I called for backup." He whistled. "This place is a mess."

She hadn't even noticed the rest of the house, her eyes drawn to the message of death. But pillows were slashed, pictures were thrown to the floor, tabletops were swept clean. Total violation of her world.

Sean directed his next question to Alan. "How long ago did you get here?"

"About ten minutes before I called Kim." Alan ran his hands through his hair and tried to pull himself together. "What if Kim had been here? What if she'd walked in when this psycho was tearing the place apart?"

Um, nice thought. Not.

"That's why she's not staying here. And I don't think you should either." Sean settled his arm around Kim's shoulder. "Get a hotel."

Alan nodded and continued to pace. "Who's doing this?"

Sean looked as angry as Alan. "I don't know."

"Well, find out," Alan shouted, "before Kim gets killed!"

Sean's arm tightened around her. "She will not die." His voice was so icy cold that she actually shivered and Alan stopped to stare at Sean.

Then Alan nodded. "Good."

Her cell phone rang then and both men stared at her.

"Don't look at me like that. You're freaking me out." She fished the phone out of her pocket and checked the number. Local, but not one she recognized. "Hello?"

"Kim Collins?" It was a man's voice.

"Yes."

"It's Will Ambrose."

Whoa. She gestured to Sean, who set his ear next to hers so he could listen.

"What do you want, Will?"

"Jimmy Ramsey. That's who tried to kill you and your sister, right?"

She tensed. "How do you know that?"

"I know who tried to murder Max. I know who's after you now."

She almost dropped the phone and Sean caught it and settled it between them again. He nodded at her to continue. Oh, sure. No problem. She took a deep breath. "Who?"

"Not over the phone. I have to show you something."

Oh, sure. Like that couldn't be a trap. "When?"

"Once I show you this, I'm taking off. Forever."

"Where are you?"

"Tomorrow morning. Nine o'clock. My house. I won't be there until then, so don't bother to come early. You set me up and I won't show."

Sean spoke then. "I'm coming with her." Nice, Sean. Way to scare off Will. She elbowed him to shut up and he gave her a look that she recognized all too well. He would not be listening to her on this one. Stubborn male.

"Who's this?" Will asked.

"Sean Templeton."

The phone was silent.

"Fine. Just the two of you. I see anyone else, and I leave." He paused. "Tell the Portland police to check out Pete Gibbs's boat. It's moored out in the harbor."

"They already did. He's not there," Sean said.

"Tell them to check the anchor at the bottom of the mooring."

Then he hung up.

BY THE TIME they made it back to Sean's house, it was almost two in the morning and Kim was exhausted. After the cops had done their investigation of the house, she'd stayed for a while with Sean and Alan to try to cover up most of the windows to keep bats and other nasties out. They hadn't even begun to clean up the destruction, which spread through the entire house.

Her bedroom had been trashed.

The hatred and desperation had been virulent.

Once they got to his house, Sean locked the door behind them and she went straight into the bathroom. Not that a shower would erase the carnage of her home, but she had to do something. She stripped down and climbed under the hot stream, making it hotter and hotter.

But even with her skin burning, she couldn't get the devastation of her house out of her mind. The words on the wall. The knife through her family photo. She leaned her head against the tile and wanted to cry. Why was this happening? How could she stop it? They didn't even know who was after her. She almost wished Jimmy was still alive. At least then she'd know who to watch for.

A light tap sounded on the door. "Kim? Can I come in?"

She didn't even lift her head but opened her eyes to check the coverage of the navy-blue shower curtain. "Yeah."

The door clicked open, then shut, and she knew Sean was in the bathroom with only a thin sheet of plastic between them. If she weren't so stressed, terrified and exhausted, she might be tempted to throw the shower curtain back and see how he would respond.

"The Portland police checked Pete Gibbs's boat."

She held her breath.

"He was dead. Shot through the head. Chained to the mooring about thirty feet down."

"Oh, God." A gun? What protection did she have against a gun?

"He'd been dead for a while."

"You think…it has to do with this whole thing?" Her

legs began to tremble and she leaned more weight on the wall in an attempt to remain vertical.

"The initial consensus is yes. The only missing file was the one on your dad. They're working on it, though. Now that it's a homicide, it'll get top priority."

Dead. Pete Gibbs was the first one who'd actually died. This wasn't only about threatening her and scaring them and stealing some money from the camp. This was now about death. Someone who wasn't afraid to kill.

"Kim? You okay?"

She shut off the water and Sean stuck his hand through the shower curtain with a towel. "Thanks."

She wrapped it around herself and stepped out. He was leaning against the sink, his arms folded, his gun still in its shoulder holster. He was frowning and looked serious. Too serious. He didn't even seem to notice that she was naked except for the towel. "What I can't figure out is the gun," he said. "A knife is personal. The hit on your dad was sloppy. But a gun?" He shook his head. "Three different methods. It doesn't make sense."

"How can I be safe against a gun? I mean, you don't even have to get close to use it." Her hair was dripping over her shoulders, the water sliding down her skin like creepy-crawlies. She tried to brush it off, but it kept dripping.

Sean grabbed another towel, turned her around and started drying her hair. "That's why I panicked when I heard you'd left the police station tonight. What if he'd been in the woods waiting for you to show up? He could have dropped you before you even knew he was there." He scrubbed her hair more vigorously. "Don't do that again, okay?"

"I promise to be safe for at least a day."

He spun her around and grabbed her shoulders. "Don't joke about it! Your dad is in a coma and a P.I. who knows how to take care of himself is dead. You think you won't be next?"

"Dammit, Sean. I know the danger!" She tried to shove him away. "I'm trying to keep from totally freaking out about it. I've been scared for a year and a half and I either find a way to deal with that fact or go crazy with fear and terror. I'm trying to cope, so back off."

He stared at her, then dropped his hands. "I'm sorry."

She sighed. "No, I'm sorry, too."

They stood in silence for a while. Then Kim said, "I'm worried about my dad. What if someone decides to finish him off?" She got cold suddenly and wished she had clothes on.

He studied her. "I have an officer on his room. He's okay."

"Are you sure?"

"You sound like you really care about him." He smiled then, a half smile. "Did you mean what you said today in the hospital room?"

"Mean what?"

"When you said you loved him?"

She shrugged. "I don't know." She didn't have the energy for this discussion right now.

But Sean caught her arm as she tried to slide by. "I've been thinking about that letter from your mom."

She stopped. "And?"

"And I can see why you left."

Kim turned back, searching his face. "Truly?"

He nodded. "If your mom had been that determined to save me, I would have believed her, too."

"Oh." Suddenly, her shoulders felt so light, so incredibly weightless. "So you...forgive me?"

"Yeah, I guess I do."

"Thanks." She blinked. Her chest felt tight, her throat achy. To hear that he finally forgave her... She wanted to hug him. Hug herself. Dance. "I'm so glad." Could her voice sound any more fervent? She doubted it. He had to realize how much his forgiveness meant to her.

He was watching her intently. "And I think if we'd gotten married, it wouldn't have worked."

She nodded. "I agree. I mean, I think we both needed to get away. Figure out life away from parents."

He touched her face. "It's just you and me today."

"No, it's not…"

He set his finger on her lips. "I want to kiss you right now and it's not because of your dad or because I've kissed you a thousand times before. It's because you're an amazing woman who nearly died to save her sister, who loves her dad despite some very good reasons she has not to. A woman who is willing to admit she might be wrong about Helen, even as she gets up every day ready to fight off a man who wants her dead." He kissed her forehead. "You are nothing like the girl I almost married, and yet I want you in a way I've never wanted you before. Ever."

Oh, wow. Package that and sell it and he'd make millions. "How is a girl supposed to resist that?"

"I don't want a girl. I want a woman, and the only woman I want is you."

As he bent down to kiss her, she recalled that all she was wearing was a towel.

Wasn't that convenient?

Chapter Sixteen

Kim let her arms slide around Sean's neck, let her body sink against his, and let his kiss melt her.

This man wanted her, and she needed him. More than anything. His lips tasted so good, minty and warm, his body firm and cut under her fingers. He wasn't a boy. He wasn't a kid. He wasn't innocent. He wasn't bumbling.

He was heat and passion and talent, and he was all she wanted. It wasn't sex, though. It was about his soul and everything that came with it. She needed all of him, and she needed him now.

His lips still caressing hers, he swept her up in his arms, opened the door and carried her to the bed. She was definitely digging the big brawny he-man thing. "When you were eighteen, you would have dropped me."

He set her on the bed. "I'm totally offended. Just because I was skinny didn't mean I wasn't strong." He propped himself on his hands and gave her a long kiss. "The difference is that when you were eighteen, you wouldn't have let me carry you."

Was that right? Even though she was so much stronger and independent now, had she also become softer in some ways? "I was just looking out for your health. Didn't want you to get hurt." She tugged at his holster and he quickly stripped it off.

Along with his shirt, his shoes and his socks.

"Let me." She wanted this to last. Wanted to enjoy every moment with this man she loved. She'd loved him ten years ago and she still loved him. The love was different, and now it was so much better. Now her love was rough and tainted and imperfect, which is what made it so powerful and strong and intense. Which is what made her so sure she was right.

She undid the top button of his jeans, kissing a line down his collarbone, over his chest and down his taut stomach. Then she unzipped his fly and he sucked in his breath. She held up her hands. "They're shaking."

He kissed the tip of each finger, then pressed his lips to her palm. "Why?"

"I don't know." Her voice was barely more than a whisper.

He trailed his lips over her wrist, along her forearm, up her biceps and across her collarbone and neck, then caught her lips in his. By the time he got there, she was nearly desperate for his touch. For his everything. She wrapped her arms around his neck and pulled him close, closer, as close as she could, kissing him as if she'd never be able to kiss him again.

And maybe she wouldn't. Who knew what would happen tomorrow? Or when this nightmare was over and she went back to L.A.?

Then she felt his hand on her knee and she tensed. "Maybe we should turn out the lights."

"Nope." He pulled back, then kissed her kneecap, his hands pressed against the sides of her thigh. "I want to see you."

She tried to tug the towel over her scarred thigh. "Cut it out, Sean. I don't want you to see it."

"Too bad." He caught her wrists easily in one hand, then pushed the towel aside, exposing her mangled thigh.

Too late.

She groaned and flopped back on the bed, covering her face with her arms. "Not like it was ten years ago, huh?" It was all she could do to keep her voice from breaking. Why had he insisted on light? She could sense that he was staring at her leg, absorbing its grotesque twists, wondering how to get out of having to make love to her now that he could see what she'd become.

He didn't answer and she tried to shield herself from caring.

Except she did care. She cared so much.

She felt his hand slide along her leg toward the scar and she tensed, waiting for rejection.

Then he laid his hand over her thigh, over the scar. Touching it. And he didn't pull away.

She moved her arms and looked at him. He was watching her face, and as soon as she looked at him, he smiled. "You're so much sexier than you were ten years ago."

"Shut up." But she couldn't stop the feeling of warmth from spreading over her.

"Fine." He bent down then and kissed the scar. She could just barely feel it, but watching him was all the sensation she needed.

"You don't care?"

He rolled his eyes and held up his arm to expose the scar on his triceps. "Does this make you not want me?"

"No." She giggled. "I think it's hot."

"Or this?" He pointed to the scar on his chest.

"Totally sexy." And it was. He was all man, and she loved him and every scar on his body.

"Then why would it be any different for me?" He slid his hand along her thigh as he pulled himself level with her face. "You're brave and strong and bear that scar as proof that you're a woman who will defend those she loves until the day she dies. I find that scar so erotic I can barely stand it." He kissed her hard and deep until she believed him.

He saw the scar as sexy, and he meant it.

If she'd had any doubts before, they were gone now. She loved him, thoroughly and completely, and there was no going back. She gripped his shoulders and held on as he stripped away her towel and shed the rest of his clothes.

Nothing between them but skin. He was gorgeous and perfect and she felt as if her heart was going to explode. Never had it been this way between them. Not with all this emotion and intensity and power singeing the air between them.

"I feel like we've never done this before." She traced her fingers over his chest. With its muscles and contours and the scar on the right side, it was a chest she didn't recognize. A man she'd just met. And that was how it should be. This was about now. The present. Today.

"I know." He kissed her, but this time his kiss was so gentle, almost reverent. "It's better than before, huh?"

She giggled as his hands slid up her thighs, drifting to the inside and sending tremors down her legs. "I don't know. I need more information to decide."

He grinned. "My pleasure."

By the time he finished providing sufficient data, it wasn't only her hands that were shaking. It was her entire body. She cupped his face with her hands as he moved over her, sliding his knee between her legs. "I've never stopped loving you, Sean Templeton."

He shook his head. "No, I don't want you to love me like you did when we were eighteen. It's not about the past anymore."

"I didn't mean it like that. I…" How was she supposed to say it? She wasn't even sure. "It's different now."

He kissed her deeply as he moved his body, slipping inside her. "It's different for me, too."

"Better?" He felt so good. Right. As if she'd been waiting a lifetime for this moment.

"No comparison."

No comparison. She dug her fingers into his shoulders and pulled him deeper, her body electric with energy and need. *I love you, Sean.* The words didn't make it to her lips, but they coursed through her body.

He shuddered against her and they clung to each other as the waves rocked their bodies.

Whatever was between them, she never wanted to lose it again.

KIM AWOKE TO the sensation of warmth and utter contentment. Sean was draped over her, nibbling at her ear and whispering her name. She smiled and felt herself relax. He hadn't withdrawn and put up walls after last night. He was still there beside her, fully embracing the change in their relationship.

They might have made love ten years ago, but this felt like the first time, as though they'd crossed a line they'd never ventured past before. And it felt right. So unassailably perfect.

She rolled over and faced him, then blinked with surprise. "You're dressed." As in blue jeans, shoes and a T-shirt. His hair was barely damp, so he'd been out of the shower for a while.

"Some of us have to keep working." He kissed her again, his fingers twisting in her hair. "I called the guys in L.A. and convinced them to send us the list of people who visited Jimmy in prison and the info they have on John Ramsey. Dead guys chained to moorings tend to get people's attention. They promised that I'd have a fax or an e-mail by two o'clock today."

So much for whispering sweet nothings or declaring his undying love.

He kissed her again. "It's almost eight-thirty. We have to leave in a little bit to go over to Will's house. If you want breakfast or a shower, you'll have to hustle."

She struggled to a sitting position. "That's it? It's all business this morning?"

He frowned. "What do you mean?"

"After last night, you can't just pretend nothing has changed and wake me up by talking about Jimmy." So much for her perception that he'd been kissing her because he was ready to be all snuggly and devoted.

He got a wary look on his face. "What do you want from me?"

"I don't know." She sighed and pushed her snarled hair out of her face. "I just thought *something*." If he couldn't figure out that he loved her, she certainly wasn't going to spell it out for him.

"Well, I don't know, either. Last night was great, but—"

She pulled the blankets around her, suddenly very aware that she was still completely naked and he was fully dressed. "But what?"

He shrugged. "I don't know."

"I thought you forgave me for leaving."

"I do. I did."

"Then what?"

"You're leaving again."

She stared at him.

"Aren't you?" He peered more closely at her.

"I guess. Yes. I have a career." But somehow, it didn't seem all that important right now. All that mattered was Sean. If he said he loved her, if he asked her to stay…this time the answer might be different than it had been ten years ago.

He nodded. "I'm not moving to Los Angeles. For the first time in years, I feel like I've come home. With your dad and his family, I belong again. I have a job that's pretty decent." He shrugged. "I'm tired of being alone."

"So once again, you choose my dad over me." She felt like screaming. Why couldn't he want her more than her family?

He didn't even ask if she wanted to stay. Just assumed she wouldn't and had already made his choice. Her dad wins again.

"It's not that—"

"Then what is it?"

He sighed. "There will always be a place for me in this town. I want that in my life."

"And you think you don't have a place with me?"

He cocked his head. "Let's be realistic. You have your high-society life in Los Angeles. I'm a small-town cop. What am I going to do out there? I'm not interested in putting on tuxes and going to meet some movie star at a party. It's not my style. I want to stay here, run the camp someday. It's where I belong."

So that was it then. "What if I stayed here?" Not that she was considering it anymore, but she needed to know.

He lifted an eyebrow. "Are you thinking about it?"

"It's a hypothetical question. If I was willing to stay here and run the camp with you, would there be a future for us?"

His face softened and he touched her cheek. "I'd be interested in trying again, yeah."

She pulled back. It wasn't enough, and she shouldn't have asked. As if she needed to torture herself that way. "So that's the way it is, then. You want me as long as I bring along my family and the camp. If the only way you can have me is to go to L.A. and give up my family, you won't do it." She lifted her chin and willed her voice to be steady. "You don't want me for me. Same as before." She wanted to march into the bathroom and close the door in his face, but she was naked. Stalking nude didn't seem to have quite the same dignity, and since he was still lying on top of the covers, it was parade in the buff or stay put.

He frowned. "I'm not interested in getting hurt again."

"No, you're not interested in taking a risk. You refuse to love me for me." She tried to shove him off the bed so she could get the covers, but it was like ramming an elephant on steroids. "Well, forget it, Sean. I didn't love you back then, not really and truly. How could I? I was eighteen. But now, I think I could. But only if you loved me for me. And since you don't, there's no point in having this discussion." Oh, forget it. A door slam was definitely needed right now.

She kicked off the covers, swung her feet to the floor and stood up. Naked or not, she was making a statement. "You may be an ex-war hero and good with a gun, Sean Templeton, but you are nothing more than a total wuss who's too wimpy to take a chance on love." She flung her hair over her shoulder with a very admirable head flip, marched across the room and slammed the bathroom door shut behind her.

And then she turned on the shower to hide the sound of her crying.

BY THE TIME they pulled up to Will Ambrose's house, Sean was in a foul mood. Kim had shrugged off every attempt he'd made at physical contact and had erected a cold barrier between them.

Just because he didn't want to move to California? Why was he to blame, when she was just as unwilling to move here? Last night was great and it had reawakened hope in him, hope he hadn't felt in years. Hope that he could have it all. Kim, her father, the camp, a home that was truly a home.

But no. She wanted him to give it all up to follow her to California and live some glam life that wasn't his style. Or, at the very least, she wanted him to reject her dad and the camp. Because he wouldn't, he was the bad guy?

And she wouldn't even talk about it. Every time he tried to bring it up, she changed the subject to Will or Helen or the message of death on the wall of her house.

Argh! Women!

"You think he's here?" Kim peered through the window

at Will's house. "What do you think he's going to tell us? You think he's going to admit that he's John Ramsey?"

"What if I told you I loved you? What then?" Not that he was sure he did, but he was pretty confident that, with time to rebuild their relationship, he could love her, really love her. How could he not? She was strong, intelligent and courageous. What man wouldn't love her?

"Did you bring your gun? Because Pete Gibbs was killed with a gun." She pursed her lips and stared at the house. "Do you see anyone in the windows? What if he's planning to shoot me without even showing his face?"

"Fine. Be like that." He threw the gearshift into Park, grabbed his gun and kicked open his car door. "Stay in the car."

"So he can sneak out the back door and get me while you walk in the front door? Sorry, not gonna happen." She climbed out of the car and stood on the sidewalk.

That's when he realized how wide her eyes were, how white her skin was. Crud. She was terrified, and he was barely paying attention to the risky situation they were in. What was he thinking?

He wasn't thinking. That was the problem. Fear gripped his spine at the thought of endangering her because he screwed up. He cursed and ordered himself to focus. *Forget Kim. Stop thinking about love. Screw California.*

He turned to face the house, his eyes narrowing as he examined every window, each bush and tree, the front door. He tensed. "The front door is ajar."

"That's bad?"

"I don't know." He readied his gun and eased toward the door, aware of every movement, sound and odor. "Stay right behind me. If I swing around, duck."

"So you don't shoot me. Nice."

She didn't sound afraid anymore. Good.

They reached the front door and he rapped the door with his knuckles.

No one answered.

He knocked again and the door swung open slightly from the force of his touch.

"Will Ambrose," he shouted. "It's Officer Templeton. Are you there?"

Silence.

Kim shifted closer to him and he could smell the scent of her shampoo.

Cut it out. Don't think about that!

Sean yelled again, tapping the door open with his toe.

The front hall loomed before them. Empty and silent.

"Something's wrong," Kim whispered. "I can feel it."

"Me, too." He eased into the front hall, taking a quick glance in the family room and dining room. Nothing looked out of place.

The stairs stretched up above them, but he ignored them, sliding past the railing toward the back of the house.

"Wish I had a gun," Kim muttered.

"You'd probably shoot me."

"That's why I want one."

He shot a glance at her, but she was looking behind them so he couldn't see her face to determine if she was joking.

The door to the kitchen was on swinging hinges, so he hit it with his hip and leaned through with his gun. He cursed. There was enough blood on the floor and cabinets to convince him that Will would never be getting up from the kitchen floor again.

Kim leaned in behind him, then squawked in surprise. "He was shot in the head?"

"Looks that way." He scanned the room and listened but heard no sounds. "Be careful in case the shooter isn't gone."

She let out another noise and moved closer to him while he called it in to dispatch. Made him realize that this was no place for Kim. If the killer was still here, Sean had just brought a civilian into serious danger. "We need to get out."

"Don't you need to check the house?"

"No." He grabbed her arm with his left hand and moved back down the hall, watching the upstairs landing especially carefully. "Keep an eye out. And be quiet." No sense in giving away their position.

For once in her life, Kim didn't protest and they made their way back out to his car without being shot at. He shoved Kim into the passenger seat and shut the door, then watched the house until backup arrived. By then, he was pretty sure that no one was still at the house, but it wasn't until his team did a thorough search of the area that they decided it was safe.

Safe for them. Not for Will Ambrose.

Sean explored the house but found nothing that could have been what Will was going to "show" them. Whatever Will knew had died with him.

"Guess that leaves Carl," Kim said, when he returned to his cruiser and delivered the news. "Tom exonerated himself. Will is dead. Carl's the only one left who could be John Ramsey."

He nodded. "I already called him and asked him to come down to the station for an interview. At this point, we have nothing on him other than that he's the right age and works at the camp. Not enough for anything." He sighed. "We called in the regional crime-scene investigators to work this scene, so with any luck, Carl left behind some evidence that will get him, but it'll take a while to get results back."

"So that's it? There's nothing you can do, even though Will is lying there dead?"

He scowled at her. "We'll do everything we can, but I can't snap my fingers and solve the crime. And until we do solve it, you're in serious danger."

She rolled her eyes. "Give me a break. I've been in serious danger this whole time. I can't be freaking out every second or I'd lose my mind."

"No, this is different." He ran his hand through his hair. "The initial contacts were planned to scare you. With the destruction of the house and the murder of Will, things are escalating. Maybe now that Jimmy is dead, John is losing control. Grief has sent him over the edge. He's becoming desperate, irrational and unpredictable. Maybe he doesn't worry about getting caught anymore. What does he have to live for now that Jimmy's dead?" He leveled a serious stare at her. "No, Kim, it's different now, and you're in danger."

"Then so is my dad. And Helen if she's innocent."

He thought of something then. "Didi was questioning Carl the other day after I filled her in. If Carl realizes that Didi knows something…"

Kim was dialing the office number for the Loon's Nest before he'd finished talking. "Is Didi there?" She frowned. "Do you have her home number? This is Kim Collins, the owner." She waited, then wrinkled her nose at Sean. "Thanks anyway." She hung up. "Didi isn't on duty until tonight and the person working the front desk doesn't have access to employees' personal files to get her phone number." She stomped her foot. "What if something happens to her?"

"Call Alan. The way they were looking at each other, I bet he didn't stay at a motel last night."

"Good idea." She hit speed dial on her phone, then visibly relaxed when Alan answered. "Alan! It's Kim. Is Didi with you?" She gave Sean a thumbs-up sign and he felt tension ease from his shoulders. "Where are you guys?" She frowned, then covered the mouthpiece. "They're at her house."

Sean held out his hand for the phone. "Alan, it's Sean. Will's been murdered." He paused. "We think it's Carl, but we have no evidence yet. But Carl might know Didi is working with us and he'd certainly know you are. So the two of you need to get out of Didi's house and get to the police station. We'll figure out a safe place for you guys to hide until we get Carl into custody." He listened. "Well, get there as fast as you can. That's where we're headed. And be careful, okay?"

He handed Kim's phone back to her. "They'll meet us there in a couple of hours."

"A couple of hours? What are they doing until then?"

"I didn't want to ask."

"Oh." She frowned. "They can think about sex while there's a murderer running around?"

"Didn't stop us last night."

Her cheeks immediately turned red. "That's all last night was to you? A little sex?"

Crud. He hadn't meant it that way. He'd just wanted to force her to acknowledge that there was something between them, even though she'd been shutting him out all morning. "No, that's not what I meant."

She held up her hand. "Forget it, Sean. I don't want to talk about it. You've made it clear where you stand and that's fine."

"Obviously, it's not."

Officer McKeen cleared his throat. "Excuse me, sir. I don't mean to interrupt, but I have Chief Vega on the line. He says he needs to talk to you."

"The interruption is fine. We weren't getting anywhere anyway." He took the phone. "Yeah?"

"Get down here now. I got the photo of John Ramsey. The most recent one they have is from when he was fourteen, so I don't recognize him as anyone I've seen around town. Maybe you or Kim can." He paused. "And someone named John Ramsey visited Jimmy in prison twice. So there's been contact between them. The last time was a week before he was paroled."

"We're there." Sean hung up and tossed the phone back to Officer McKeen. "We have an identification to make," he said to Kim.

God, he hoped they could match the photo. If not, more people would die.

Chapter Seventeen

Kim's gut was twisted in such a knot by the time they walked into the police station, she was sure she'd never be able to eat again. What if she couldn't match the photo to someone she knew? What if this lead failed entirely, then what? Where would they start? How long could she keep hiding? Will Ambrose had known what was coming, and he hadn't been able to escape.

They walked in and a trio of cops were huddled around a desk, all of them staring at something on top of it. The picture?

Chief Vega glanced up as they walked in. "We can't match it, but we don't know the folks at the camp that well." He gave Sean a look. "It's not anyone on the force."

What was that scowl for? It wasn't exactly hostile, but it wasn't friendly, either.

Sean simply nodded. "Good."

"Damn right, it's good."

Kim realized that the chief had been worried that someone on his team was actually John Ramsey, despite his insistence that his team was innocent. Guess Chief Vega wasn't the big, tough guy he pretended he was.

Sean approached the desk, and after a moment, Chief Vega stuck out his hand and Sean accepted it. They shook hands once and Kim felt an immediate easing of tension between them, strain she hadn't realized was there.

The chief picked up the photo and handed it to them. "It's an old photo, but maybe you can make a match."

Sean held it where she could see it and they both inspected it. It was a photo of two teenage boys. The taller one had his arms folded across his chest and looked angry, and the shorter one was standing a distance away from him, his eyebrows tweaked so he looked wary.

The boys looked completely opposite; no one would have considered them brothers.

She pointed to the taller boy. "That's Jimmy." She shivered. "Those eyes never changed."

Sean set his hand on her shoulder, and she wasn't in the mood to shrug it off.

"What about the other one?" Chief Vega asked, and there was no mistaking the hope in his voice.

Kim studied it and frowned. "There's something familiar about him."

Sean nodded. "I swear I know him, but I can't place it...."

At that moment, Kim recognized the picture, and her world shattered. "Oh, my God." No, no, no. It couldn't be him. She had to be wrong.

"Who is it?"

She grabbed the picture out of Sean's hand and stumbled across the room, staring at it. "Magnifying glass." She had to be wrong. Wrong. Wrong. *Wrong.*

"Kim? Who is it?" Sean's voice sounded so far away, tinny and distant, and she ignored it.

Someone set a magnifying glass into her hand and she almost dropped it, her hand was shaking so badly. She sank into Sean's chair, turned the lamp on, set the picture on the desk, pulled out the magnifying glass and then closed her eyes.

She felt Sean's presence before he spoke, his breath hot on her neck. "Who is it?"

Right. She could do this. Totally. "Give me a sec." She

positioned the magnifying glass over the boy's face and she knew instantly. There was no doubt. She felt sick. She set it down, spun around in the chair and faced Sean. "It's Alan," she whispered.

He grunted in surprise and touched her shoulder. Then he took the magnifying glass and examined the photo.

She leaned back and waited for confirmation, which was coming. There was simply no other conclusion.

Sean set down the magnifying glass and looked at Kim.

She managed a tight smile. No time to fall apart. But her mind was reeling, spinning, spiraling downward in a mass of heartbreak and confusion. How could Alan be John Ramsey? How could he have betrayed her like that?

No wonder Jimmy had been on his way out here. Alan had told him exactly where to find her.

Sean set his hands on her upper arms. "You can deal with this."

She nodded. Not a good time to try to speak.

He studied her for a minute, then squeezed her arms. "I'm here."

Earlier in the day, she might have been tempted to kick him in the shin for assuming that she cared whether he was there for her, but at the moment, it sounded pretty good to her. Sean might be a lot of things, like more in love with her dad than with her, but he was who he was and he'd never lied about it.

Honesty was something that seemed kind of important at the moment.

He didn't remove his hands, but he turned his head to address Chief Vega, who by some magic of transportation was now standing by their side. How did he get there?

"It's Alan Haywood, Kim's friend who is visiting from California."

Triumph lit up Chief Vega's face. "Are you positive?"

"Yes." She'd managed to speak. Good for her! Almost

made it seem as though she hadn't been ripped to shreds by the man who she thought was her best friend. "He's on his way to the police station." Double bonus. An entire sentence. She felt kind of wobbly though, as if she might topple off the chair at any moment.

Chief Vega addressed his question to Sean. "Is she right? He's coming here?"

"Yeah. I told him to come here with Didi so we could arrange to protect them from Will's murderer." Sean grimaced. "I told them I thought it was Carl."

"Good. Then they won't think it's a trap, and they'll show up." Chief Vega turned away, barking orders to get prepared for the arrival of John Ramsey.

AN HOUR AND A HALF later, Kim dialed Alan's cell phone, with Sean and the rest of the Ridgeport Police Department positioned strategically around the station, ready for him to appear. Sean was the one with his head next to hers so he could listen in on the conversation.

Could she do this? She felt as though she was betraying her best friend, but hadn't he deceived her already?

Alan answered on the first ring. "Hey there."

She had to take a moment to regroup at the warmth in his voice. "Just checking in on your status. Sean and I are at the station now and if you're not going to be here for a while, we were going to grab something to eat." Liar, liar, liar!

"We're pulling up outside the station, alive and well. We haven't seen or heard from Carl, so that's good."

"Yeah."

"You okay? You sound down."

Sean set his hand on the back of her neck and rubbed gently. "I'm a little stressed," she admitted.

"I can't believe you saw Will's body. What was Sean thinking, letting you in there?"

Okay, that was it. She could take being manipulated only

so long. "I'm sick of you putting down Sean, so cut it out. I walked in, so it's my fault, not his. Quit trying to make me doubt him. It's not going to work and you're ticking me off." Then she hung up on him.

"That was subtle," Chief Vega said.

She glared at him. "Don't even get me started."

"Not even a fraction of what he deserves," Sean said.

"They're here." A rookie ran in the front door and everyone took their places. So many cops being industrious at their desks. Yeah, right. Every other time she'd been in here, there'd been one cop in the office at most.

Would Alan bolt?

A part of her wanted him to realize it was a trap and run. The smarter part of her kicked herself in the head and reminded herself that he had just murdered Will and probably Pete Gibbs and maybe even set up her dad's accident.

She felt sick again.

No time to run to the bathroom, as Will and Didi walked in. Poor Didi. Her previous boyfriend dead, her current one a murderer. Talk about bad luck in love.

Alan waved at her and Sean. She managed a smile. "Hi, guys. Good to see you."

"You look like hell," Alan said, reaching out to give Kim a hug.

She ducked out of his grasp and moved to the other side of the desk, prompting a frown to mar Alan's face. "What's wrong?" He narrowed his eyes at Sean. "I get it. You're responsible for her outburst on the phone, right? Somehow you've managed to convince Kim I'm the bad guy." He flashed anger at Kim. "How can you listen to him?"

"Shut up, Alan!" She threw the photo at him. "Just shut up."

He caught the picture and looked at it. Expression left his face until it was carefully blank.

Yeah, nice try.

"What is this?" he asked.

"A picture of Jimmy Ramsey and his brother, John, when they were teenagers," Sean said.

"No, let me." Kim set her hand on Sean's arm. She wanted to do this. She *had* to do it. "Recognize the boy on the left?"

Alan looked at her. "Should I?"

"I do."

She saw the instant when he realized she knew who he was. The pain shackled his face and panic flew into his eyes. "You told them?" He nodded at the roomful of police officers who were pretending not to listen.

"Yes."

Betrayal flickered in his eyes. "How could you? You know what they think."

"That you murdered Will and Pete Gibbs and tried to kill my dad? Yeah, I know what they think."

"You think that, too?"

"What else am I supposed to believe?" She clenched her hands around the back of Sean's chair. "Did you destroy my house? Write that horrible message?"

"No!" He slammed his fist on the table and Sean moved closer to him, his body tense and ready. "Don't you remember how angry I was that the vandal blamed John Ramsey? Because I knew I didn't do it!"

"Oh, come on, Ramsey. You expect us to believe that? You lied to Kim for a year and a half. Why would you start telling the truth now?"

Alan spun around to face Sean. "I hate Jimmy. I know what he's capable of, and I've been trying to expose him for years. He killed our mother. Did your records search show that? They said it was an accident, but I know the truth. When I saw the engagement announcement in the paper for him, I knew what would happen to Cheryl, so I decided to get in there and do what I could." He turned to Kim. "I swear I was trying to protect you and Cheryl. I haven't seen Jimmy in fifteen years, so I made sure I wasn't around when he was, but I did it to keep you safe!"

"And you did a damned fine job of it, too, didn't you?" Sean said. "You've seen the hospital photos of Kim and Cheryl?"

"I was there! I saw it! And I saw him get off in that court-room." Alan's voice was enraged now and shrill, spiraling wildly. "How can he go free when he's done all that?"

"But why did you go visit him in prison?" Kim asked. She wanted to believe him. More than anything, she did. But how could she?

"To try to convince him to leave you and Cheryl alone. I visited when he first went to jail and he blew me off, but I tried again right before he got out." He wiped the sweat off his brow. "He laughed at me. Told me to help you so he'd have a reason to kill me, too."

"Nice try, Ramsey, but we're not buying the vulnerable little brother thing." Sean nodded at one of the other cops. "Take him into the interrogation room for a chat. I'll be in later."

Alan didn't move as one of the young cops took his arm. "Kim, if you don't believe me, your life is in danger. I'm not the one doing this, I swear. You have to trust me."

No way could she stand there and accept his story. And no way could she refute it. "Prove it to me," she said. "Please, please, please, prove it to me."

His face fell. "I can't. But you can. If you keep digging, you'll find out who it is."

That wasn't the answer she wanted. "How come you lied to me about who you were?"

"Would you have ever trusted John Ramsey?"

"Of course I would have. But I can't trust you anymore." She turned away then, unable to stand the look of despair on his face. Despair at being exposed before he could avenge his brother's death? Or despair at not being believed when he was telling the truth?

"Where were you between the hours of ten last night and nine this morning?" Sean asked. The window between when they'd spoken to Will and then found him dead.

She closed her eyes and waited for an answer that would exonerate him.

"I was with Didi for part of it."

"What about the rest of it?"

"I was alone."

Kim picked up her purse and walked out of the station, not even stopping to console Didi, who was standing by the door, a look of utter shock on her face. Yeah, poor Didi. At least she'd been victimized by his lies for only a few days, not a year and a half.

"HANG ON A SEC," Sean said to his team. It would be good for Alan to sit in the interrogation room anyway. Kim was more important.

He jogged out of the station to find Kim in his car starting the engine. "Hey!"

She glanced at him, then rolled down the window. "What do you want?"

"Just checking in. You okay?"

"No, of course I'm not okay. The man who slept on my couch during the trial is actually a liar and potentially a multiple murderer. How do you think that makes me feel, huh?"

He squatted next to the car, his arms resting on the door frame. "It sucks."

She looked surprised. "Well, yeah. It does."

"He deserved more grief than what you gave him."

She managed a half smile. "You think?"

"Definitely. You took it easy on him. You should have kicked him in the nuts and then shot him."

"Shut up." But she was smiling. "How can you joke about this?"

"Because it's the only way to survive." He grinned. "I cracked a lot of jokes after you left."

Her smile faded. "Are you going to make a lot of jokes when I leave this time?"

"Why leave? Why don't you stay here and run the camp? You have all of us here."

She touched his cheek, let her finger trail over his jaw. "Sean, you just don't get it, do you?"

He felt as though she was slipping out of his grasp and he couldn't stop it. But he didn't know why he was losing her. "Get what?" Frustration made his tone harsher than he intended. "Tell me."

"Never mind." She reached for the gearshift, but he caught her hand.

"Don't drive away without telling me the truth." He tightened his grip on her wrist. "Not again." He couldn't handle not knowing again.

She looked at him. "I can't be with a man who loves me for my family."

"So you want me to reject your family?" He frowned. What did she want from him? "Hurt them to make you happy?"

"No." She sighed. "Forget it. I guess I'm not making sense."

He sighed and rubbed the back of her hand with his thumb. "Are you going back to L.A. now? Since we've caught John Ramsey? The threat's over."

She lifted an eyebrow. "What if Alan's telling the truth? What if he didn't do it?"

"Do you really believe that's possible?"

"Yes."

He didn't understand her. "How can you have such loyalty and confidence in a man that you've known for a year and a half, yet refuse to forgive your own father? Reject your own family?"

She frowned. "It's not like that—"

"Yes, it is." Sean pressed harder. "Alan's guilt is practically a given. He's John Ramsey. He visited Jimmy in prison. Yet your only evidence on your dad is what your mom wrote in that note and what she told you."

"Leave me alone." She yanked her hand off his, jammed the gearshift into Reverse and began backing up.

Sean stepped back, even though a part of him wanted to reach through the window, yank out the keys and force her to stay. Make her face him and what was going on between them. But he didn't. He wouldn't know what to say to reach her. To bridge the chasm between them. "Where are you going?"

"Somewhere. If you're right and Alan's the bad guy, then I'm not in danger anymore, am I?"

She had him there. But if he was wrong…

"See ya." She pulled away and left him standing in the parking lot. He had a feeling he'd just screwed up again and he wasn't sure what he'd done or failed to do. All he knew was that the clock was ticking on Kim staying in town and he was getting less and less happy about the notion of her leaving. His chest felt heavy and tight, and a heaviness weighed on his shoulders.

Like he needed to be thinking that way. He wasn't going to let her break his heart twice. She was the one who hadn't loved him enough to try. Not before, and not this time. She was running, and he couldn't stop her. He stalked back into the station to talk to Ramsey, passing Didi on the way out. Her cheeks were flushed and she looked agitated. "Didi." He caught her arm as she brushed by.

She jumped at his touch, then looked at him. "Sean."

"I'm sorry about this. We had no idea that Alan was John Ramsey."

Didi nodded. "Me, neither. Guess Carl's no longer a suspect, huh?"

"No, he's not. I'm really sorry," he said again. Guess he'd been right to worry about Didi's safety, even though he'd thought the danger would be coming from Carl instead of Alan.

She lifted her chin then. "I'm not sorry."

Okay, so he was confused now. "What do you mean?"

"Alan's a good man, and I believe him. Just because he was born related to some psycho doesn't automatically mean he's bad, too."

"Kim said the same thing."

"I like Kim." She met his gaze. "You don't believe him, though."

"No, I don't." He'd been getting a vibe from Alan all along and now he knew what it had been. "Alan's a smart man. He's manipulated Kim and he's using you. Don't get sucked in, Didi."

"I'm going to go post bail for him."

He grimaced. "Don't let him fool you. He'll burn you in the end."

"No, he won't. He loves me."

"He doesn't love you! He's known you for two days and you're his key to getting out of here."

"He loves me, and I love him," she insisted.

What did they know about love? "You don't love him. You just met him."

"And I was with him all night last night."

A ping of warning sounded in Sean's head. "But he said you weren't together the whole evening."

"He was trying to keep me out of it, but I won't let him protect me. I was with him, so you've got nothing to hold him on. He'll be out by the end of the day, and if he's not, I'll bail him out."

He cursed under his breath. So much for matchmaking.

It was seriously backfiring. "Didi, lying to provide an alibi can get you thrown in jail."

"I'm not lying." She met his gaze and didn't flinch.

Damn. Was she fibbing or not? His instincts seemed to be shot to hell in this case.

She was covering for Will's death. She had to be. Alan was not the good guy in this mess. He'd been manipulating for too long to be considered an innocent.

"Don't jeopardize your future for the wrong man."

"I'm not. Good day, officer." She flounced down the steps toward the parking lot and Sean had to let her go.

It was time to talk to Alan and get some answers. He thought of Kim out there by herself and a trickle of fear gripped him. If he was wrong and Kim got hurt, he'd never forgive himself. If he was right and Didi got injured... He shook his head. Now was no time for ambiguity. He had to find out the truth before anything else could happen.

Chapter Eighteen

Kim walked into her dad's hospital room. The curtains were open, letting in the afternoon sunlight. Despite the flowers and the cards, there was no cheer here. Just stupid machines beeping and her dad looking pathetic and weak.

She practically threw a chair down next to the bed and sat down, glaring at him. "What happened with Mom? I need to know."

Silence.

"Did you know Sean loves you more than he loves me?"

Silence.

"I don't think he even loves me. It's the same thing as before. Sean loves you, not me. I want Sean to love me and you wanted Mom to love you." She frowned. "Or did you even care if she loved you? I don't know." Kim realized what she'd said. Did she really want Sean to love her? Like really love her?

It wasn't even worth thinking about because it wasn't going to happen. Why torture herself?

"I loved her."

Kim's gaze snapped to her dad's face at the sound of a very rusty and gravelly voice. His eyes were closed, his lips still. Had it been her imagination? "Dad?"

"I loved her." He said it again, and this time she saw his lips move.

"Dad!" She grabbed his hand and squeezed it, tears blurring her vision. "Oh, my God. You're awake!" Tears gave way to heaving sobs as she clutched his hand to her chest. "I thought I was never going to talk to you again."

His hand twitched in hers and then squeezed ever so slightly. "I felt the same way." A single tear trickled out of his eye and she cried for both of them.

After she ran out of tears—and energy—she sat there quietly, gripping his hand as though she'd never let go. He'd fallen asleep without saying anything else, but he was back. She knew he'd returned to her.

They had so much to talk about, so much to say.

A light tap sounded at the door. "Kim?"

She blinked to try to clear her vision, then turned to the door. "Hi, Helen."

The older woman took in Kim's tearstained expression and her face literally crumpled as she clutched the door. "What happened?"

Kim managed to smile. "He talked to me."

"He…woke up?" Helen stared at her. "Don't lie to me."

Kim shook her head. "He's asleep now, but he woke up."

"Oh, God." Helen fell to her knees beside the bed, tears streaming. "Max, Max, Max. Can you hear me?"

He moved his head slightly and a faint smile curved his lips. "My love."

Kim decided to give Helen some privacy. Or was it she who needed the privacy? The tears were starting again and she wanted to be alone. She slipped out of the room and shut the door behind her, giving them a moment.

How could she have doubted Helen? Maybe there was stuff going on, but it certainly didn't include Helen stealing from Max or trying to kill him. She leaned against the wall and wiped her cheeks.

Her dad was awake.

Soon they would get a chance to talk, really talk, about

things that should have been discussed a long time ago. It was time.

But before she did anything, there was someone she needed to tell. She pulled out her cell phone and made a call. "Sean? It's Kim. My dad's awake."

SEAN EASED HIMSELF into Max's hospital room while Kim and Helen waited outside, giving him a chance to be alone with Max. He paused when he saw Max's eyes open. "Hi." His voice felt rough and sounded strange, so he cleared his throat. "Good to see you, Max."

"Don't be a fool…. Come hug me." The words were slow and halting.

Sean blinked hard. "Yes, sir." He walked across the room and did as ordered. He felt sort of awkward until Max held him tight and didn't let go. After a few moments, Sean gripped the older man right back. When they finally released, Sean was annoyed to find the old man's tears reflected on his own face.

He wiped them off and sat next to the bed. "How do you feel?"

"Like hell." He paused to take a few breaths. "How did you get Kim…back here?"

"She came because of your accident."

"Really?" Max rubbed his chin and it seemed as though that small action took so much effort.

"You haven't asked her why she's here?"

"Doctors have been…bugging me…since I woke up." His voice faded by the end of the long sentence. He lay back on the pillow and closed his eyes. After a few moments of silence, he spoke again. "You going to…marry her…this time?"

Sean studied his fingernails. "No."

"Why not?"

"Because." He wasn't about to tell Max that Kim was leaving again. Kim could tell her dad herself. "I'm sorry."

Max opened his eyes a crack. "Why are you sorry?"

"Because I know you want me to marry her."

Max snorted once, so weakly, but it was still a glimmer of the old Max. "I'm too old…to worry about who you marry… I'm just—" he struggled to find the energy to continue "—glad you're back in town."

Sean frowned. "You don't care?"

"You're here. That's enough." Max shut his eyes again. "Glad you're back, son."

"Me, too." They sat for a few more minutes until Max's even breathing told him the man was asleep.

Son.

Max had called him *son*.

And Sean wasn't even going to marry his daughter.

Suddenly, Sean's chest felt tight and his eyes started to act up again.

He stood and cleared his throat. Time to get back to the interrogation of Alan, which had turned up not a single shred of usable evidence against him so far. The man was good, Sean would give him that, but he would break him.

THIRTY-SIX HOURS LATER, Kim and Sean were sitting beside her dad's bed and Alan had been released.

According to Sean, Alan hadn't coughed up any useful evidence during the interrogation and Didi had been waiting outside to pick him up. Alan seemed surprised to hear that Didi had been so supportive of him, but accepted her ride anyway. Something wasn't right there, but neither Sean nor Kim could figure out what it was.

Which was why they were in here to grill Max on what he knew. Yeah, he was still weak, but they simply had to find out the truth. Max was propped up, eating Jell-O, and he had some sparkle in his eyes. The doctors deemed him recovered enough to sit for an official interrogation.

Kim watched Sean prepare to begin the interview. He

hadn't been home in a day and a half, interviewing Alan around the clock to try to get him to admit something. The first time Kim and Sean had seen each other again was outside this room five minutes ago, even though she'd continued to stay at his house. Sleeping in his bed. Wondering when he'd come back and unsure what she'd say when he did. She should have gone to a hotel. But she hadn't been able to make herself. It felt right to stay at Sean's place, so that's what she'd done.

She missed the fool. Or was she the fool? Either way, when he'd approached the hospital room, she'd wanted to throw her arms around his neck and hug him. Oh, sure, he probably would have embraced her if the look on his face was any indication, but what would that accomplish? It wasn't as if it would change anything, make him decide that she was more important than her dad. Or, at least, equally important. She could settle for equal billing, couldn't she?

"You guys an item again?" Max asked them.

Kim wrapped her fingers around the arms of her chair and didn't look at Sean. "No."

Max didn't look as though he believed her. "Why not?"

"Because."

Max looked at Sean. "You not doing right by her?"

Sean shifted in his seat and looked uncomfortable. "I don't know."

Max turned back to Kim. "He loves you."

She met his gaze. "No, Dad. He loves you." Sean didn't deny it.

Max grinned. "I love him, too. Great kid."

"He's not a kid. And see? That's the problem. He would choose you over me and I can't marry someone like that." She frowned. "I couldn't before and I couldn't this time. Last time, Mom was the one who saw it, but this time I figured it out on my own."

Sean still said nothing, but he was looking at her with a

thoughtful expression on his face. What was he thinking about?

Max's smile faded. "Helen said you had some questions about Mom."

Kim hesitated. Somehow, it didn't seem so important to bring up the past. Except that she still didn't forgive her father, and the little girl in her wanted everything to be all right with Daddy. And part of her wanted to know the truth. No, she didn't *want* to know. She *had* to know.

"Show him the letter," Sean said.

She looked at him and saw in his eyes the same need to get closure on unanswered questions. Just as she had believed her dad was a murderer for so long, Sean had held him up on a pedestal. Maybe it was time for both of them to learn the truth.

"What letter?"

She unfolded the envelope from her purse and gave it to Max. "I received this a few days after Mom died."

Sean handed Max his glasses. Then the two of them waited while he read. She almost reached out for Sean's hand but stopped herself. What would be the point? They had to learn to go their separate ways.

Yet when he took her hand, she didn't resist. They curved their fingers together and waited. Was he also wondering if his world was about to collapse?

By the time Max finished reading, there were tears in his eyes. A month ago, Kim would have dismissed it as show, but now? Maybe they were real. She didn't know.

Max looked up. "I'm so sorry you didn't tell me about this. Is this why you left in the first place?"

"Yes."

He sighed and leaned back against the pillow, suddenly looking very tired.

She took his hand. "I'm sorry, Dad. I'm sorry for leaving."

Sean's grip tightened on her other hand.

Her dad squeezed her fingers. "And I regret so much that I didn't chase you across the country." He sighed. "Your mom was clinically depressed. She'd been on medication for years, but sometimes she stopped taking it."

What was he talking about? "Are you serious?"

"I'd taken her to so many different doctors and we found medication that would stabilize her for a while and then she'd go off again." He rubbed Kim's hand, staring off in the distance as if he wasn't even aware of Kim and Sean in the room. "I loved her so much and I blamed myself for her depression. It was Helen who helped me see that it wasn't my fault."

Kim tensed. "So you *were* dating Helen before Mom died?"

Her dad looked at her. "Yes, I was."

She pulled her hand free, all her old feelings of anger and resentment resurging. "Did Mom know it? Is that why she killed herself?" She caught a glimpse of Sean's face and he looked absolutely shocked.

Her dad sat up. "I gave everything to your mother until there was nothing left of me, either. Helen saved me. Without her, I would have fallen with your mom. I needed a woman who thought I was actually worth something. You think that letter was awful? Try living with a woman you love more than anything who tells you how horrible you are whenever her medication stops working. She's the one who killed me, and Helen saved me."

Kim stared at him. "You take no responsibility for cheating on Mom?"

"Of course I do. It was wrong. I actually broke it off with Helen three months before Mom died. Once Helen showed me I was worth something, I decided I was strong enough to save Mom." He met her gaze with an unwavering stare. "I wasn't. No one was. Not you. Not me. Not anyone."

"So when she died you ran to Helen's arms without another thought?"

"I had plenty of thoughts, but I'm human. I needed her."
He shook his head. "And now look what I've done. I almost
lost Helen because I couldn't stop thinking about Mom and
wondering what I could have done differently." He looked
at her. "Helen has stood by me for ten years while I blamed
myself for everything. Did you know she was in the process
of filing for divorce when I had my accident?"

Sean sucked in his breath, and when she glanced at him,
the lines around his eyes seemed deeper than before. "Was
she embezzling?" he asked.

Max nodded. "She told me about it. Said you two would
figure it out soon."

Oh, *wow.*

"She admitted it?" Sean sounded dumbfounded.

"Yes. After the accident, she realized she didn't want to
lose me, so she figured the only thing that would save me
would be to destroy my past and make me live for the
future." He shrugged. "I think she was right."

"You do? You're not mad?" She'd been so certain that
losing the camp would destroy him, which is why she hadn't
believed that Helen was guilty. "I don't understand."

"I'm selling the place. You and Cheryl get first dibs and
if you don't want it—" he looked at Sean "—you can have
it. Otherwise, it's going on the market at the end of the
summer."

Hope flashed across Sean's face, replaced almost instantly with the heaviness of despair. "I can't afford it."

"Don't be ridiculous. We'd work out a payment plan."

"Even though I'm not married to Kim?" A hint of fire
flashed in his eyes. A fire she hadn't seen since she'd been back.
It was the energy of hope for a future, for a home, for his
deepest desires to come true. How could she compete with that?

Max looked aggravated. "Who the hell cares if you're
married to Kim? You're still my only son."

Kim stared at her father, her mind reeling. He considered

Sean his only son. By giving Sean the Loon's Nest, Sean would never need her. He had everything he wanted.

Loneliness surged through her and she fought to keep the corners of her mouth from turning down. She didn't have to be lonely. Not anymore. She had her dad back, and that was something, right?

In some ways, Max was exactly the man she'd imagined. He'd cheated on Joyce. But he carried so much pain she'd never imagined, she actually found herself feeling sympathetic. He'd suffered as much as the rest of them. She lifted her hand, hesitated, then touched her dad's shoulder, her fingers lingering for only a moment.

Sean cleared his throat and she glanced at him. His jaw was locked, his eyes cold. His gaze flicked briefly at her and she saw the hurt deep in his soul. She had just learned that her dad wasn't as horrible as she'd thought, and he'd had the opposite experience. His idol had fallen.

"Did Helen arrange for your accident?" Sean's voice was harsh as he blew off the personal discussion and focused on the investigation. Too much for him to deal with?

Max shook his head. "She says she didn't, and I believe her. Why try to knock me off when she was already filing for divorce?"

Sean hunched his shoulders and Kim realized that Sean didn't know what to believe anymore.

"Why did you hire Pete Gibbs?" Sean asked.

Yep. He was in denial.

She should be annoyed with him or feel smug because all his harsh judgment of her had been proven unfair, but instead, she felt his pain. He hadn't been right about Max and Helen and her mom, but then again, she hadn't been entirely correct, either. It was a mess, and she was probably the only one who understood what he was feeling. She moved toward him until her shoulder was brushing against his and he immediately leaned into her, as if they were drawing strength through their touch. Did her father's fall from heaven change anything between them now? Did she want it to?

"Pete Gibbs." Max shook his head. "The man took my money and then disappeared. What a thief."

"He's dead."

"Really? Dead?" At Sean's nod, Max rubbed his chin. "Well, I guess that's a good excuse for not returning my calls. Heart attack or something?"

"Gunshot to the head."

Max's hand stopped moving. "Oh. Why?"

"The only missing file was yours," Sean said. "We think he was killed because of the investigation he was doing for you. What did he turn up? Was it Helen?"

"Stop with Helen. Just because she stole some money doesn't mean she's a murderer." Max resumed rubbing his chin, a contemplative tilt to his head. "I hired him because I was getting worried. I was hearing rumors that someone was asking questions about Kim and Cheryl and that scum she married. Someone searched my office and my house. When I looked into it and found out that Jimmy was getting out on parole, I decided to have Pete look into things." He shrugged. "Then Pete disappeared and I went to my office to meet someone and I got clobbered on the head. Next thing I knew, I woke up here."

"Who called you?" There was an edge to Sean's voice, desperation for answers he didn't have.

"Will. He was working the front desk that night and said he'd found a discrepancy in the payroll system he couldn't reconcile."

Poor Will. He'd been manipulated, then killed.

Sean leaned forward and handed him a mug shot of Alan. "Did you ever see this guy around the camp?"

Max peered at it. "Nope. Good-looking guy, though. Who is he?"

"Jimmy's brother," Kim said quietly. *And my former best friend.*

"The scum has a brother?"

Sean filled Max in on all the details while Kim leaned back in the chair and watched them together. They were a perfect match, bouncing ideas off each other, finishing each other's thoughts. They should be father and son. They were far more alike than she and her dad were. Except there was an undercurrent of tension between them now—a new one—and it was coming from Sean. The man he'd idolized no longer existed. How would he take it?

Welcome to her world.

Then her dad smacked his head. "I can't believe I didn't think of this."

She sat up and Sean leaned forward. "Think of what?"

"Did you pull down the overhead light fixture in my office?"

Sean shot a look at Kim and she shrugged. "What are you talking about?"

"Pete was going to install a digital camera in there in case someone broke in again. It was supposed to feed to my computer. I figured he didn't do it because he never called to confirm. But maybe he did it before he died and hooked it up."

Sean snapped his notebook shut. "I'll go check it out." He looked at Kim. "Walk me out?"

Her heart immediately jumped. She didn't know what to say to him in private. Heck, she didn't even know what to say to herself. Both their worlds had been ripped to shreds. "I'll be right back...Dad."

Max nodded and she followed Sean into the hall, where there was an officer reading a newspaper on a chair next to the door. Kim frowned. "Is he here because Alan is out of jail?"

"Yes."

She pressed her lips together. Alan couldn't be a murderer. He couldn't. But what other options were there? Helen?

"Listen, I want you to stay here until I get back. I don't like Alan being out," Sean said. He didn't touch her. Didn't try to bond. Just threw on his cop persona and ignored the rest. Why wouldn't he let her in? "I'm also worried about Didi. If she stops by, try to detain her until I get back. She's going to get herself in trouble if she hangs out with him."

Kim nodded, her head spinning. "Sean…"

"What?" He pulled out his keys.

"Be careful." Maybe it wasn't Alan, and maybe it was. But either way, there was a murderer out there.

He gave her a half smile. "Yeah." He hesitated. "I think we need to talk."

She nodded before he could take it back. "Definitely. We have to talk. Are you doing all right?"

He shrugged. "I don't know. I have no idea what to think." He shook his head. "I can't believe your dad had an affair on your mom."

"It's hard when the people you idolize let you down, isn't it?" The empathy was heavy in her voice and she knew he heard it when he let out a shaky breath. She could see the aching sadness in his eyes. "I've been living with it for ten years, Sean. I know it sucks."

He touched the hem of her shirt, his fingers trailing softly over the material, as if he were reluctant to let go. "You'll be here when I get back?"

She nodded, unable to speak over the lump in her throat. What did her dad's revelation mean for them? She didn't know and she had a feeling Sean didn't either. Where did that leave them? Too burdened by an ugly past to move forward, or finally free to become themselves? "I'll be waiting."

He caught her wrist, then pressed her hand to his chest,

right over his heart. She flattened her fingers and felt his heart beating. How much did she want to throw herself at him?

He pulled her close and kissed her, deeply and hard until she was almost ready to declare that it was enough to be second place to her dad. He released her slowly, his gaze dark. "Stay safe." He kissed her again and then left.

Whew.

She watched him leave and wondered what kind of mess she was headed for. Maybe he didn't want her to go, but even if he got down on his knees and begged her to marry him, how could she say yes? She'd been his pathway to her family and the camp. Now that his confidence in that was shaken, she was all he had left of his childhood dreams.

To him, she represented other people, other things he wanted and couldn't have. If she married him, she'd spend her entire life wondering if he ever really loved her. Seemed to her that was the fast track toward the depression her mom had endured.

No way could Kim do that to herself.

Chapter Nineteen

Kim nodded at the officer guarding the door, then walked back into the hospital room. Her dad was sitting up, his eyes alert and sharp, like the dad she remembered from so long ago. "How's Sean?" he asked.

"Fine." She walked over to the window and looked out. Bright sunshine, trees, grass. So pretty. Prettier than the cement views she had from her office in Los Angeles. Funny how even now, in the face of her dad's infidelity, she still had absolutely no desire to go back to Los Angeles.

"Kimmy?"

"Yes?"

"I love you."

Her throat tightened, but she didn't turn back to the room. "I love you, too. But I don't think I can forgive you."

"I can't forgive myself, either. Maybe Helen will have to have enough forgiveness for both of us."

"I'm not sure I like Helen."

Her dad chuckled then. "She's what I need. She's tough and caring at the same time. You'd like her."

"She stole from you. She had an affair with you while Mom was suffering."

"Without her, I wouldn't be here. Either way, your mom would have died. I know that now."

Kim bit her lower lip. "Why couldn't you just have been a jerk? It would have made it so much easier."

"Life isn't easy."

"No kidding."

They were silent for a few minutes.

"I'm glad you came back," he said.

She hesitated, her heart thudding heavily in her chest. "I guess I am, too."

"Are you staying?"

Something deep inside her wanted to say yes, but it was a part that she couldn't succumb to. A girl's foolish dream. So she started to say "No," then realized she didn't know if that was true, either. What did the woman in her dream of? A home. Wherever that was. "I don't know."

"Is Cheryl coming back?"

She turned around then. "I don't know. I haven't called her yet to tell her anything."

"Why not?"

"Because I don't want to endanger her. Until we know it's safe, I don't want to." She should let her know Max was okay, though. Surely that kind of news would be worth the risk? After all, she'd e-mailed her the staff photo and so far, that hadn't backfired. Of course, she hadn't gotten a reply on it yet, not that it mattered. They knew who John Ramsey was.

She felt weak suddenly. Two men who'd lied to her. Alan and her dad.

Only Sean was honest. He was who he was. That had to be worth something, right?

A light knock sounded at the door and Didi stuck her head in. "Oh, sorry, I didn't realize you were here. I just wanted to go over some camp issues with your dad."

She remembered Sean's request to keep Didi safe. "Please come on in. Are you okay?"

Didi pursed her lips as she stepped inside and shut the door. "Of course. Why wouldn't I be?"

"Sean was worried because you were with Alan…."

"You believe Alan murdered those people?"

"No. Well, I don't know…."

"He's a good man." Didi smiled at Max. "How are you doing, boss?"

"Great. I'll be back at work tomorrow." But he looked tired, wan.

Revisiting his past for her and Sean had taken its toll and now she felt guilty. She might not be able to forgive him, but she didn't want anything to happen to him. Okay, so she was a little messed up. Who could blame her? She sighed as Didi approached the bed and sat next to Max. "Didi? Where's Alan now?"

Didi shot her a look of disdain. "Why don't you call him and find out? He's pretty hurt that you don't believe him. You haven't even called him to ask his side of the story. Judged him and tossed him out."

Sadness cascaded through her. "He lied to me."

"So? He had good reason." Didi nodded toward Max. "But maybe we should discuss this later."

Shoot. Didi was right. It was unfair of her to burden her dad with her personal issues when he was still fragile. "I agree."

"Discuss what later?" Max yawned and faded into his pillow. "Who's Alan?"

"I'll fill you in later. Right now, why don't you talk to Didi about the camp and then get some sleep?"

"Yeah, that might be a good idea. I feel fine, but the nurses keep telling me I gotta sleep." He rolled his eyes and relaxed deeper into the bed. "They're so annoying."

Kim couldn't keep from grinning. "I know. They're so overprotective, aren't they? Coddling you when you should be out at the camp, huh?"

He winked. "You bet." Then he nodded at Didi. "What do you have for me?"

Didi started to talk about the camp and Kim decided to throw some cold water on her face. After all the emotions of this morning, she was sure she looked like hell. "I'm going to the bathroom."

Neither of them reacted as she headed into her dad's bathroom, flicked on the light and shut the door. She could still hear them talking.

She should really let Cheryl know. One quick phone call had to be okay, right? She called her number quickly and moved toward the back of the bathroom, away from the chitchat of Didi and her dad, though she could still hear them clearly.

Her sister answered on the first ring. "Where have you been? What's going on? How's Dad?"

Kim smiled. "He's awake. He's good."

"Oh, my God. Really? He's okay?"

Cheryl's relief made Kim realize that she'd done the right thing by calling her. "Sorry I haven't been in touch, but I was afraid to contact you." She tried to keep her voice quiet, but the silence in the other room told her that Didi and her dad could hear her. No doubt, her dad knew who she was talking to. She let her voice carry. "Dad said he loves you."

"Oh, tell him I love him, too. Can I come visit? Is it safe?"

"No, not yet." She lowered her voice again. No need to stress her dad out or risk invoking Didi's wrath again. "Alan's out of jail again."

"Alan? Why is Alan in jail?"

"Because he's John Ramsey, Jimmy's brother."

Cheryl made a noise of disbelief. "Impossible."

"I swear. So you don't need to worry about that e-mail I sent you. We were hoping you'd be able to identify Jimmy's brother from the photo, but it isn't necessary anymore."

"You didn't get my reply? I sent it last night. Sorry it took so long, but my computer was down."

"No, I haven't checked. Why?"

"I did recognize someone from the photo. One of the women looks exactly like this psycho ex-girlfriend of Jimmy's. She was stalking him the whole time I was with Jimmy. Crazy woman. Even Jimmy thought she was a lunatic."

Kim's heart stalled. "A woman? Which woman?"

"The one in front, holding the Loon's Nest sign."

Didi had been holding the sign in the photo. "I gotta go." She hung up on her sister and gripped the edge of the sink.

It was Didi. Didi, who had loved Jimmy so much she'd do anything for him, including track down the women he wanted to kill. Didi, who had dated Will and then killed him. Didi, with the keys to her dad's office. Didi, who had insinuated herself with them so she could keep track of what they were uncovering. Didi, who was out there with her dad. Oh, God.

Kim lunged for the door, then froze as she heard her dad's chuckle. They had resumed talking, so at least he was alive. For the moment.

She needed a plan to get Didi out of there. Now.

Sean. First she had to call him.

But what if Didi heard her? Knew she was exposed? Would she whip out a gun and kill them both right then?

Damn.

Her fingers shaking, she text-messaged Sean that Didi was Jimmy's ex and in the hospital room now.

That was enough. He'd be on his way in a heartbeat.

Kim shoved the phone into her pocket and flung the door open. Her heart was racing so hard she was certain Didi would be able to see her pulse thrusting against the skin in her throat. Didi was still sitting next to her dad, chatting, and Max looked weary. No gun in sight. No knife.

"I'm just going out in the hall for a second." Her voice was shaking.

Didi looked at her curiously but nodded.

"Was that Cheryl you were talking to?" Max asked.

"No. It was Helen. She said to tell you she'll be over soon." Oh, *no*. If Didi knew she was talking to Cheryl… Kim made it to the door and pulled it open.

No police officer. Just a newspaper on a chair.

This was so bad.

She glanced down the hall, but it was quiet. No one to help. Had to get Didi away from her dad. She took a trembling breath. "Didi? Want to go to the cafeteria and get some lunch? We could talk about Alan."

Didi cocked her head and studied her. "Yeah, okay. I guess we're done here."

Lunch in the cafeteria. Plenty of people around. Didi wouldn't try anything, especially if she didn't realize she'd been exposed. Just get her into the lunchroom. "When Sean arrives, Dad, tell him that Didi and I went to the cafeteria. We'll wait there for him."

"Sure." He yawned again. "I'll tell him."

Didi stood up slowly. "See you later, boss."

"Yep."

Kim held the door open and held her breath while Didi slipped past. Once they were out in the hall and her dad was no longer in view, she let out a heavy sigh. "So I think the cafeteria is on the first floor," she said.

"Basement, actually." Didi punched the elevator button. "Elevator okay?"

Better than an abandoned stairwell.

The elevator came and they got on, along with a nurse and tech.

Safety in numbers.

Kim shoved her hands in her pockets to keep them from trembling.

"You all right?" Didi asked. "You look a little strung out."

"Fine."

"Helen doing well?"

"Fine."

The nurse got off on the third floor.

Silence.

On the second floor, the tech departed and Carl from the camp got on. He nodded at Didi and smiled at Kim. Phew! Carl. He could fend off Didi. Never had she been so happy to see a man with muscles. Corded strength that could crush Didi's throat without a thought. She was so not letting him out of her sight. "What are you doing here, Carl?"

He frowned. "Trying to find your dad. I thought he was on the second floor, but I can't find him. I was going back to the first-floor reception to ask again."

"He's on the fourth floor," Didi said.

"Come to lunch with us," Kim interrupted. "My treat."

Didi shot her a look again and Kim tried to float a serene smile across her face. "I mean, if you want to."

Carl shrugged and moved behind them to lean against the back wall. "Who am I to turn down a free lunch?"

Big relief. She even managed to smile at Didi.

Didi smiled back.

Then Carl threw his arm around Kim's chest and pressed a cloth up to her face.

She had time only to realize that she'd made a horrible mistake, and then everything faded to black.

SEAN CALLED KIM'S cell phone for a tenth time as he sprinted down the hall toward Max's hospital room. Why wasn't she answering her phone? He blew by the cop sitting in the hall and flung the door to the room open.

Max was in there watching television, but no Kim, no Didi.

He grabbed the officer's arm. "Where's Kim? Where's Didi?"

The cop looked at him and shrugged. "I didn't see them."

"How could you not see them? They were in here."

The rookie's cheeks began to turn pink and Sean cursed. "You left your post, didn't you?"

"Didi gave me a gift certificate for the snack cart. Said she'd keep an eye on the room, so I ran down there. I was only gone for fifteen minutes."

Sean cursed and ran into the room. "Where's Kim? Where's Didi? Were they here?"

Max flicked a weary gaze toward him. "Yes. Kim said to tell you she and Didi were going to the cafeteria for lunch." His brow furrowed. "Why? What's wrong?"

"Apparently, she's Jimmy's ex-girlfriend."

Max's eyes widened. "You think she's the one?"

"Sounds like it." He went out into the hall. "If Didi shows up here, detain her until I get back. Do not, under any circumstances, let her out of your sight. She's a possible murderer."

The officer froze in mid-chew of his chocolate croissant. "You serious?"

"Get on the wire and send out an APB on her." Yeah, sure, he didn't have all the evidence he needed for that, but he'd be damned if he took any risks at this point. "And get some guys over here. I think Didi's in the cafeteria."

The officer jumped to his feet, hand on his gun. "Want backup?"

"No! I want you to stay here and guard Max. I think she came here to kill him this morning and you weren't around to stop it."

"I was only gone for a minute…."

Sean took off. No way was he standing around waiting for an explanation.

He was in the cafeteria in less than two minutes and it took him another four minutes to realize that Kim and Didi weren't in there. He cursed and his gut tightened. No, it convulsed into total fear and panic. He swore viciously and dialed Kim's phone again.

Nothing.

TWO HOURS LATER, Sean, Bill and the rest of the available police force were gathered in Max's room with Helen and Max.

"My girl's okay," Max insisted, but his skin was as gray as it had been when he'd first woken up. "We'll find her."

No Kim.

No Didi.

And they couldn't even find Alan. He wasn't answering his phone, either.

They'd checked Didi's house.

Alan's hotel room.

Kim's house.

Every inch of the camp.

Nothing.

Chief Vega was leaning against the doorjamb, looking way too relaxed. Only the clicking of his jaw gave away his stress. "Okay, let's regroup. How did we find out about Didi anyway?"

Yeah, probably late to be debriefing, but the search had taken priority. "I don't know. Kim text-messaged me," Sean said.

Max turned to Helen. "Did you tell her? She took off with Didi after talking with you."

Helen frowned. "When was this? Today?" At Max's nod, she shook her head. "I didn't talk to her today."

Sean groaned. Was Helen lying again? Crap. He didn't even know who to believe anymore.

But understanding was dawning on Max's face. "Then it was Cheryl. She was on the phone with her sister."

Sean's head snapped up. "How do you know?"

"We could hear Kim talking in the bathroom and it

sounded like she was talking to Cheryl. But when she came out and I asked her, she looked at Didi and then said it was Helen." Max smacked his fist into the palm of his hand. "She lied because she realized who Didi was."

"So let's call Cheryl." Sean looked at Helen and Max. "Please tell me you have her phone number."

"Of course." Helen pulled out her cell phone and handed it to Sean. "It's filed under Martin Timlin." She shrugged. "We aren't supposed to do anything that could compromise her, so I filed it under Martin."

Sean took the phone and hit Send.

Cheryl answered on the fourth ring. "Hi, Helen. How are you?"

"It's Sean Templeton."

"Oh, hi. Are you the one who's meeting me?"

Sean frowned. "Meeting you where?"

"My flight is about to leave."

"Flight to where?"

She hesitated. "I got a call from Chief Vega that Didi had been apprehended and I was needed to identify her. Chief Vega said an officer would meet my plane and take me to the station."

He knew the answer, but he asked anyway. "Billy, did you or any of your team contact Cheryl today and tell her to come out here?"

Billy raised an eyebrow. "Nope."

He got back on the phone. "Cheryl, it's a trap. Didi probably got your number from Kim's phone…." Oh, *hell*. Kim would have done anything to keep Cheryl's number from getting into Didi's hands. If Didi had gotten it…not a good sign. His pulse whirled and he felt sick. "Don't get on the plane. Go home."

"Does Didi have Kim? Is that what you're saying?"

"I think so."

"She's crazy, Sean! Even Jimmy thought she was a

wacko. She was so obsessed with him, she'd stop by the house in the middle of the night and bang on the front door until he went downstairs to talk to her. When he was away, she'd stalk me, waving a gun whenever no one was looking. You have to get Kim out of there!"

"I know." God, he knew.

"I'm coming. She's using Kim to get to me, so use me to find Kim."

Sean's fingers curled around the phone. "I can't do that. Kim would kill me if I put you in danger."

"And I'll kill you if anything happens to her. She saved my life more than once and I owe her."

Sean couldn't help but smile. "You Collins women are a pain in the butt."

"So are you. This is the deal, Sean. I'm getting on this plane and I'm coming out there. Some fake officer is going to be there to meet me and probably take me to Kim and Didi. You can help me or you can sit back. Either way, I'm coming. My plane boards in ten minutes. Call me back and let me know what to expect." Then she hung up.

Sean set the phone in his lap and looked at the room. "We have a decision to make."

Chapter Twenty

"Wake up."

The sound of Didi's voice jolted her awake and Kim jerked her head up. Ow. Pain. Brain felt fuzzy. Heavy. Thick.

She struggled to focus. She was in a small, unfinished room. A cabin maybe? She could see trees out the window and the walls were raw wood. She was lying on a mattress, her wrists tied behind her back, her ankles bound and yanked up behind her, apparently attached to her wrists.

Didi was standing at the foot of the bed, a smile on her face that made chills shiver down Kim's spine. "Your sister is on her way here."

"What?" Kim tried to sit up, but the ropes took that option away from her. How long had she been tied up like this? Her shoulders were screaming, her legs numb.

"I called the last number on your cell phone. She was more than happy to come out and identify me so I could be sent to prison." Didi's smile vanished. "Now I have both of you."

"Why do you want us? What did we do to you?"

"You killed Jimmy."

Kim allowed disbelief to show on her face. "How?"

"Your sister forced him to marry her, then you both set him up for a crime he didn't commit and then you stole his career by sending him to prison. And then he died coming out here to get you." She pulled a knife out from behind her back and slammed it into the bedpost.

Kim flinched and black dots flickered across her vision. Not again. Not the knife. As the fear trickled into her mind and started to yank her sanity away, Kim slammed her eyes shut and fought it. The psychological battle between them wasn't over. It hadn't been Jimmy trying to weaken her with mind games. It had been Didi.

Screw Didi. She wasn't going to win.

Kim forced herself to stare at the knife, to think. Assess. The way Sean would. How many knives did Didi have? That was the third one Kim had seen. Assimilate information. Find an opening.

There had to be one.

"You stole the man I love and you'll die for it. You and your sister. For Jimmy, you will pay." Then Didi spun on her heel and left, yanking the door shut behind her.

Kim had to get away. Had to get out. Had to save Cheryl.

"Kim."

A groggy groan from the corner made her jerk. She managed to roll to her other side and then gasped. Alan was lying on the floor, curled up in a ball, covered in blood and bruises. His wrists were handcuffed behind him, his face swollen and nearly unrecognizable.

"Oh, my God, Alan!"

"Carl's in on it, too. Jerk hits hard."

"Oh, Alan, I'm so sorry."

He closed his eyes. "When she heard that I was John Ramsey in the police station that day, I became the final piece in her little game. She wanted me to kill you, thought I should be avenging Jimmy's death. When I wouldn't, I became the perfect scapegoat. You and Cheryl are going to die and I'm going to be set up for it." He groaned. "She's a sick woman, Kim. You need to get out of here."

"Oh, Alan. I'm so sorry I didn't believe you." It was her fault. All her fault. She hadn't trusted him. She'd even set him up with Didi. "I'm so sorry."

"It's my own doing. I went with Didi just to tick you off. I was stupid. I didn't even like her that much, and I thought it was strange when she declared herself my savior after you and Sean didn't believe me. But I was too angry at you to question it." He shook his head. "I'm the fool, Kim, not you."

"We were both stupid."

"And now we're going to die." He let his head fall to the floor. "Jimmy's going to win, even though he's dead."

"No!" She tugged at her ropes and pain shot through her shoulders. "We're not going to die! Cheryl's on her way here. We have to get free and warn her!"

Alan managed to open his eyes slightly. "How? Every time I move or speak, Carl beats the hell out of me. What kind of boots does that man wear anyway?"

Fierce anger raged through Kim at the thought of Carl and his boots. No one had the right to steal the people she cared about from her! "Can you walk?"

"Broken ankles. No, I can't walk. You?"

"Tied up." *Think, Kim. Think.*

Alan cursed. "You don't happen to have a gun on you, do you?"

"Sorry. Left it at home." They were in deep trouble.

Very, very deep.

SEAN SPOTTED CARL just before the passengers began to deplane. He was wearing a Ridgeport police uniform, including a badge. Looked legit, too.

He met Billy's eyes across the terminal. Billy was dressed like a vagabond, with long hair, torn jeans and faded sneakers. Sean was dressed the same, with sunglasses covering his eyes.

Carl didn't know them that well, but he might be looking

for cops, so Sean and Billy decided to have the rest of the officers out of sight, on call to respond, but not on the front line. They were rookies and too much of a liability.

But Carl wasn't scanning for threats. He was staring at the passengers, watching them get off.

Sean saw Cheryl before Carl did. She was walking with a slight limp, her shoulders erect and her blond hair done up in a smart bun. Her face looked wan and worried, but there was a defiance in her eyes.

He knew she hadn't changed her mind, and God help him if he failed her.

She walked right up to Carl and introduced herself, and Sean had to force himself not to rush up there and rip her away from him. They needed her to find Kim.

Something ached deep inside him at the thought of Kim at Didi's mercy, but he shoved it aside. Now was not the time. But what if this didn't work? Maybe they should close in now. Not give Carl a chance to walk away….

"Let her go." Billy's voice crackled through his earpiece.

Sean looked across the crowded terminal toward his friend. How had Billy known Sean was about to march over there and grab Cheryl and take Carl into custody? They'd decided it was too risky. If Carl didn't talk or didn't know enough, they might never find Kim until it was too late.

But it was so much more difficult than he'd imagined to sit back and let Cheryl walk into danger, to let time pass while Kim was missing.

His fingers twitched over his gun as Carl set his hand on Cheryl's back and guided her through the crowd, slinging her carry-on bag over his shoulder. Sean melted into the throngs of travelers just behind the couple, but he was aware of Billy lurking on his right somewhere.

They reached the door to the airport and Carl led Cheryl toward the short-term parking lot. Billy followed them.

Sean went to his junker that ran like a dream, slipped

behind the wheel and headed toward the exit of the parking garage.

He'd been there a couple of minutes when Billy reported in. "They just got into a 2002 Toyota 4Runner. Maine plates, 692 XYG."

Sean waited until the car in question pulled out of the garage. "Got 'em."

He fell in behind them and radioed their position to Billy until he caught up.

Carl might be able to lose one of them if he was trying, but not both of them.

The two of them traded off trailing Carl, so neither car was in sight for an extended period of time.

Two hours later, they were still playing the game and Sean was at the end of his patience. It was time to act.

"ALAN!"

He twitched, as if he'd fallen sleep. "What?"

"You have to untie me. Before Didi comes back."

"I can't move."

"I can." She wiggled across the bed, biting her lip to keep herself from yelping from the discomfort. "I'm coming over." She rolled off the bed, landing with a crash on the wooden floor. No way to stop the moan. Screaming pain wrenched through her shoulder and she had to lie there for a few moments to catch her breath. She was pretty sure she'd dislocated her shoulder. The room was spinning and she was sweating from the pain. "Alan?"

"I'm here," he said from behind her. "I need to adjust. Hang on."

He groaned with pain and she felt him thud against her. "Alan?"

"Got it." His fingers touched her wrists. "I can feel the knot."

She held her breath while his handcuffed hands went to work on the rope binding her. "Hurry."

"Shut up."

"Right." Didi could walk in at any second. Carl could arrive with Cheryl. How would Sean ever find them? It was up to her and Alan.

What would she do if Alan succeeded in untying her? She hadn't gotten that far yet.

WHEN CARL TURNED OFF onto a dirt driveway, Sean pulled up into the woods up ahead and Billy coasted to a stop in front of him. They met at the hood of Sean's car and checked their weapons. "Through the trees?" Billy asked.

"You take the front door. I'll go around back."

Billy nodded, then clapped him on the shoulder. "We'll get them."

"Damn right."

"DO YOU STILL HAVE feeling in that scar?"

Kim jerked at the sound of Didi's voice. *She was back.*

"Not talking, huh?"

"Kimmy?"

Kim lifted her head to see Cheryl standing in the doorway. Her hands were behind her back and her cheek was bruised, but her eyes were dry. No tears from Cheryl anymore. She wasn't the same girl Jimmy had beaten up. Well, neither was Kim. "Did you have a nice flight?"

Cheryl blinked, then nodded. "A little turbulence, but nothing too bad."

"Shut up." Carl shoved Cheryl into the room. She stumbled and smacked into the corner of the bed frame, dropping to the floor in a crumpled heap.

Unconscious, hopefully in the same way Alan was, which was not at all.

Carl walked over to Alan and kicked him in the ankle. Kim flinched, but Alan didn't move or make a sound. She had no idea how he managed to avoid reacting. "Still passed out? No tolerance for pain."

Didi held a knife up so Kim could see it. That made number four. "You're sure those knots are tight enough, Carl?"

"Yep. She won't be able to get away from you."

Didi grinned at Kim. "You ready for some payback? We'll start with you, then when your little sister wakes up, we'll take care of her. It's no fun to carve up unconscious people."

"No, I can't imagine it is," Kim said. "No screams of agony to enjoy."

Didi flicked the knife toward Kim. "Pretending not to be scared, eh? I don't believe you." But she looked annoyed.

Good.

"Want me to tie up the sister while she's out?" Carl asked. "Yes."

Carl left the room to retrieve some cord and Didi curled her lips in a creepy imitation of a smile. "He's such a good little boy. Amazing what men will do for a great lay, isn't it?"

Amazing what Didi did to the men she seduced. "Did you kill Will because he broke up with you?"

Didi snorted. "You think that's why I was crying? I was crying because your boyfriend told me Jimmy was dead. Dead! You killed him!" She clenched the knife tighter. "Will died because he was going to show you a picture of me and Jimmy he found in my purse. Thought he'd play hero just because I kicked him out of my bed. Dumb male."

Didi waved the knife and moved to the side of the bed, tracing her knife over Kim's jeans, right above the scar. "I think we'll start in a new place. How about your stomach? Nice and soft. Lots of important body parts to spill out. Sound like fun?"

"Tons." Kim gritted her teeth and forced herself not to move. Not yet....

Didi lifted the knife and wrapped both fists around the handle for full power.

Not yet....

She reared back and brought it down.

Now!

Kim rolled to the right and the knife sliced the side of Kim's leg and ripped into the bed. Before Didi could tug it free, Kim swung with her left hand, smashing the knife Didi had left in the bedpost into Didi's hip. *Too many knives, Didi.* She'd been banking on the fact that Didi would bring in yet another knife and not miss the one in the bed.

She'd guessed right.

Didi screamed and fell to the floor, blood turning her fingers red as she clutched her side.

Cheryl jumped to her feet and Kim crumbled to the mattress. "I hoped you were faking it." Could her shoulder hurt more? It was definitely dislocated. Carl must have been messing around while she was unconscious. Jerk.

And her leg. Blood was rushing out of it, just like before. The pain was so intense. So bad. She licked her dry lips and tried to focus on her sister, but the room was starting to waver. "Tie her up. My shoulder is shot."

"Is that your blood?" Cheryl grabbed the ropes and Didi kept screaming.

"Not all of it." Her vision began to blacken and she fought it. It wasn't over. Couldn't give up yet. "Carl…"

At that moment, the door flew open and Carl jumped through it, aiming a gun at Kim's chest. "You die now." He cocked the gun and pulled the trigger.

Gunfire exploded in the room, Cheryl shrieked, Kim ducked, the wall behind her exploded and Carl fell to the ground.

Then Sean rushed through the door, his gun in his hand. "Kim!"

Sean. She collapsed back on the bed. "About time you made it. What kind of a cop are you, anyway?" Was that her voice? It was some awful grating whisper that didn't sound like her.

He dropped next to her on the bed, his fingers brushing her, skimming over her leg, her mangled shoulder, her face. "Oh, God. Your leg. What happened to your shoulder?"

She was vaguely aware of Chief Vega entering the room, of Cheryl going to talk to him, but all she wanted to concentrate on was Sean's face. It was going in and out of focus and he looked sort of gray and fuzzy, so it wasn't easy. "We won."

"Yeah, we did." His forehead furrowed. "Kim?"

No need to fight it anymore. It was over and Sean could clean up the mess. She let the blackness take over this time. Sean would take care of her.

HER SHOULDER WAS killing her.

And her thigh.

And someone was holding her hand.

Kim wrenched her eyes open to find Sean leaning over her, holding her hand against his lips. He smiled. "Hey."

"You were late." He looked so worried, so tired. She wanted to touch his face, but she was too exhausted.

"Sorry. You forgot to leave a map."

"My bad." She looked around the room. "I'm at the hospital?"

"Yep." He caught her chin and made her look at him again. "You scared the hell out of me, passing out with all that blood gushing out of your leg."

"Really?" Somehow, the thought she could scare him sounded okay to her. "Cool. How's Cheryl?"

"Fine. Everyone's fine. Didi's going to live, but she's going to jail. Same with Carl. They killed Will and Pete and tried to kill your dad. But that doesn't matter."

"It doesn't?"

"No. See, here's the thing. You're wrong."

She frowned. "Maybe it's the painkillers—" which weren't working all that well, by the way "—but I'm really not following you."

"Your mom was right. When I was eighteen, I wanted you *and* your family. And I still do, but I want you more."

She blinked. "What are you talking about?" She had a feeling she didn't want to misinterpret this one.

"When you were off with Didi, I realized I couldn't lose you again. If you left this time…" He shook his head. "Nope. I can't allow it. If you won't stay, I'm coming with you. After all, they probably have an open spot in Ramsey's department, don't you think?"

She stared at him. "You're going to move to L.A.? What about the camp?"

"The camp doesn't matter. Cheryl doesn't want it, so your dad's going to sell it."

"You're not going to buy it?"

"No." He gripped her hand tighter. "Don't you understand what I'm trying to say?"

She smiled then. He was so going to have to say it. If he didn't, she'd never believe it. "No, tell me."

"I love you. More than the camp. More than your dad. More than your family. I'll ditch this town and move to California if you'll marry me this time." He let his breath out. "So? What do you say?"

She couldn't wipe the grin off her face. "You really love me?"

"Yes." He kissed the back of her hand. "Nothing like seeing the woman you love collapse in a pool of blood to make you realize what's important in life."

"That's so romantic." It was, actually. Maybe she should swoon. The stubborn man finally loved her. Really loved her.

He shrugged. "I didn't have time to get romantic. I was too worried that you'd yank out your IV and march off to the airport before I had time to declare my undying love and devotion."

Okay, so that made her smile grow even bigger. "Undying love and devotion? I like that."

He groaned and pressed her hand into his forehead. "Stop teasing me. I've had enough stress lately." He looked up and she saw the vulnerability in his eyes. "Will you marry me? And leaving me at the altar doesn't count as a yes."

She shook her head. "I can't. Not under those terms."

His face fell. "But I thought—"

"That I loved you?" At his nod, she smiled. "I do. But I'm not into this whole idea of you moving out to L.A."

His brow puckered in consternation. "Why not?"

"Because I'll miss you too much."

Now it was his turn to look confused. "What are you talking about?"

"I'm staying here."

He looked shocked. "You are? Why?"

"Because I don't want to grow old without my family. When Cheryl walked in, I realized how much I'd missed out on with her living so far away. And I have a dad again. Yeah, we still have a lot to work out, but if I leave, I'm afraid we'll never get it sorted out." She met Sean's gaze. "I lost my mom, but it's my fault if I lose out on everything else." She smiled. "I fell back in love with you the minute you walked into my house to chase away a prowler, but I was afraid to love a man who didn't love me the way I wanted to be loved."

"And now?"

"You've convinced me."

"So you'll marry me?"

"As long as we stay here. And I think Cheryl's wrong about the camp. She's going to want it later on in life, so it's my job to buy it for her."

Sean grinned. "You can't lie to me. You're buying it for yourself."

"For us, Sean. For us."

He leaned forward and kissed her gently, careful not to rattle her shoulder or touch her bandaged leg. "Your family is in the hall. I kicked them out. Can we bring them in and make the announcement?"

She grinned. "Only if you promise to get me out of this hospital room today. I want a little privacy with the man I love."

"Deal."

He tightened his grip on her hand, then turned toward the door. "You guys can come in."

The door flew open, and in marched Cheryl, pushing Alan in a wheelchair, Chief Vega, Eddie, and Helen, helping Max with a walker.

It had taken ten years to find her way, but finally she was home.

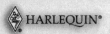
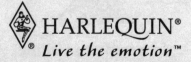

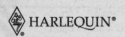

HARLEQUIN®

INTRIGUE®

COMING NEXT MONTH

#897 CRIME SCENE AT CARDWELL RANCH
by B.J. Daniels
Montana Mystique
Former lovers reunite to dig up their families' torrid pasts and reveal the secret behind the skeleton found in an old dry well.

#898 SEARCH AND SEIZURE by Julie Miller
The Precinct
Kansas City D.A. Dwight Powers is a street-savvy soldier in a suit and tie. His latest case: saving the life of a woman caught up in an illegal adoption ring.

#899 LULLABIES AND LIES by Mallory Kane
Ultimate Agents
Agent Griffin Stone is a man that doesn't believe in happily ever after. Will private eye Sunny Loveless be able to change his mind?

#900 STONEVIEW ESTATE by Leona Karr
Eclipse
A young detective investigates the murderous history of a hundred-year-old mansion and unearths love amidst its treacherous and deceitful guests.

#901 TARGETED by Lori L. Harris
The Blade Brothers of Cougar County
Profiler Alec Blade must delve into the secrets of his past if he is to save the woman of his future.

#902 ROGUE SOLDIER by Dana Marton
When Mike McNair's former flame is kidnapped, he goes AWOL to brave bears, wolves and gunrunners in the Alaskan arctic cold.

www.eHarlequin.com

HICNM0106